Buchan

A contemporary crime thriller written by five members of Hinckley Scribblers

Biography

Norma Bowen
Retired journalist and member of Hinckley Scribblers.

Brent Kelly
Retired early to follow my interests in writing, particularly poetry, football and walking and member of Hinckley Scribblers.

Carol Mogano
Retired school teacher and Secretary of Hinckley Scribblers.

John Trott
Treasurer of Hinckley Scribblers. Retired after serving for ten years in the Royal Marines and thirty in the police.

Rita Wilson
Retired school teacher and member of Hinckley Scribblers.

The above five members of Hinckley Scribblers are the authors of Buchan.

Copyright for the following content is held by the various writers accredited to the work © 2023.
All rights reserved.
ISBN: 9798862749182

Prologue

'The exact percentage is not known but the vast majority of parents die before their children.'

He always expected to outlive his parents but had imagined they would grow old together and pass away peacefully when their time was up. Nobody could be ready for this kind of nightmare.

His eyes become misty as he recalls his mother nursing him after his motorbike crash resulting in a broken leg. He would never forget the look of pride on his father's face as he took him to their local for his first pint of beer on his eighteenth birthday.

They had always been there for him with advice and encouragement when he needed it. 'Where was I when they needed me?' he thought with a lump of guilt coming to his throat. Surely his parents would have been safely tucked up in bed and asleep by eleven o'clock but suddenly his mind is filled with all sorts of other possibilities. His military training has taught him to stay hopeful but prepare for the worst. The uncertainty is making his head spin.

He desperately rubs his eyes and drags his hands through his hair. His palms are sweating yet his knuckles look cold and white. Distracted by a loud rhythmic bass he wonders begrudgingly who is partying at this time of night. As he stops to draw breath he is suddenly aware that what he can hear is not coming from a distant night club but is the frantic beating of his own heart.

Stumbling over a large stone he kicks it fiercely into the gutter as he rushes towards the scene.

Osman

At a glance the dilapidated back street looked deserted. This part of Stretford had long since ceased to be a desirable area of Greater Manchester and was well overdue for demolition. In the meantime it served as a perfect area for the low life of that region to do business. Wayne Osman had pressed his bulky frame as far back as he could into a crumbling doorway. His long, grey jacket concealed the gun tucked into his waistband. Only the tips of his size 12 black studded boots protruded into the street. He peered round the warped doorframe to the corner on the left hand side of the street. His lookout guy, a thin under-nourished looking figure, was lighting a roll-up. This was the sign that the next person to round the corner on the opposite side was Osman's prey.

A lean, lanky youth came into view. Averting his eyes from his phone he appeared to check the guy lighting a cigarette and then swept his eyes down the street. He must have considered it safe as he walked on confidently, his eyes focused on the phone again as he selected a number.

Osman swiftly pulled out the gun as he stepped into the street and fired two shots. There was a sharp cry of pain from the youth as he dropped the phone and automatically reached for the knife he always carried in the pocket of his jeans. His hand did not even make contact with the knife. With a gasp and a guttural groan he fell forwards. There was a sharp crack as his head smacked onto the grimy flagstones, a young life over in seconds.

A female voice could be heard coming from the phone, "Hello, hello. Is that you?" One of Osman's large black boots silenced the phone in an instant, the sun catching on his shaven head as he did so. With a smug look of satisfaction his glance moved to the body, blood already seeping into debris along the gutter, turning it bright red. From the corner of his eye, Osman caught a slight movement at the top of the street and then heard what sounded like a heavy door slamming shut.

Shoving the gun under his jacket, he ran the few yards up the street. He looked to the right and left, nothing. He looked behind him, only his stumbling lookout relighting his roll-up. On the other side of the street running perpendicular to the back street was an old building with several bins outside. Next to the bins was what he surmised was a Fire

Exit door, firmly shut. He became aware of another noise, a light tap tapping. A slight breeze was causing dozens of paper cups to roll in different directions along the road. His eyes returned to the bins. In front of the recycling one was an empty cardboard box, probably discarded in a hurry as it was still intact. Osman grabbed his lookout by the arm.

"What's that building?" he snarled.

"Back of Hope Church," was the shaky reply. "Main entrance is at the front, down that alleyway. Some days they have old folk in and give 'em dinner."

Osman brought his face close up to the lookout, the snake tattoo winding round his neck adding to his menacing look. "Well you'd better get round there fast and find out who clears up after the old folk. We have ways and means of dealing with lookouts who fail to look out. Understand?" The lookout discarded his roll-up and wasted no time in distancing himself from Osman and disappeared down the alleyway.

Osman waited until he was in his car parked several streets away before he got out his phone. He hesitated knowing what the question would be. There were to be no mistakes, the shooting was to serve as a warning to all the small time dealers stupid enough to invade the boss' territory.

Osman made the call. "Job done, Boss," he said.

"Any witnesses to the demise of the little shit?" Even in those few words a steely Glasgow accent was apparent.

   A slight pause before Osman answered, "None I saw."

"Mmm, sounds like job not done to me. Sort it." The same voice in a steady matter-of-fact tone.

"I'm on it," said Osman but the line was already dead.

Buchan

It was a dark night, and the threat of rain was in the air. The quiet residential street appeared deserted until the dark shadow of a slim young man moved quietly through the darkness. He paused only to observe if he was being watched. He was wearing a black balaclava helmet and gloves. In one hand he carried a Squeezy washing up bottle and in the other a bunched newspaper. The bottle contained not washing up liquid but petrol.

Rather than walking along the pavement he sidled past doors until he reached number 7 Hale Road. He looked around one last time and satisfied he was not being watched, silently lifted the flap of the letter box and inserted the nozzle of the Squeezy bottle. He squeezed the bottle and moved it from side to side to spread petrol. Crouching he placed his ear to the letter box and listened, there was no sound inside, he had not disturbed the occupants. He pushed newspaper partly through gap and used a camping ignitor to set fire to the newspaper. As soon as it caught and flames appeared, he leaned his head away to avoid any flashback and pushed the flaming paper through the gap. He was rewarded by a soft whoomph as the petrol inside the house ignited. Job done, he retraced his steps and before leaving the road looked back and nodded with satisfaction. The front door was already burning.

Rosemary and John Buchan slept on as the fire tightened it's grip. Flames passed through the open sitting room door and crossed the ceiling, setting fire to the curtains. Another tongue of fire advanced along the hallway and entered the kitchen. Soon more fire was making its way up the stairs and smoke poured into the upstairs rooms.

Rosemary and John woke up coughing and wheezing. John rushed to the door and turned round, "Come on Rose, the house is on fire, have you got your mobile?"

Rose cried out," No it's downstairs."

"Aye so is mine. We're never going to get down the stairs, I'll shut the door and open the window, we can shout for help."

John Buchan forced the door shut and rushed to the window, he opened it and leaning out started calling, "Fire, Fire, get the fire brigade. Help. Fire." But there was nobody in sight and no sign of lights being switched on. He knew they were on their own. It was up to him to get help.

Rosemary hugged him and sobbed, "John, are we going to die? I don't want us to go like this. John shook her by the shoulders, "We're not dying if I've got anything to do with it, get all the bedding on top of yourself. I'll have to go downstairs, I'll get help, just cover yourself up."

They were both now continuously coughing and struggling for breath, and they could see flames licking under the door, which was smouldering.

"But John, you'll die, don't leave me, please don't leave me."

John pulled the duvet from the bed and threw it over his wife while pushing her to the floor. Shouting," Stay there, keep covered up, stay down low." He then rushed to the door and opened it. Invigorated by the flow of oxygen from the window the fire exploded into the room and both quickly perished in the inferno.

Annie Gray

Annie Gray's latest court story had given her a front page lead. A week later she was on the way to an incident she knew would again hit the headlines in the local newspaper. She was unaware, however, of the sinister connection between the two.

She had been asleep for just one hour when her mobile rang. She slapped her hand on the iPhone, dragged it under the bedclothes and in a hoarse voice whispered, "Hello."

It was her taxi driver friend, George Sparrow. "You might want to get over to Stretford Annie. There's a house on fire and it's raging," he said in earnest.

Using her free hand to lever herself into a sitting position and with her eyes still closed she cleared her throat and asked, "What's that, George?"

Raising his voice he repeated, "A big fire Annie, in Hale Road. I saw several fire engines and police cars and, an ambulance is just going by." Annie heard the whining siren even as George was speaking.

She rubbed out the sleep from her eyes, threw aside the duvet and, when her feet landed on the cold, laminate floor, she was awake enough to confirm, "Hale Road, Stretford. Thanks a lot George, I owe you one."

George, a Greek fast food vendor by day and a taxi driver at night, contacted Annie whenever he came across anything he thought was noteworthy to the local newspaper.

At weekends he worked into the early hours of the morning, picking up and dropping off Manchester's night revellers.

Annie was not always grateful for George's tip offs, especially if it was just about brawling drunks, unless knives were involved, in which case her ears perked up. She returned the favour by using his taxi for any work-related trips.

*

Sitting on the edge of her bed, Annie pulled on her Fat Face top and jogging bottoms over her T-shirt and shorts, grabbed a shorthand notebook, there was always one within reach, and ran downstairs. She slid her bare feet into a pair of suede Skechers and snatched her car keys from the hall table before slinging a roomy bag over her shoulder and jumping into the red Fiat Panda that was parked outside her house.

The car was not the raciest of its type but it was a no-nonsense, cheap to run model that she inherited from her father. It was chunky and reliable, just as he had been. It brought many a smile to her face. She had been very close to her father and, though the car had been valeted several times since his death, the smell of his Old Spice aftershave lotion still lingered. Annie liked to think it was his way of telling her that he was still close by.

Annie did not mind losing sleep for a good story, especially one she knew would give her a byline, which was the reward for actually being at the scene of an event as well as producing a well written piece of work. She believed the incident she was on her way to would at least make it to one of the early, right hand pages, if not the front page.

She was excited and her heartbeat quickened when the adrenaline kicked in as she motored through the neon-lighted streets of Manchester, which was patronised by the good and the bad

She smiled as she passed a happy group of people having a laugh as they made their way home. Her expression changed to one of pity, however, when she saw the sorrowful sight of a drunken, scantily clad girl sitting on the pavement outside of the entrance to a nightclub. She was holding in her hands a pair of high-heeled shoes. Annie, who had covered too many court cases for alleged rape, felt sorry for the girl she believed was easy prey to the city's lowlife.

*

She arrived in Stretford in good time and parked a little way from Hale Road, which had in part been cordoned off. She walked towards a crowd congregating around the police tape and was staggered at the searing spectacle before her. George had been right, it was a serious, destructive fire. He had not mentioned, though, the fire and rescue appliance that was also standing by.

Annie noted the glow from the flames reflected in the eyes of the horror-stricken faces of a gradually growing crowd, which watched incredulously as fire-fighters tackled the blazing house.

Devouring black smoke billowed from smashed windows, blown out by the fierce heat. Glass littered the ground and the smell of charred wood licked by the flames made the air toxic, causing onlookers who were gagging on the acrid smoke to cover their noses and mouths. Slowly Annie mingled among them and, using her iPhone, she discreetly photographed the shambolic scene.

"The old couple, have they got them out?" called a woman from the crowd, her face creased with concern.

"I think they must still be in there, they would have been in bed," cried another, who pitifully explained, "The fire was too far gone when Robbie noticed it on his way home from work. Please God if they are dead I hope they died in their sleep," she added as she clutched her hands together as though in prayer.

Annie made a mental note of what she heard. She did not want to make a song and dance about who she was, knowing the less savoury residents of Stretford were often featured on the wrong pages of the Stretford Star and were not enamoured of journalists.

She knew the area quite well. It was known to be riddled with vermin, the two-legged sort. Drug addled gangs terrorised the neighbourhood that was plagued with soaring knife crimes and shootings as they fought for supremacy in a turf war. Some parts of the town were no-go areas for the police, even though most of the criminal element were known to them.

*

Only last week Annie's front page lead featured Wayne Osman, who had been arrested in relation to a shooting in Stretford. There had been talk of threats and intimidation to anyone thinking they might help the police with their enquiries.

Annie herself had been a victim of intimidation when Osman appeared for his first hearing at Manchester Magistrates Court. A shiver ran through her when she recalled that day. She had been sitting in one of the press seats and tried in vain to evade Osman's grasping glare, which had compelled her to glance up at the dock. His powerful stature had conflicted with the court's authority. It had been all over his smirking face - I know who you are.

Butterflies had stirred in her stomach as the bald-headed aggressor, displaying a snake tattoo on his neck, blatantly held up two fingers. He first pointed to his menacing eyes before sharply directing the threat towards Annie. She had been unable to hide her fear.

Osman and his hostile followers, who had been sitting on a bench in the public gallery, had enjoyed the show. One of them put his hand under his hoody and pretended to wipe away tears from his eyes. Another exaggerated the gesture of licking the tip of a pen and writing on a notepad. It had been a flagrant display of contempt for the court's authority.

Two stone-faced, burly looking police officers had been standing either side of the court room's exit door. They had expected trouble from Osman's friends, who had left the building shouting their support for him with threats of vengeance as he was taken back to the cells.

There was an element of hostility within the crowd watching the fire. Annie thought it was worse than hostile, it was a shocking display of anarchy, when thugs in hoodies pulled down over their faces, heckled the fire-fighters.

One of the thugs held his hands between his legs and called out, "Can I help? I've plenty of water in my bowser." His mocking mates doubled up with laughter and followed suit as they threw plastic cups filled with stones at the fire-fighters. The thugs had come prepared to cause mayhem.

Annie was not surprised to see more police cars and a police van arrive, which saw the thugs running in different directions. Her eyes followed one of them when she noticed a lone figure on the perimeter of the crowd. He appeared to be over-seeing the activities. He casually stood with his hands in his designer track suit pockets before slowly fading into the shadows. Annie felt the threat in his chilling expression. If he was noticed by her she was in no doubt that he would have been clocked by the police. Annie now suspected there was a lot more to the fire than the flames that were engulfing the property.

She sought out from the crowd Robbie George, who she had heard raised the fire alarm. He was willing to talk to her but not until she promised she would not mention his name in the article. He told her the families from two houses either side of the fire had been evacuated and that Robbie and his wife lived in one of them.

He explained he was returning home after a late shift at around midnight, when he noticed flames coming from Mr and Mrs Buchan's living room. His voice cracked with emotion as he said, "I ran towards the front door to alert them but the heat was so bad I couldn't get close enough to it. I fear the worse, I mean, the fire was well on its way by the time the fire service arrived." Annie thanked him and asked him why he did not want his name mentioned. He said, "I don't want any come back on me or my family. I'll leave it at that if it's all the same to you." He cocked his head to one side and raised an eyebrow to emphasise the point, which Annie acknowledged.

She made notes about the number of fire-fighters and appliances that were on site and nodded to a policeman she knew. His expression told her she would get short shrift if she tried to approach him for information so she changed direction and wandered among the bystanders asking if any of them knew the Buchans.

"Yes, I do," called a man, standing close by.

"What are they like?" asked Annie.

"Rosemary and John are well known round here. They are a friendly, community minded couple, who will help anyone," he said.

He then focussed on Annie's eyes and, raising his voice in condemnation, added, "Rosemary was so fed up with the thugs terrorising residents to the point they were afraid to leave their homes she set up the Multi Faith Lunch Club in the Hope Church Hall." Annie saw the pain in his eyes as he explained,

"She wanted to bring something nice to the community so she advertised for

volunteers prepared to make soup and a pudding on a fortnightly basis. I was one of the volunteers. It took a while to get things going but eventually it became popular, despite the rising crime wave."

With a small smile on his face and pride in his voice he continued, "Rosemary is a stalwart, she isn't afraid of the gangs that hang about intimidating us residents. She used to say that she wasn't going to be beaten by a load of no-brain druggies."

People standing within earshot nodded in agreement with his sentiments. His name he said was Arthur Plant and, as if taking a leaf out of Rosemary's brave book, he agreed to be quoted in the newspaper.

Annie was touched by his courage and felt sorry for the decent, law abiding residents living in a ravaged part of Manchester. She could not help thinking, though, that she had a brilliant story.

The fire was finally brought under control. The crowd waited with their hearts in their mouths knowing the worst was yet to come. Some linked arms for support as they gravely witnessed two bodies being carried from the blackened remains of number seven Hale Road.

Walking alongside was an agitated man, who was being supported by a compassionate looking WPC. Annie, even from her distant view point, could see how distraught and pale he was. Arthur Plant pointed out the man was Paul Buchan and said, "Rosemary and John were very proud of him. He was their only child, though he didn't visit them much."

A stillness hung in the air and the silent, outpouring of sympathy was almost tangible. Knowing what it was like to have lost both parents, Annie could empathise with Paul Buchan but to lose them in such a horrific way must be unbearable, she thought.

Their lonely demise brought to mind a saying her father once said on hearing about the death of a friend, "The most painful goodbyes are the ones that are never said and never explained".

Paul Buchan, with his knees buckled beneath him, was eventually persuaded to get into a car, which then followed the ambulance carrying his parents

The silence from the saddened crowd was deafening as people slowly went on their way. Annie also made for home knowing that later on in the day she would be knocking on doors and contacting the police and fire service before settling down with her laptop.

*

At thirty one she was the proud owner of a two up two down mid terrace house that was built in the early 1900s. Every house in the street looked the same. When she moved in all the rooms had been painted in a dull shade of cream. They were screaming for colour and Annie had lavishly obliged by hanging three bold coloured, abstract paintings she had bought cheaply from a craft fair.

The house became her home in no time at all. As a lover of history she had often wondered about the lives of its previous occupants as they sat in harmony or otherwise around the fireside in the small living room. She was happy to live among them and had not wanted to erase any memories that might be pervading the walls.

Pleased though she was to be on the first rung of the property ladder, her prosperity was sadly linked with the death of her parents, first her mother then a year later her father. It was he who had supported Annie's wish to become a journalist.

She was determined and ambitious and, though currently working for the local newspaper, she aimed to progress to a national daily. For now, however, her bed beckoned.

Buchan

Buchan was taken from the fire to the local police station, given a mug of coffee and told a detective would be with him in a few minutes. He stared at the blank walls, grimy chairs and metal table in the harsh light and slumped forward, resting his head on his arms. He was confused, who did he have to tell, aunts, uncles, cousins, friends who he had never met. Where did he start? How do you arrange a double funeral? His mind was whirling, when there was a soft knock on the door and a woman walked in.

She gave a tight smile and held out her hand.

"Mr Buchan, I'm Detective Constable Maria Ross. May I first offer my sincere condolences. This has obviously been a dreadful night for you. I'm here to take you through what has to be done now. Please call me Maria."

He studied her before replying. A tall slim black woman in her late twenties or early thirties. She was wearing a damp khaki raincoat, open at the front, a dark blue trouser suit and dirty wellington boots. He could smell the smoke on her. He took her hand and was surprised by the firmness of her grip.

"What happens now?"

"I'll take you to the mortuary and ask you to identify your parents to me, then we can sort out somewhere for you to stay while we investigate the fire."

Buchan frowned, "Look, I think I should tell you now, my father would never have gone to bed and left anything switched on, it's something he never did."

"Don't worry, if there is anything suspicious, we'll find it."

*

An hour later he was sitting on a bed in the local Travelodge, still trying to banish the image of his dead parents from his mind. He had identified first his mother and then his father to Maria Ross. He had managed to keep control of his emotions while he did this but as he walked from the mortuary his stiff upper lip crumbled and he fell against the hospital wall sobbing. Maria Ross had comforted him, holding him tightly until he regained control and then she drove him to the Travelodge.

Knowing he would never be able to sleep and on impulse, he telephoned for a taxi to take him to collect his car. When he arrived, he saw his car had not been moved and beyond it could see the smouldering ruin of his parent's house. There were still people standing and staring. A few police were there and a couple of fire engines. The sour smell of burning blended with the rain and it saturated his senses.

A voice called out, "Paul, Paul is that you?"

An elderly man rushed towards him, it was Robbie George.

"Thanks for calling me Robbie."

"Yes well, it's just as well they left your number with me. Look, it's freezing out here, come back to my house and have a hot drink, or something stronger if you want. There's something I need to tell you."

A few minutes later Buchan was seated in the tidy living room of Robbie's house, two doors away from the smouldering ruin.

"You had something to tell me Robbie?

"Aye, this fire was no accident! It was me called the fire brigade, I was returning home from my late shift at the garage and the first thing I saw was the front door and hallway were blazing and there were flames in the front room. I tried to get near the door but it were too hot so I rang 999."

"You say the front door was on fire?"

"That's right, like I said it were blazing, so I ran round the back but I could see the kitchen was on fire as well but not as bad as the front but I still couldn't't get into them."

"You did everything you could Robbie and I'm grateful." He grasped the old man's wrist.

"But that's not all, I told a fireman what I'd seen and he said they could smell petrol as soon as they got inside, some evil bugger set it on fire."

"Why would anyone do that to Mum and Dad? They've never harmed anyone."

"It were that court case, I told her not to get involved but you know what she were like. She would always do what she thought was right but she didn't understand some of the people who live round here now. They killed them, I'm sure of it."

Buchan remembered his last conversation with his mother. "She told me she'd seen something and had to go to court but she wasn't bothered about it, just said it was a local lad had got into a bit of trouble."

"It was more than just a bit of trouble. That Wayne Osman from the end of the road, he shot a lad, tried to kill him by all accounts."

"I didn't know that and I wish I had, I could have done something about it, something to protect them. What was it all about?

"Oh, the usual I expect, drugs, the streets round here are paved with drugs, it's so open, they stand in the street selling them and the police do bugger all."

As Buchan walked back to his car it was daylight. His head felt like it had been tumbled in a spin dryer and he had an appointment to see Maria Ross at eleven, he would have a lot of questions and would insist on some straight answers.

*

Buchan arrived early for his meeting with Maria and found she was already at the station waiting for him. He was ushered into the same bleak interview room he had only left a few hours before. Waiting for the door to close he stared into Maria's eyes.

"Before you say anything, I can tell you this fire was no accident. I've spoken to Robbie George and he tells me the front door was ablaze and a fireman told him they could smell petrol as soon as they entered the house. My parents were murdered."

"That's exactly what I was going to tell you. We have opened a Murder Incident Room upstairs and Detective Chief Inspector John Morgan is the SIO, that's Senior Investigating Officer. If you are in agreement, I will be your family Liaison Officer. That means I'll be your point of contact with the investigation, I'll keep you informed of the progress of the inquiry and if you have any questions you want answered please come to me and I'll do my best to answer them. Are you happy for me to act as your liaison officer?"

Buchan relaxed, "Yes I am and I'm relieved you all seem to be treating it as murder and not some unfortunate accident."

The next hour was taken up by the two of them exchanging contact details and an introduction to DCI Morgan who appeared pale, listless and not very communicative. He shook Buchan's hand with his own, which was limp and damp. He said there had been a great deal of interest from the media and Buchan readily agreed to speak at a press conference.

*

The next job on Buchan's list was to contact the army. He was due to take terminal leave in one month and finish his twenty-two -year army career. This was not how he imagined it would be. He had visions of visits to old friends and a monumental last night in the Sergeant's Mess before bidding farewell and embarking on his new life.

The army can be a harsh unreasonable master at times but in the event of a real emergency they will pull out all the stops and act swiftly and humanely. Buchan spoke to his Commanding Officer who said, in the circumstances, Buchan could report to HQ, sign the necessary papers the following day and the remainder of his time in the army would be written off as compassionate leave.

*

He was then introduced to Assistant Chief Constable Freeman and together they were soon seated in the glare of lights in front of the gathered media. After a few words from the Assistant Chief Constable, Buchan made what has come to be a routine appeal in these circumstances. More lights flashed and a few reporters shouted pointless questions that did not get an answer. He was then able to walk away from the hubbub and link up again with Maria Ross.

He turned to her." I'm going back to my flat now. Tomorrow I'll report to HQ to sign all the papers needed to finish with the army. I'll come back up as soon as I've done that. Keep me posted."

She hesitated, "Look Paul, DCI Morgan was not himself earlier, I don't know what's wrong but I've never seen him like that before. He looked ill to me."

Buchan nodded, "He certainly didn't impress me. I hope he pulls himself together before I see him next time. If he doesn't, I'll be complaining but for now I'm going back to camp to get out of the army."

*

Buchan had not slept for well over twenty-four hours. He kept his driver's window open and made the journey out of Manchester and back to his flat slowly and safely. On arrival he stripped, fell into his bed and was instantly asleep. Suddenly he was awake. His body saturated and his sheets wet with sweat. The nightmare had returned. Now it was even worse than before.

Buchan had been attached to the SAS when serving in Iraq at the height of the fighting. He'd accompanied them on a raid with orders to collect all data storage devices and anything written. They would have to fight their way into the target premises, which were used by Al Qaida, quickly gather anything that looked as if it could be of use and leave as swiftly as they arrived. The raid had been successful. The troops had blown a hole in the wall and thrown grenades into the space inside. The SAS moved through the building to the accompaniment of short, efficient bursts of automatic gunfire. Buchan followed behind ignoring dead Al Qaida while cramming hard drives and papers into a backpack. The grenades had set fire to the room and it was spreading fast.

Buchan heard a groan followed by a whimper and saw an Al Qaida fighter he had believed dead looking up at him. The man had no weapon and was staring, his eyes pleading. He was young, very young, no more than sixteen.

An SAS trooper slapped Buchan on the shoulder. "Come on, time to go."

The Al Qaida fighter was screaming now, obviously unable to move and the fire was licking around his feet and legs. Buchan took a step towards him but the Trooper grabbed his shoulder and threw him out of the door. As he ran towards the Land Rover he could hear the terrorist's screams getting louder and he was screaming even louder as they drove away.

Buchan had seen a great deal of action in Iraq and Afghanistan but the screams of the wounded young terrorist being burned alive remained with him and disturbed his sleep far too often. He never sought treatment and in time they faded. Tonight; they had returned with a vengeance. Now it was not a terrorist he saw but his mother's pleading eyes. Her piercing screams jolting him awake.

Splashing cold water over his face and knowing he would never be able to get back to sleep, he donned a tracksuit and trainers and went out into the breaking dawn. He ran ten kilometres through parkland and along the canal. Exercise was the only cure he knew for the nightmares.

*

The rest of the day he spent signing discharge papers and handing in his accumulated army kit. By the time he drove away from the camp for the last time he had shaken the Commanding Officer's hand and was in receipt of a modest pension and a useful lump sum to support his return to civilian life.

Back at his flat his phone pinged, a text message from Maria Ross. "DCI Morgan has been taken off the case. He's been rushed into hospital with kidney stones. He's been replaced by DI Mick Kinkaid. I'm not happy about this and need to speak to you but not at the police station. Can you meet me at Starbuck's tomorrow morning?"

Buchan texted back, "Yes I can, I'm intrigued. I'll text you when I'm back in town."

He wondered. "Who is Mick Kinkaid and why is Maria Ross so worried?"

*

The following morning he was with Maria Ross in Starbucks.

"Right Maria, what's the story with Mick Kinkaid?"

"I'm going to tell you something that could get me into a lot of trouble. Before I say anything, I want your promise that you will never ever tell anyone what I've told you. I could lose my job and a lot more besides if it ever came out."

"Now you really have got me intrigued. I promise and I can assure you, I know how to keep my mouth shut."

Maria stared into her coffee for a moment. "I'm not sure Mick Kinkaid is honest. He's a very effective detective, seems to know everything the local villains are up to and he clears up a lot of major crime. But there is one gang he's hardly ever touched and that's the one Wayne Osman worked for until he got arrested."

"Which gang would that be? I don't know anything about crime or gangs up here."

"It's a family firm called Scilacci. The main man is Dominic. He controls the drug trade in this area of the city and the brothels and we think he brings in illegal immigrants. A lot of them are girls for his brothels. He's an odious man but very powerful and violent with it."

"All right, so he is the local 'Mr Big'. How does this impact on my parents' death?"

"Wayne Osman is one of his enforcers and your mother was the main witness against him, Scilacci can't risk Osman getting a long sentence. He needs Osman outside where he can keep an eye on him. There's always the chance if Osman is convicted, that he may turn on his boss and try and do a deal in exchange for a lighter sentence."

"This sounds more like Chicago in the 1930s not Manchester. Where does Kinkaid fit in?"

"I think he has been feeding information through to Scilacci. We've raided his brothels and drug houses and they always know we're coming. He might let us find a minor dealer or something but we never find any of the heavy stuff. I got to know one of the girls and she told me she'd seen Scilacci meeting a man they know is a cop, she described Kinkaid to a tee. Short for a copper, blond hair and always very well dressed, Scilacci called him Mick and they seemed to be the best of mates."

"Have you tried telling anyone you know, in your job?"

"I put a confidential report in but it never even got acknowledged and I think it might have been intercepted. He's got someone covering for him. And there's more, he's already saying the fire was probably just some local toe rag who attacked your parents' house, that's because round here the local culture is very anti-police and they all think of her as a grass. He says there's no conspiracy, just one brain-dead idiot taking the law into his own hands."

Buchan slouched forward for a moment and then straightening up said, "If the police won't find who killed my mother and father then I will. It might not always be legal doing it my way but whoever's behind it is going to suffer."

"Don't tell me about what you're going to do, I don't want to know but think about it, do you have the sort of skills, equipment and backup you'll need to even start investigating on your own?"

"I served in Northern Ireland, Iraq and Afghanistan in army intelligence for the last twenty-two years, I know how to find the information I need and I know how to present it in a file of evidence. To settle your nerves, I'm going to try the legal route. I'll send video and sound recordings of the Scilacci's gang breaking the law, I'll send it direct to the Chief Constable. If that doesn't work, I'll have to think again."

"While you're staying legal, I'll be happy to point you in the right direction. It's about time Scilacci got sorted but, if you decide to take the other route, leave me out, I won't want to know."

"I can understand and respect that but I'll tell you now, I will track down whoever killed my parents."

*

Walking away from the meeting Buchan hoped he had not disclosed too much to Maria Ross. She was obviously an astute detective and he did not want to scare her off by even hinting about a violent response. He would, as promised, stay legal while he gathered evidence of the crimes of the Scilacci gang and also, as promised, forward it to the Chief Constable. What he would not do is tell Maria of his intentions if that approach failed. In that event he would arm himself. He knew how to use his army skills and cause chaos amongst the Scilaccis and their friends. He not only knew how to use weapons but also knew exactly where he could obtain them illegally.

Kerry Blazer

All twelve screens on the west wall of her flat on Blackfriars Street showed similar and unfortunately familiar scenes. Most of the images, although grainy, were still clear enough to show the depressingly bleak scenes. Drab, grey rooms haunted by seedy men and needy girls. Kerry hit return and the screens changed to views of Sparkle Street at the junction with Chapeltown, an area known to the locals as the Jane Austen gobble zone, so called because £10 would buy the said service.

On the corner two men were involved in an illicit deal. She zoomed in. Three clear packets of a tacky brown substance, almost certainly heroin. Kerry froze the image and opened the facial recognition software on her Lenovo Thinkpad laptop. In less than twenty seconds she had a name, Peter Chivers, a nasty piece of work known to the criminal community as Nine Cube. She flipped the Thinkpad to a split screen view and hit the Liaison icon. As she thought, the facial recognition matched a hit at Lena's Massage parlour.

Kerry had no idea whether this meant anything but if her knowledge of computers had

taught her anything it was that coincidences are usually the result of something that was not a coincidence. She saved the images as a thumbnail in a file buried deep within another file each containing over five thousand documents, which themselves consisted of more than fifty thousand thumbnails.

She swapped to a second laptop, a Voodoo Envy and inputted the name Peter Chivers. The only hit was a deleted Facebook account. Bypassing the security hurdles she quickly transferred any posts he had ever been involved with. She did not expect to find anything significant but had long since discovered any information can open up into as yet unknown opportunities.

She typed the name again and hit Amazon. It asked for username, password and security number. Within a minute Kerry had opened the PayPal account belonging to Peter Chivers. The account was linked to Lloyds bank. She opened another screen which was bright red and had hundreds of tiny black **X**'s filling the top half of the screen, that to an untrained eye all looked the same. She clicked the 9th **X** on the fourth row and a black horse galloped from the **X** and exited the screen right. As the horse left the screen a new one popped up, filled with lists of names. Quickly scrolling down them, she slowed down at the Chivers, coming to rest on Peter Chivers. A double click and his current account details filled the screen.

Kerry opened up the latest statement scanning any deposits that might lead her back to the massage parlour. She then trawled the history but found nothing linking Chivers but unfortunately for Peter, Kerry held a lifelong hatred of drugs and the people who pedalled them. The account had a balance of £12,688.22. One click reduced this to £88.22 The money quickly passed through dozens of offshore accounts before it ended up as an anonymous donation to the Just Say No charity.

*

The screens were back showing images from Lena's 'lazy relaxation' rooms. Lazy was quite an apt term. In the two years that Kerry had been observing this and five similar premises across inner Manchester, she had never seen a cleaner. She could almost smell the sweat and strains of stale semen emanating from the waste bins brimming with used condoms. Kerry had hacked the CCTV at the premises more than two years ago, after Suzy Bute, an old school friend had confessed to her how she now made a living. Suzy now owned her own beauty salon on Deansgate, still unaware how the money that got her started had arrived in her account.

Every so often a face would pop up who was known to Kerry. It was one of the few perks of the job. On one occasion she had recognised her old maths tutor, Mr Cundy, a man she despised. A girl young enough to be his granddaughter had been performing a sexual act on him. Two days later plain brown envelopes containing the sordid images had arrived at the Cundy household and the office of St Abigail's Academy. Kerry never attempted to extort money, the knowledge of exposure was more than enough.

The screen in the bottom corner showed a man getting dressed after finishing his fulfilment. Kerry was about to flip screens again when the bottom corner blurred into action. Even observing second hand, it was brutal. The savageness taking Kerry by surprise. The woman ended up cowering on the floor next to the wall sink where the man was washing his hands, the terror burnt on her face. He turned to the door giving

Kerry her first view of the man's face. She would not be requiring the facial recognition software. The man in the picture blew a kiss to the girl. It was Dominic Scilacci, owner of this and at least five more similar establishments across Manchester.

Kerry was keenly aware that hacking into Scilacci's accounts would achieve nothing. The real money was securely hidden in faceless accounts that as yet she had been unable to infiltrate. Scilacci obviously had his own 'black hat' assisting him in his manoeuvres along the information highway. It would not be easy to gain access through the multiple electronic gates and firetraps but Kerry had always fancied being a highway woman and she would not even require a mask...

Scilacci

Dominic Scilacci was in a bad mood. He scowled at his reflection in the bathroom mirror, a very bad mood. He had woken up early to find a text telling him that two of his 'girls' had tried to make a run for it after being forced to work into the early hours. They had been at a small, seedy hotel Scilacci used for his illicit business, situated on the edge of Stretford. Their minders had been busy doing a drug deal, for their own financial benefit, giving the girls an opportunity to take off.

Of course, worn out from at least ten hours of submitting to the whim of customers, they had not got any further than the car park. He grinned to himself as he imagined his minders dragging them by the hair back to the car, slapping them about their faces and threatening to scar them for life if they shouted for help. Slim had been on duty, he was particularly good at making threats, and carrying them out if necessary. Scilacci was in a bad mood because this sort of incident had a habit of making the other girls restless.

Stupid bitches, why didn't they realise they did not stand a chance? With his connections their complaints would not make it past the front desk even if they did make it to a police station. He made it clear to them, they had no paperwork, no identity. Having entered the UK illegally the authorities would not be lenient. They would be locked up and the key thrown away.

It was not as if any of them had been living a good life from wherever they came. His touts on the continent had instructions to procure vulnerable girls, or boys, desperate to get out of their situation, looking for a better life. It suited him not to have parents looking for their offspring. Even better was when they were in on the deal. Idiots, did they really think 'better lives' were handed out on a plate?

Although the incident had been dealt with he knew that news of it would spread through his premises like wild-fire, creating unrest. This he could do without, especially as he had just lost one of his top earners, Cutie Suzy. She was not one of his foreign imports but it was still a mystery how she had managed to convince someone to put money upfront to set up her own beauty salon. Enquiries as to who it was had proved fruitless. He had decided to let it go but it still niggled him, the deal had been done right under his nose, without him even suspecting.

after reading the text, he had got up and vented some frustration in his home gym. Twenty minutes hard rowing and ten minutes with his weights. Not being particularly tall in stature, he had become focused on body-building in his teens. Now in his forties, he still took it seriously. He flexed his right arm making his bicep pop up. Rock hard, ready to throw a punch if required. In his business he always had to be ready. He checked himself in the mirror, his clean-shaven face had sculpted features, the receding black hair flecked with a few strands of grey. The chilling glint in his brown eyes determined it was time to make his presence felt.

He was grateful that his younger sister, Francesca, was not at all squeamish when it came to keeping the girls in tow. He flinched now as he remembered some of her methods but he had to admit, they were effective. Possibly she had inherited her sadistic streak from their father, he was a mean bastard, especially after a heavy drinking bout. His mother had been a small, timid woman. She had not coped well with the climate change from Southern Italy to Glasgow and died when Fran was only five years old. Then they moved to Manchester and, with a twelve year age gap, he had not been around much as she grew up. His father had drunk himself to an early grave. 'Good riddance 'Scilacci had thought at the time.

*

Today he would need a driver, most of his properties were in obscure places with no parking facilities and he intended to make a day of it. He had called his number one henchman, Chunky, whilst in the gym. By the time he had finished his protein enriched breakfast, Chunky had the latest top-range Mercedes waiting for him on the drive. Half an hour later they had left the green pleasantness of Cheshire and were heading into the less pretty metropolis of Manchester.

"Which one first, boss?" asked Chunky.

"We'll keep away from the hotel in case any nosey neighbours were on the lookout last night. We'll start at Sheffield Street. Half an hour should do it."

As he got out of the Mercedes, the front door of the small terraced house opened. He strode in and looked into the kitchen. Two girls were spreading thin jam on toast. They froze at the sight of Scilacci.

"Where's Walt?" Scilacci asked.

They both flicked their eyes upwards. Scilacci always had at least one minder on the premises. Walt was upstairs making sure the girls were getting ready for work. Scilacci found him seated on a stool in the bathroom watching a young, blonde Hungarian girl, barely out of puberty, drying herself. Walt, a middle-aged gay man, looked inoffensive enough but had a short temper and vicious mean streak if any of the girls tried to get the better of him. Scilacci indicated for him to leave the bathroom and plonked himself on the stool. The girl, Jazmin, tried to cover herself with the threadbare towel. Scilacci grabbed it and flicked it across her back leaving a wide, red welt. She winced and held her breath, bracing herself for more. Scilacci laughed.

"Not this time, you can get dressed and make me a coffee." Jazmin grabbed her clothes and ran downstairs.

Scilacci barged into one of the bedrooms. The two girls in there stood rigid. One girl was partly dressed in a short, black skirt and pink bra, the other girl wore a tight-fitting, gold lurex dress. She had been applying foundation make-up to a bruise just below her left eye.

"Get that covered up," Scilacci ordered, pointing to the bruise. He left the room and returned to the kitchen. Jazmin had managed to put on a pair of denim shorts and a red, lacy top while the kettle boiled.

"Sit down," said Scilacci nodding to a chair next to his. She sat down, her body trembling, eyes downcast. Scilacci put his hand under her chin and pushed her face upwards, roughly, so she had to look him in the eyes.

"Now that's better. You have nothing to fear if you do your job." He laughed, enjoying the power he had over these young girls.

"Mmm, nice cup of coffee," he said, smacking the girl hard on her bare right thigh, leaving another red welt. She winced, fighting hard to hold back tears.

"You're learning fast, bitch," Scilacci called out as he opened the front door. Walt shut it and locked it after him. Chunky was already waiting outside, the engine running.

*

A run down end-of-terrace house in the city centre was next. The minder let him in after hastily gathering up evidence of a Mexican takeaway. The smell, however, still lingered. Scilacci glowered at him. This was the house where the failed runaways were living. All was quiet upstairs. Scilacci went to check. He thrust the bedroom door open noticing the body shapes on the bed stiffen as he went inside. Even in the gloom, he noticed spots of

blood on the girls 'clothing strewn across the floor.

"Sluts," he shouted, "get this mess cleaned up." Considering they knew now not to mess with him, he went back downstairs and called Chunky to say he was ready to move on.

"It's your job to see all the girls are ready to start work at one o'clock. Customers will be waiting at the hotel. So get moving now!" Scilacci barked at the minder. "Otherwise there will be consequences."

*

Two houses in the Chapeltown area were visited with Scilacci throwing his weight around sufficiently for the girls to know he was boss. Next was a two bed-roomed apartment where four Romanian girls had just been brought in. He had no appetite now to take part in the 'settling in 'period as he liked to call it. That was a 'perk 'he could use to his advantage. He did, however, still want ultimate control.

One of them was not a looker, a disfigurement made her mouth lop-sided. He wondered how the hell she had got picked up. To cover his costs he would have use her, at least for now. There were always bathrooms to scour, kitchens to scrub, bed sheets to wash. One of his cleaning sluts was due to be replaced. She did not seem to know one end of a mop from the other and had not grasped the idea that bins needed emptying. Time for an 'accidental 'overdose to be arranged, Slim was good at that too.

"We'll finish at Lena's," he told Chunky, you can have a bit of a breather for an hour.

"Thanks boss," Chunky replied. Having to keep alcohol and drug free on a driving day was a bit of a strain but a flutter on the horses would make up for it. He knew there was a

Ladbrokes on the next street with a couple of parking spaces outside. One of them would soon become available when they spotted whose Mercedes was outside.

Scilacci entered the so called 'massage parlour 'with a swagger in his step. A few of his more experienced girls worked here, girls who knew the business, girls who knew how to please a man and did not pass out with the first pang of pain. The sound of music and conversation greeted his ears, evidence that customers were on the premises. A mousy-haired woman, in her early thirties but looked ten years older, sat at a work-top in the kitchen. She got up when Scilacci entered, handing him the appointment book. Her left arm hung loosely by her side evidence of an M and S session going badly wrong a while back. He had kept her on though, thought Scilacci, who said he didn't have a heart? He glanced at the book relieved to see that business was good. His accounts had been showing profits were down for the last two months.

Scilacci could hear raucous laughter and a high-pitched squeal from upstairs. The walls in these cheap properties were so thin there was no chance of real privacy. He had to take whatever was available when it came to renting premises, never paying more than a month's rent in advance. Sometimes a property had to be vacated immediately.

Three girls sat in the lounge area wearing tight, provocative 'work-gear'. Their make-up was thick enough to cover stress lines and wrinkles caused by drugs and working for several years in this hellish profession. They all had long, sparkly earrings dangling from their multi-pierced ear lobes. The fake gems caught the light from two table lamps when the girls feigned laughter to the men's obscene jokes. A young, muscly Asian man and a grossly over-weight older white man sat amongst them drinking coffee from small cups. The older man's flabby hand was finding it difficult to hold the dainty handle of the cup and coffee spilt into his lap. The red-haired girl sitting next to him wiped it away with her hand, pressing into his groin as she did so.

"Time for your massage sir," she said, attempting a flirty, come-on wiggle in front of him. The sound of his wheezing as he went upstairs could not be ignored. Let's hope he doesn't have a heart attack thought Scilacci. It had happened before causing a lot of inconvenience and loss of two hours earnings while his men had collected the body and dumped it in a public place.

Heavy footsteps coming downstairs indicated it was time up for that customer. A few minutes later the Asian guy was led out by the buxom blonde, also attempting a seductive wiggle. This left a striking looking dark-skinned Nigerian girl, Mimi. Scilacci's interest was aroused, she looked like she could take a real man. She knew the score and led the way to the top floor, an attic room converted cheaply into what they called 'the penthouse'. Customers paid double rate for this room, it was the only one to contain a king-size bed, although it was actually just a mattress on the floor. A silky, gold cover had been thrown over it and several faux fur cushions. In one of the corners a stained wash basin was attached to the wall, an un-emptied bin positioned underneath, almost full of used condoms and body wipes.

Mimi took off her dress and lay on the bed, scrunching up the cover around her and patted one of the cushions. Scilacci wasted no time in removing his clothes. "Get rid of these," he said pulling at her matching white, lacy underwear. "No need to be coy."

With no further conversation, he pressed his heavy body on top of hers and immediately began pounding into her. She moved her arms to try and ease him away from her breast so that she could breathe. Scilacci stopped momentarily then pinned down her arms with his body. Grabbing her by the throat with his right hand he snarled, "You move when I say so, black bitch." Then he pounded harder and faster.

When he had finished and rolled to the side, it was obvious she was in pain. Blood trickled down her neck from the earring which had been pressed forcefully into her. Scilacci got up from the bed. Reaching over he grabbed a handful of Mimi's thick, black hair and pulled her across the mattress. He tried to get her to stand up so that he could look her in the eyes, show his power but she collapsed in a heap by the washbasin. Scilacci laughed at the terror in her eyes. He was satisfied, his bad mood gone. He washed his hands at the sink then left the room turning to blow her a kiss from the doorway, completely unaware his cruelty was being observed.

Annie Gray

Weeks on from the fire Annie walked along Hale Road, where still the smell of death hung in the air. She saw the charred remains of Mr and Mrs Buchan's house had been encircled with police tape, a constant reminder of the harrowing incident.

The community had striven to return to normality. Children in their uniforms walked to school, residents drove their cars to work, others caught buses and trains. The local shops opened for business and shoppers joined the queue at the post office, where stilted conversation was made about the degradation caused by the criminals infesting the streets like feral rats. The public feeling was one of hopelessness.

There was evidence, however, of a slight relief to feelings in the outpouring of sympathy and appreciation for the Buchans' community service. A dishevelled carpet of floral tributes, made pale and lifeless by wind and rain, lay next to the remnants of the building that once had been the home of the endearing couple. Annie read some of the messages written on cards attached to the bouquets. "Rosemary, John, you were beacons of light in our dark, troubled days", said one. "Your devotion to social justice will always be remembered", declared another.

Annie made notes of the messages before carrying out a Vox pop on the current situation. She approached residents as they went about their business and asked how the rise in crime was affecting their lives. Consensus of opinion was they were heartily sick of the ferocious feuds between drug dealers, who were targeting vulnerable young people, and the soul destroying aftermath of crimes committed to feed a self-harming habit.

An elderly woman said she was afraid to go out after a certain time and a young mother pushing a pram commented she had stopped taking her children to the park because of the used needles littering the playground and the intimidating youths hanging around in groups.

Annie bumped into Robbie George, who she had spoken to on the night of the fire. He agreed to talk but again on the understanding his name and address would not be published for fear of reprisals. With a knitted brow above staring eyes and a clenched jaw he blurted out, "Crimes are committed under the noses of the police yet they do sod all about it. They are all mouth and no trousers. Yes, they have stepped up their presence with a few more plods patrolling the streets but I'm not holding my breath."

Wearily he added, "We don't give a monkeys if junkies go round shooting each other but when it affects ordinary law-abiding citizens, it's a different matter."

Annie felt Robbie had a lot more to say but was feeling nervous so she handed him her card in case he later wanted to add to his comments.

The ordinary law-abiding citizens he referred to were the Buchans, who after a police and fire investigation, were said to have died as the result of arson.

Annie had covered the story when she attended the inquest, where the coroner had reported that investigating fire officers had found evidence of flammable substances around the front door and the hall of Mr and Mrs Buchan's house.

*

Immediately she had left the coroners court Annie had telephoned Manchester Police Media Relations Office and spoken to Will Bush, who Annie had contacted on many previous occasions.

He had praised her for being quick off the mark, so while things were going her way she had ventured, "Now that arson has been established does this mean an investigation into murder is under way?" She had guessed the information would not yet have been divulged, which Will Bush had confirmed. He had then politely asked Annie if she would repeat in the Star the police appeal for information regarding the shooting that had previously taken place in Stretford. In a questioning tone she had asked, "Is there a connection between the fire and the shooting then?"

There had been a pause before he replied, "We are widening our investigations and would appreciate your cooperation as usual."

"Take that as read, officer Bush," said Annie, who had then asked, "You will let me know as soon as there is anything available for publication won't you?"

"Take that as read, Annie," he had replied. She had noted his sardonic snub.

*

Following the in depth stories on the shooting, the fire and the coroner's report of arson, news about Stretford had dried up. Annie was certain there was a lot more to be had and, with this in mind, she had convinced her editor the Vox pop would be a good idea. It had made half a page in the tabloid and Annie had been given a credible byline.

Days after the Vox pop had appeared in the Star Annie was pleasantly surprised to hear from Robbie George, who said, "We're re-opening the Multi Faith Lunch Club at Hope Church and I wondered if you could give us some good publicity for a change?" He went on to explain, "Rosemary Buchan was the founder of the club, which closed down after she died, not only as a mark of respect but because she was the main organiser."

There was more positive news when Robbie told Annie he had stepped in as a volunteer to help run the club. "That's great," said Annie, who made a date for her and a photographer to go along to the re-opening.

"There is something else," Robbie nervously said. "I'd like to talk to you about another matter but not over the phone, so can we meet up?" She was intrigued and tingled in anticipation about what it could be that Robbie was unable to say over the telephone. She arranged to meet him on the following day at Hope Church.

*

In the church kitchen over a cup of coffee Annie was given all the details regarding the re-opening of the club. She could see Robbie was finding it difficult to say what it was that Annie was dying to hear. She sat quietly and watched as he diligently folded and put away in a drawer a pile of clean tea towels. In a sudden move, which suggested to Annie that he had finally come to a decision, he turned to face her and said he had something to say that must be off the record. Annie gave her word that anything said off the record would stay that way.

Patiently she waited for Robbie to unload. He began to fidget and shuffle from one foot to the other. Not wanting to disturb the mood and risk Robbie changing his mind about opening up, Annie remained silent. Eventually and in a hushed tone, Robbie revealed, "Rosemary confided to me that she was a police witness to the Stretford shooting. I had to swear not to say a word about it to anyone, which I haven't until now." Looking Annie in the eye, he added, "Now do you understand why you can't mention my name?" Warmly squeezing his shoulder Annie reassured him of her trust.

*

Returning to the office she tapped out the story about the future re-opening of the Stretford lunch club and zapped it to the editor in time for it to be inserted in the next edition of the newspaper. Annie then set about digging out the articles the Star had on Wayne Osman and found that his appeal for bail had been rejected because the court felt there was a high risk of witness interference.

Valeria

Valeria looked at the calendar. Tomorrow she would be sixteen. Tambula, the small village near Balti in Moldova, no longer seemed big enough. She felt sure there was a wider world waiting for her. It had been two years since her mother had vanished. Presumably she had fled the violence that defined her marriage. Her two elder brothers had disappeared soon after leaving only Valeria and her drunken father.

She ran a finger gently along her bruised ribs. The broken chair leg that had caused the injuries still lay on the threadbare rug in front of the fireplace. As she stroked she thought of the suffering her mother and brothers had endured. She understood that the beatings had eventually driven them away but she would never forgive them for leaving her behind.

Initially she had thought things would improve when she left school to work at a local farm but the full horror had not even started. Her father had then tried to make their relationship sexual. Once she had dreaded her father's drinking, knowing the beatings that usually followed but now his drinking was her ally. It left him incapable, an alcoholic shield against unwanted advances.

Her wages from the farm only served to fund her father's drinking. She was unsure if the farmer suspected anything but he continued to give her extra cheese, milk and eggs on top of the small wage. Once, to her delight, the farmer had tentatively suggested that perhaps it would be easier if she were to come to live on the farm. His wife had looked at him very strangely and beckoned him into the kitchen. They had returned within minutes to say they had decided the current arrangement was best after all.

A passport lay on the kitchen table.

"Pick it up!" Her father's malicious dark eyes challenged her.

To her amazement she heard him saying she was free to go. She grasped the table as a wave of dizziness and suspicion took hold of her. How could she believe him? She stood there speechless as he continued to inform her that he had paid the fare and she would be leaving for England tomorrow. She waited to hear what her side of the bargain would be but when nothing more was said she went silently to her room. After stuffing the few possessions she owned into an old cloth bag she lay down. She could not sleep. Her mind was racing. She did not consider herself religious but now felt the urge to pray.

*

In the morning her suspicions remained as she accompanied her father to the local bus station. Seeing a group of young people standing next to a silver Ford Transit minibus gave her hope. She watched as her father hurried over to a middle aged woman waiting in the doorway. He returned with documents bearing her name. While she checked the papers, her father surreptitiously stuffed a wad of Lei notes into his pocket. Valeria would never know how glad he was that she had repelled his advances. A virgin was worth so much more.

It was unbelievable that he was allowing her to leave and even more so that he had paid her fare. She pinched herself to make sure she was not dreaming. As she climbed into the bus she noticed her father had disappeared without saying goodbye. As soon as they were all on board the bus drove away. Some of the passengers started a conversation but the woman who had spoken to her father at the bus station was driving and told them to shut up, she needed to concentrate. The man in the front passenger seat turned and glared threateningly but said nothing. Suddenly Valeria was reminded of a creature from a book her brothers used to read to her. Capcaun was an ogre who kidnapped children and had always terrified her.

After a little while she found herself yawning, nodding off and unable to keep her eyes open. It was warm in the bus and the hum of the engine lulled her into a deep sleep. When she awoke they had crossed the border into Romania and had stopped in a place called Vatra-dornei for lunch. The woman explained that they would be given pizza and beer and she would pay the bill but they would have no time to talk. Just eat, drink, use the facilities and get back on the bus. The pizza was excellent but Valeria who hated alcohol gave her drink to the young boy sitting next to her. As they returned to the bus the woman driver threw the keys to the man Valeria now thought of as 'Capcaun' saying it was his turn to take the wheel.

*

Back on the road she studied the driver in the mirror and felt a frisson of fear. He made Her feel very uneasy. She sat still not wanting to draw his attention and glanced sideways at the other passengers. The boy who had gratefully accepted her beer was not only asleep but looked like her father when he was paralytic from drinking too much. She could not remember how many times she had knelt by her father's inert body hoping to find he was not breathing. She was puzzled that all the other passengers were sleeping soundly and she herself was wide awake. She knew that alcohol could make you sleepy but they had only been given a small bottle of beer each.

Something was not right. Could the beer have been drugged and, if so, why? From what she had heard they were being taken to a language school because they needed to speak English proficiently if they were to work in England. No more had been said because the woman had told them to be quiet. Now they were all silent. She tried to quell the ominous thoughts buzzing around in her head. It is natural to be nervous she told herself and tried to imagine the wonderful new life she would have in England. Determined not to look at the man in the driver's seat she gazed out of the window.

As they approached a built-up area she caught sight of a sign on a bank saying Transylvania Beyond. This did nothing to soothe her nerves. Isn't Transylvania the home of Dracula? She remembered her brothers frightening her with stories of vampires. Next she spotted a clock showing 5pm. So, it must be four hours since lunch and they were all still asleep!

The bus drove into a square milling with people who were clearing away market stalls. The driver stopped and got out but none of the passengers stirred. Convinced now that they had been drugged and something sinister was going on, Valeria decided she had to escape. Not wanting to wake the woman who was snoring softly, she carefully slid the door open, tiptoed out and very gently closed it. Clutching her cloth bag she ran to one of the remaining market stalls and slipped under the table, her heart pounding.

She hoped the bus would leave before anyone missed her. She was hidden by the canvas skirt covering the front of the stall but she knew she had been spotted when she heard feet approaching. She felt she would burst from the effort of keeping completely still until the owner of the feet spoke.

"I saw you get out of that bus. Why are you hiding under there?"

Valeria gingerly peeped out. A tall, attractive young female smiled back at her.

"The bus has gone. It's safe to come out now." The girl took her hand and introduced herself.

"My name is Ramona."

*

Ramona was fascinated by Valeria's story. After hearing her plan to get away from Moldova and work in England Ramona invited Valeria to stay with her and her mother until she worked out what to do next. Both girls were surprised that, coming from different countries, they could understand each other. An instant bond forged between them and they quickly became good friends.

The poster in the job centre said JOBS IN ENGLAND and the small print underneath explained that anyone interested would do an intensive English course at a Language School in Manchester after which a job would be found for them. This made Valeria feel foolish. If she had stayed in the bus would she now be in England learning the language?

Ramona's mother listened to their plan to go to England together and offered to help financially. One week later she waved as they were driven away with their dreams and their passports and their luggage. The Ford Transit minibus parked outside the job centre convinced Valeria she had been wrong about the previous one. The vehicles obviously belong to the Language School and were used for picking up the students and taking them to Manchester. This time the drivers were an English man and his wife. They looked quite friendly. Every four hours or so they stopped for a toilet break, something to eat and drink and took turns at the wheel.

Their first stop was near a sign to Budapest. Four Hungarian girls joined the group making the numbers up to twelve, all female. Having learnt some English at school they decided to practise by introducing themselves to each other.

They all fell in love with Austria. On crossing the border it immediately struck Valeria how clean everywhere was and how good the roads were. The bus was comfortable. The roads took them through Germany before reaching the French border. It was dark as they drove through France and most of the girls were asleep by the time they reached the Eurotunnel. Their passports had been collected earlier by the woman who would show them en-bloc to the customs officer at Le Shuttle. Tomorrow they would wake up in England on their way to Manchester.

Today's journey seemed like a beautiful dream. She looked down at the papers she had been given. Even the name at the top seemed romantic. She tried rolling it around her mouth with her tongue, Scilacci...

Kerry Blazer

The battered transit van had arrived early. Two months early. Usually it would turn up every three to four months, loaded with its tragic cargo unaware of the hellish existence they would soon be facing. Kerry watched as the back doors were folded open and two of the terrified girls were forcefully wrenched out. Although hard to tell the age of the girls, some of them looked to have barely reached puberty.

In the early days of her CCTV vigil on Scilacci's Brothels, her naivety had led Kerry to make the mistake of contacting the police, believing that their integrity was beyond question and the girls would be saved from their fate worse than death. She quickly came to realise that money comfortably supersedes morals.

Kerry fired up the Voodoo Envy and opened up the file in a folder named World Foods. Buried deep in the file was the document Pastas. A long alphabetical list of pasta types filled the screen. She scrolled down the pasta types until reaching the Ss:

Sacchettini
Sacchettoni
Sagne'ncannulate
Sagnette
Scialatelli
Scilacci
Sedani
Spaghetti

She highlighted Scilacci then double right clicked on the mouse. She had discovered long ago that the reorientation of a computer mouse is a simple but effective way of wrong footing ninety nine percent of the population. An image of a bowl showing hundreds of flattened triangular pasta shapes filled the screen. Below the image was a resume of recipe ideas that used Scilacci pasta. Kerry let the cursor hover for ten seconds over one of hundreds of the tiny pasta parcels, it started to glow red before a screen opened to reveal the face of Dominic Scilacci.

The face Kerry had grown to hate filled the screen. She right clicked on the stud in his left ear and the file containing everything two years of surveillance had unearthed opened. The file was enormous, every business Scilacci had owned or had dealings with. Friends, acquaintances, colleagues. Bank accounts, club memberships, travel details, including destinations. Criminal connections, police files, arrest history.

The item interesting Kerry today was police contacts. She opened it up. All the officers on this list had links to Scilacci. But who if any were clean? Kerry switched to a split screen and began the laborious task of working through the names methodically.

Superintendent	Bruce Foxley
Det Sgt	Mark Havers
Chief Det Insp	Judith Rawls
Det Constable	Maria Ross
Det Insp	Mick Kinkaid
Det Cons	Terrence Cross
Det Insp	William Stanniforth

She started from the top. Bruce Foxley was fifty two years of age. No immediate overt signs of illicit gains. A typical five bedroomed house in the suburbs that his wage warranted. A wife of twenty seven years. Two adult children state school educated. The car on the drive was a twelve month old BMW. Nothing standing out.

Kerry decided to check the money. She hit return and the bright red screen appeared along with the black **X's**

Foxley banked with Nat West and Salford Building Society. He also possessed a decent shares portfolio. His current account with Nat West was showing £27,495.25. High but not especially excessive. She logged into his savings account with the Salford Building Society and immediately found herself on more fertile ground. Foxley was sitting on savings of £565,728.84. The large amount was not necessarily an indication of illegal activity but everything would have to be double and then triple checked.

Mark Havers was 27 years of age. Still single and not in a current relationship. He seemed to Kerry as an unlikely ally or confidante of Scilacci but still followed through on everything she had. The banking details revealed next to nothing, no significant deposits in the past two years, no steady trickle of money spread out over the year to try and avoid unwanted attention.

Kerry moved onto Judith Rawls. 42 years of age, marked down for promotion to Acting

Superintendent and a possible future Chief Constable. Once again there was nothing jumping out and Kerry was about to leave the page when something connected in her brain. It was regarding Rawls' education. St Abigail's Academy. Why did this resonate with her? And then it came back, Cundy her old maths teacher had, until recent events came to light, taught there. Did this mean anything? Kerry had to admit, it was thin but it was as yet the first hint of any anomaly. More than likely an insignificant coincidence but are they not usually the result of something not coincidental?

Kerry's probing was now beginning to enjoy more success. Next was Maria Ross 33 years of age. It was the schooling that once again bore fruit. Educated at Lower Salford Comprehensive School. Kerry did a quick scan of past alumni and hit gold. For three years Ross had shared a classroom with Francesca Scilacci, Dominic's younger sister. Kerry was tempted to ditch the rest of the list and concentrate on Ross and Rawls. But her instincts kicked in and diligently she carried on down the names carrying out the necessary checks...

Buchan

Buchan had had enough of waiting for the police to act. Maria Ross told him Mick Kinkaid is still telling all who would listen the fire was caused by a lone youth, probably drunk or drugged, who on the spur of the moment decided to scare the only witness to the shooting. His theory, in public at least, is that the offender, terrified at the thought of being convicted for murder, has gone to ground and told nobody about his actions.

There are no useful lines of enquiry but he said he will of course persevere.

He met with Maria Ross again, as usual in Starbucks.

"Maria, I've waited long enough, we both know the police investigation is going nowhere, how can it with the man in charge doing everything he can to obstruct it?"

Maria looked out of the window before turning towards him. She had tears in her dark eyes, "How do you think I feel? I'm supposed to be working with the investigation, I want to find out who killed your parents and I'll do everything in my power to do just that. You may not realise it but being family liaison officer doesn't mean I'm expected to just hold your hand and keep you up to date. I'm part of the investigation. I'm supposed to watch you and report back on your behaviour and whether I think you could be involved and pass on anything else that's useful to the team. For what it's worth I've given you a clean bill of health."

"Now we both know I had nothing to do with it, I'm going to go out and find the evidence that show your lot it was Scilacci and his gang."

Maria reached across the table enclosing his hand in both of hers, "I told you I would point you in the right direction and I will, next time we meet I'll have a list of places where you will be able to get the sort of proof you'll need."

*

Buchan knew he would be working virtually on his own from now on and in circumstances very different from when he had carried out surveillance in the Army. In Iraq he had been able to insert a camera inside or outside a suspect building and video would be sent direct from the camera to his senior officers via satellite. Here in

Manchester he would have to rely on basic military skills and equipment he would have to buy himself. First on the list was a good quality camera capable of operating in low light. He would also need to use camouflage clothing, which he fortunately still had in abundance from his time in the Army.

He carried out a google search for a suitable camera and, following the on-line recommendations he settled on a Nikon FX SLR DF camera together with a Nikon 55-300 lens which would enable him to record 4K Ultra High Definition stills and video. With further exploration of Google he was able to track down a dealer in Liverpool who had both items in stock, at a cost of over £5,000. He told the dealer he would be able to drive over the following morning and pay in cash.

Three days later after collecting the list from Maria Ross and familiarising himself with the camera he set out on his first evidence gathering operation.

*

He walked from the hotel to Rosswell Street, a road of red brick, terraced and semi-detached Edwardian houses. Maria's list showed that number 23, an extended semi-detached house, was being used as a brothel and that customers would arrive from midday until around midnight. Dressed in clothing that suited the area, jeans and a black hooded top, he walked slowly along the road looking for somewhere he could use to video and photograph those using the brothel and hopefully some of the people who managed and worked in it. He soon saw that number 28 was either unoccupied or with perhaps an elderly person living there on their own. Paint was peeling from the window frames and the windows had a thick layer of grime, overgrown shrubs and brambles had taken over the front garden. Rubbish was scattered along the frontage, Macdonald's debris, sweet wrappers and dog crap. He returned to number 28 in darkness and saw a faint light in an upstairs window, as he had thought earlier, it appeared likely a very elderly person lived in the house alone. He would return before dawn and observe from the overgrown garden.

He had spent the afternoon preparing himself. He would wear loose camouflage clothing and a loose-fitting camouflaged hat with strands of green string and sacking to break up the silhouette of his head and shoulders. He would also carry a camouflaged net to drape over his himself, a supply of water, sandwiches and an empty bottle to urinate in if necessary, plus of course a large plastic bag in case he had to pass solids. The camera would be in a dark backpack together with secateurs for trimming back obstructive growth.

He set out at 5am, walking openly as if he owned the town, the loose items were in his pockets. He arrived in Rosswell Street and, although in a highly built up area, it was in almost total darkness with just a few dim lights shining from doorways. He stood for a few minutes letting his eyes adjust and then walked quietly along the road. Seeing nobody nearby slipped into the garden of number 28. He dropped to the ground and listened, hearing nothing more than the rumble of distant traffic. Crawling forward through undergrowth, still wet from earlier rain, he eased himself under a large shrub and used the secateurs to cut back some of the growth and a vicious bramble that had already tried to gouge his eye. He could see the front door of number 23 at a reasonable angle and settled down to watch, observe and record the activity for the next twenty hours.

As dawn was breaking he saw the first signs of movement, people on their way to work walking past and cars, that had been parked overnight, starting up and driving away. There was no movement at number 23. From 8:00am children passed by, pushing, shoving examining their mobiles, senior pupils at first followed later by junior school children and parents.

He was unable to see into the house, either curtains or blinds filled all the front facing windows. Buchan was used to this. In Northern Ireland he had spent many hours watching the everyday activities of people in an area whilst staying hidden, observing and recording.

The overcast sky must have decided he was too comfortable and a steady drizzle started, saturating him and the foliage around him, he covered his camera with a plastic sheet and waited, not moving.

The rain ceased and more people appeared. One elderly woman stopped directly in front of him, looked up at the upstairs windows and waved before walking on. He sighed and sank deeper into the undergrowth. The occupant was obviously in the house and looking out from the window.

Then elderly dog walkers were next to appear. Most of them seemed to know each other and called greetings across the road. A white van drew up outside number 27, a parcel delivery, the gig economy in action. It was getting close to midday and he hoped to see some action soon.

The sky had now cleared and the sun put in an appearance waking up the flying insects, hover flies, a wasp and a couple of bees. Ants were marching back and forth a few feet in front of him.

Twelve fifteen and the first action at number 23, the door opened and a Mediterranean looking woman of about thirty walked to the edge of the road. She was wearing black jeans and a close-fitting black top. Her black hair was pulled back in a ponytail, she was smoking and looking up the road. Within a few minutes a mini-cab came crawling along the street and stopped near her, there was a brief conversation and two well-dressed Asian men got out and followed her into the house. Obviously the first customers of the day. Buchan recorded the whole incident.

More followed during the afternoon and as customers left Buchan caught glimpses of a tall heavily built man ushering them out of the door. He had the appearance of a body builder and had obviously been in the house all night or entered through a back entrance.

School children returning home and dog walkers began to appear again. One small terrier leapt onto the garden, cocked its leg and started sniffing round the shrubs. It soon detected the scent of Buchan, who lay flat facing the ground, praying. The dog was now pushing his nose into Buchan's face. He blew air straight into its eyes. The dog backed away barking, ran back to the edge of the road, turned and carried on barking, everybody was looking. Then Buchan heard a voice, "Come on Toby, you daft bugger, get over here." Then after a pause, "He must have seen a cat, he really hates cats."

Buchan breathed again and continued watching and recording. The trickle of men continued, mainly white, some Asian and a couple of blacks. Buchan felt sorry for the girls inside, they were being kept busy.

He was now longing for darkness to fall. His back was aching, his thighs felt numb from the contact with the cold ground and he wanted to move. His blood needed to circulate. If he were disturbed now he doubted he would be capable of running.

At last darkness fell and customers kept arriving, Buchan could still see them in the reduced light and his recording continued. The only light visible from the front of the house was a dim glow in the front entrance. At 8pm a large Mercedes stopped outside and a burly man in his late thirties or early forties stepped out. The front door was opened and the body builder and woman he had seen earlier walked out to greet him. The woman kissed him while the bodybuilder stood respectfully to one side.

Buchan wondered if this could be Scilacci. After an hour the Mercedes returned and the man walked from the house, turned and waved to the Mediterranean looking woman and left.

Business at number 23 tailed off after midnight and at 1:00am Buchan noted glimmers of light were visible in windows set in the roof and thought attic rooms were being used, possibly as bedrooms.

He eased himself out from the shrubs and brambles, ensured he had all his equipment and quietly hobbled away from the garden, feeling relief as blood and life returned to his legs. He made his way back to the hotel totally exhausted and texted Maria Ross for a meeting the following day. He fought off the urge to review the recordings, had a hot bath and crashed onto the bed.

*

He woke six hours later, Maria had replied, she would meet him as usual at Starbucks.

Maria grasped Buchan's arm as soon as he sat down." How did it go, did you get anything?"

"I got cold, wet, sore, scratched and a video of about forty or fifty men walking into the house. I think I may have also got Scilacci going in, we can't watch it here, let's just have a coffee and go to the library or somewhere."

"To hell with the coffee, let's go back to my flat. I want to see exactly what you've got, I'll even get you a coffee, come on."

They hurried away and were soon in Maria's flat drinking coffee and examining the footage on Maria's smart TV. Buchan had only operated the camera when there was activity at number 23. Maria was the first to comment.

"This is bloody good quality, I wish we had the same."

Buchan refrained from replying, knowing the military had much better.

They watched as the woman with the pony tail walked from number 23 and stood waiting at the edge of the road.

Maria gasped, "That's Francesca Scilacci, bloody Dominic's sister, she's an evil cow, worse than her brother, at least that's what that girl told me. Keep going let's see what else happens."

Maria again, "Where were you? This looks as if you're standing next to them all."

Buchan laughed, "Not standing, laying under a bush not daring to move and zooming in for close ups."

Maria smiled, moved closer, grasped his arm and leaned against him. They continued to watch as customers, Maria referred to them as punters, moved in and out of the house.

The recording moved on and as it showed the Mercedes approaching the house, Buchan nudged Maria, "You might find this next bit interesting."

"Bloody Scilacci, it is him. We've got him, his sister and that thug Aaron Melrose all in the picture together."

"What's the story with Melrose?"

"He's hired muscle but not thick, Scilacci brought him down from Scotland."

They watched through to the end of the recording.

Maria stared into his eyes, "If we, I mean the police, had had this years ago we could have finished Scilacci then. The question is, what are we going to do with it now?"

Buchan said, "I've been thinking about that and I think we should make a two-pronged attack. We can send one copy to the local Chief Superintendent and one to a journalist. The one I have in mind works for the Stretford Star, her name is Annie Gray. She's written a lot about the fire and she seems to know what she's talking about, I'll ring her from one of my burners."

They both stood up and Maria took a step forward, "I'm so excited we are actually doing something positive." She put her arms round him, stared into his eyes and pulled him towards her. "Now we can get the bastards and get the girls out of that brothel."

Buchan started to respond but Maria broke away, "Sorry about that, I just got a bit carried away."

Paul smiled, "Nothing to apologise for," and had the thought that he had rather enjoyed being cuddled by Maria Ross.

*

Buchan walked away from Maria's flat and found a quiet place to make the phone call to the Stretford Star.

He was put through to Annie Gray, he adopted the tone of an outraged local.

"Look Miss Gray, I'm sick of what's going on round here, so I've decided to do something about it. I've just posted a memory stick to you, it shows men going in and out of a brothel at 23 Rosswell Street. I'm sending another one to the police and I expect you to make sure they don't just put it in a drawer and forget it."

Annie asked him for his name and phone number but he refused to give it, saying he wanted to stay anonymous. He warned her he was using a burner phone, so she would not be able to trace him. He went on to say she could expect to receive more video of crimes being openly committed on the streets of Manchester in the near future. He finished by telling her he expected her to publish the evidence and hold the police to account if they did not take action.

He posted an identical memory stick to the local Chief Superintendent with a note saying the press already had a copy of what had been recorded. While waiting for the police and press to respond he would continue his evidence gathering by recording drug dealers at work.

Kerry Blazer

She watched expressionless as the scissors in the reflection she was facing struggled to keep pace with the real event happening on her scalp. This was her first professional visit to the 'Bute-iful' salon on Deansgate. Normally Kerry visited Percy Reeds on Great Portland Street London once every five weeks. The discretion, service and quality of cut there were unequalled, even at a three hundred miles round trip and £300 plus tip for a basic trim. But today was about more than a haircut.

Suzy was clearly expecting the question when it came.

"When did things start to change?"

She could see Suzy building herself up to reply. That life, that existence was in her past and she was reluctant to revisit it now, not even with Kerry. She would know better than anyone just how far the Scilacci tentacles could reach. Even after two years she probably still woke at night with terrible dreams all too real.

"Why now Suzy? After all that time, why the change?"

Before she came here Kerry had thought long and hard about involving Suzy, even though the involvement would be peripheral. But the CCTV images of the girls' faces as the realisation hit home just what they had come to had given her little choice.

"Have they never been in contact?" She asked realising that she had not followed Suzy's story at all once she was out of Scilacci's grip. "Not even protection?"

Suzy shook her head, "No. And that's how I want it to stay."

Kerry could see Suzy fighting back the tears of frustration as she picked up a hairdryer. Her sleeve rode up giving Kerry a glimpse of an angry red weal on her forearm, a reminder if Suzy needed one, of the brutality the Scilaccis were capable of. But she pressed on, "I just want to know, why did they swap from local girls to foreign dupes? Surely the hassle of trafficking and everything it involves would outweigh any financial benefits?"

"Control and compliance," Suzy shook her head, "As simple as that."

*

It came down to a choice between a pangolin and a turtle. She finally decided on the pangolin and then got to work finishing the artwork on the screen. She looked at the logo she had created it was as innocent as it gets. The armour plating on the beast representing security. The email screamed from the screen 'your money is safe with us.'

The sight of Suzy's livid scar had angered Kerry impelling her into a swift retaliation. Above the pangolin she typed Burley Financials before quickly deleting. It did not look or sound right. She tried again this time in bold print **WISLEY HOLDINGS** then underneath the title in twelve point font she added Global manpower solutions for the modern company.

*

The trap was now fully baited and all Kerry had to do was sit back and wait for the deadly combination of doubt, curiosity and greed to work their magic. She knew that they would get their expert to vet the missive and the purported company. But she had made certain that any such probe would lead them chasing ever expanding but never ending circles.

Valeria

Suddenly the Ford Transit was turning in different directions, first a left hand bend and then a right hand bend. This jolted Valeria awake and she looked sleepily out of the window to discover they were in Calais. She had never been to France before but she knew from her Geography lessons at school that Calais was a ferry port in Northern France and it was only a short distance across the sea to the English coast. She was confused. There was not a boat in sight. They had arrived at a large car park and joined a queue of other vehicles. When the queue moved forward they stopped at a kiosk. The English lady handed all the passports to the man in the kiosk who checked them and looked at the passengers. He then produced a piece of paper to hang in the front window of the minibus and waved the driver on. They were all wide awake now and curious as they drove into a tunnel and stopped. There were vehicles parked in front and behind them. None were moving. Luckily the tunnel was brightly lit or it would have been scary.

They were told to remain in their seats, they would soon be in England but if they needed to use the toilet they could do so. An illuminated sign showed where the facilities were. They could get out and walk there if necessary. They all remained in the bus waiting to see what would happen. About thirty minutes later when nothing had happened they heard engines starting up and the vehicles in front moved forward. At that point Valeria was amazed when she realised that they were driving out of a train. They were stopped by an official but after a brief conversation with the driver he allowed them to leave. Before they drove out onto the road the woman spoke to her husband who pulled over and waited while she removed some stickers from the headlights.

A mixture of excitement and apprehension made Valeria's stomach churn as they sped along the M25. She had never seen so many cars so close together on one road. It was made more frightening because they were all driving on the wrong side of the road. She took Ramona's hand in hers believing that she must be having the same thoughts. Closing her eyes, she forced herself to breathe deeply and remain calm.

*

Everyone was relieved when an hour and half later they pulled into a service station for a toilet break and a late breakfast. The woman accompanied them and paid for the food and drinks.

Back at the minibus they found the driver talking to a man in the next vehicle. It was an old, battered VW minibus with numerous dents and scratches. Apparently this would take them on the rest of their journey.

They were surprised when a woman jumped out from the front passenger's seat and told them in Romanian to collect their belongings. She also told them she would be accompanying them to Manchester and her name was Carmen. Valeria guessed she was about the same age as Ramona's mother but the lines around her mouth made her appear older. Her dyed black hair was too harsh for her colouring. One of her eyelids seemed to droop and the heavy make-up she wore emphasised rather than disguised the disfigurement.

As goodbyes were said Valeria saw a thick envelope being handed over in exchange for the passports She was sorry to see the English couple go but there was a look of relief on the man's face as he stuffed the envelope into his breast pocket.

Clinging onto her old cloth bag she climbed into the VW. It was not as spacious as the previous minibus, they would be more cramped. Ramona was already sitting on the back seat and was looking very pale. Valeria sat beside her and whispered. "Not long now."

Soon the speed and the boredom of the road lulled the girls to sleep until they were aware of the VW slowing down and then coming to a halt at a huge service area Valeria looked at the brightly lit buildings, the neat rows of parked cars.

"Is this the Language School?" she asked the driver.

"Language School?" He shrugged his shoulders and laughed towards Carmen.

"It's not far now," she said. "But we stop for toilets, stay close it'its busy and English people are not very nice if you get lost."

*

The dishevelled group of girls alighted onto the car park and followed Carmen to the toilets hardly noticing the shops full of 'must-haves'. Valeria thought the people looked friendly but the girls huddled together hardly speaking to each other as they lathered their hands with pink soap before washing them in the sparkling hand-basins.

Back in the minibus the driver hoisted a couple of brown boxes in the air "Pizza," he shouted. He took a huge slice then passed the boxes back for them all to help themselves. The aroma of melting cheese and hot dough filled the minibus. "Coca Cola," he shouted triumphantly and passed back ice cold cans of the brown nectar. Valeria smiled encouragingly at Ramona as she passed her a can. It seemed so long ago now since they had said goodbye to Ramona's mother, Adriana, as they drove off in the Ford transit. She thought for a moment and realised it was probably only twenty four hours ago.

Stuffed with pizza and coke, Valeria dozed again until she felt the minibus filter off the motorway onto smaller roads. These roads were more like the ones she was used to in Moldova although these were lit by street lights. After ten minutes or so they came to a halt again. Valeria reached across Ramona to clear the steamed up window with her hand. She could see they had parked outside a tall building with lots of windows and a main door. Lights were on in some of the rooms but curtains and blinds were drawn so tight she could not see inside.

"Wake up Romana," she said," I think we're there!"

At the front of the minibus, Carmen was reading a text message. Turning round to face the girls, she nodded to the four Hungarian girls to get off, which they did warily.

"Is this the Language School?" asked Valeria.

"Not yet," laughed the driver. Valeria did not understand why he found any mention of the language school so amusing.

By the time they reached the main front door, it was open. Valeria could see a woman inside dressed in tight-fitting jeans and a multi-coloured low-neck top. She was wearing more makeup than Valeria had ever seen on a face before. The girls and their meagre belongings were ushered in quickly then the door slammed shut, no words of greeting, no goodbyes. Carmen returned to the minibus, took out her phone and began texting.

*

The next stop was in front of a house. Valeria switched places with Ramona so she could get a better look. There was a small path to the front door, several bins seemed to be in the way as Carmen escorted three of the Romanian girls into the house. Again, no exchange of greetings. Almost the same scenario was repeated at another house a few streets away. This time Valeria saw a blind at an upstairs window move and a girl's face peeped through. Five of the Romanian girls were quickly dispersed inside the house before they drove off again.

Several streets later, they stopped in front of, what appeared to be, an older narrow house with several floors. Carmen indicated that Valeria, Ramona and the remaining Romanian girl Alina, should follow her into the house.

Valeria's first impression was of an overpowering smell of perfume, cigarettes and other smells she was not familiar with. Carmen pointed to the narrow staircase and gave an upward wave. On the first landing one of the doors was open, Ramona and Alina were shown in. Valeria felt other people were on that floor but there were no signs of them. Carmen indicated that Valeria should climb the next flight of stairs. When she started to protest and tried to follow Ramona, Carmen grabbed hold of her arm and pushed her upwards. On the next landing, Carmen opened a battered looking door and pushed Valeria inside a small room.

There was barely space for a single bed and a bedside table on which sat a small lamp emitting a dim yellow light. Under the tiny window was a lop-sided cane chair.

"Where is the Language School?" asked Valeria nervously, Carmen's aggressive behaviour had taken her by surprise.

"Language School." Carmen almost spat spitefully. "You have cost my employer, Scillaci, a lot of money to get you here, the passport, the transport, food and drinks." She nodded towards some cheap toiletries on the bedside table and flimsy nightwear on the bed. "Your things, you have to pay for everything."

"But I don't have any money," said Valeria, " How do I pay for them?"

"You work for them" snapped back Carmen, "like I had to."

"Work? What do I do?" asked Valeria

"Oh believe me, a pretty girl like you will have plenty of work." She nodded towards the nightwear on the bed. "Get changed and I will see that your clothes are washed. Come, I'll take you to the bathroom."

She accompanied Valeria back down the stairs and showed her a small bathroom. From her pocket she produced a wrapped toothbrush and a small tube of toothpaste which she handed to Valeria. "Put your clothes into the plastic bag and leave them there." Valeria was allowed to close the door but aware that Carmen was listening.

She was as quick as she could be and stood on the empty landing. "Ramona," she called out softly, "are you OK?"

Carmen rushed out from a room. "Shush," she said. "They are asleep, you will see them tomorrow." She indicated the stairs again and followed Valeria into her room. "Manchester can be a very dangerous city. The door will be locked to keep you safe."

Valeria heard the key turning, then all was quiet. Weariness took over as she sat on the edge of the bed surveying the tightly shut blinds, the chipped bedside table, her bag unopened on the chair. She felt the thin, floral duvet cover beneath her. She had always wanted a flowery bed-cover but not here, not like this. Her body started to shake at the realisation that she had escaped from one violent situation only to be landed in another. But this was worse, she was in a foreign country, locked in, her passport taken from her. Curling herself into as small a shape as she could, she lay on top of the bed cover, the silent tears started to fall and within seconds the thin pillow was soaked through.

Carmen

Carmen handed toothbrushes and toothpaste to Ramona and Alina before allowing them five minutes each in the bathroom. Then, giving them the same reason that it was for their safety, she locked the door and went downstairs. She pushed the door of a small sitting room open, there was barely room for an imitation black leather settee, two matching chairs and a tiled coffee table holding two large ash-trays. At least they had been emptied but the table had not been wiped, stray ash and rings from beer bottles were evidence that business had been conducted there.

As soon as she sat down on the settee, weariness set in but her instructions had been to send word as soon as all twelve girls were delivered and under lock and key. Scilacci's henchman, Slim, was the contact number on her phone. She cringed as she texted her 'mission accomplished' message. With weeping sores on his hands and face from years of drug use, Slimy was the name the girls secretly used. Slim replied quickly to her text message, almost as if he were sitting waiting for it. Carmen's instructions were to stay up and wait for him.

Carmen knew that both men would be particularly interested in the stunning girl from Moldova on the top floor. She had already blanked out any feelings of guilt, there was no place for sentimentality in Scilacci's world. It was survival of the fittest. She had discovered that in her first few weeks here, almost ten years ago. Then, she was the beauty on the top floor, bringing in much cash to Scilacci, barely seeing any of it herself. Now she looked almost twice her age, she knew, men did not want to pay for her services. But Scilacci used her in another way, to recruit new victims, always that elusive carrot that he would release her passport and she could return home to Romania. Her father had not long to live, hard work and poverty had taken its toll. If it were not for the money she and her sister managed to send him, he would have died long ago. Her mother, her dear mother hobbling to church every day to pray for her daughter's return.

Carmen gently touched her drooping eye-lid. She knew it was suicide to force the issue with Scilacci but she also prayed she would be accompanying her sister, Madelina, on the return journey soon. She was sure Madelina's marriage to the English guy was not by chance, and it certainly was not the happiest partnership but it did mean she was spared from the humiliation of working in a brothel. For now, she had to content herself with the knowledge that they had been paid in dollars for their part in the transportation.

It was quiet upstairs, she knew it would be quiet, even if the girls had not used the toothpaste impregnated with the drugs, they would have used the soap, also impregnated. Carmen dozed on the settee for an hour or so then woke when she heard a faint tap on the door.

Carmen opened the door to Slim and the two girls from the house who had been working that night. Both girls, teenagers, looked tired. Their skin already had an unhealthy pallor about it, their eyes semi-glazed. Maybe they had been given a fix after their night of adding to Scilacci's wealth.

Carmen was struggling not to be dependent on drugs since the new role she was being used in. She did not need to be transcended into oblivion to make her unaware of the men she was serving, their lack of hygiene, hideous bodies, all shapes and sizes. But with no chance of attending a clinic to enlist on a rehabilitation programme it was an uphill battle and one she did not know if she would win. Scilacci did, at least, not force the drug issue now. He already had complete power over her, why would he waste money on drugs?

Slim pushed the ashtrays aside, set his wares on the tiled coffee table and prepared syringes for the girls upstairs. Carmen led the way into Ramona and Alina's room. Both girls lay peacefully on their beds, as well they might after several days of travelling. Carmen held one of Ramona's arms steady while Slim injected the heroin. The procedure was repeated on Alina. Slim put the used needles into a bag and they both left the room without a second glance at the girls. Carmen locked the door and they headed upstairs to Valeria's room. Carmen held an arm ready but before Slim injected, he lifted her nightwear to have a good look at her body, nodding approvingly.

The front door was locked and bolted after Slim had done the dirty work ordered by Scilacci. Carmen was relieved to collapse in her room next to Valeria's. It was not much bigger but she had acquired a few furnishings to make it look a little cosier. It was 3:00am, she worked out she could have five hours sleep.

She was awoken by someone calling out, someone vomiting violently? Carmen hurried downstairs and unlocked the door to Ramona and Alina's room. Alina sat huddled and shaking on her bed. Staring ahead, she knew she should do something but her body just would not function. Her eyes were partly glazed over. Ramona was lying very still, vomit had soaked her nightwear and seemed to be still spilling out of her mouth onto the pillow. The stench made Carmen heave but she had seen this before and knew she had to act fast to avoid reprisals from Scilacci.

Banging fiercely on the door of the two girls who had returned earlier, she ordered them to take Alina into their room as Ramona needed to be taken to hospital. There was, of course, no way Carmen would be summoning an ambulance, instead she called Slim and told him to get over here, quick. None of Scilacci's girls ever go to hospital, well not for treatment. Slim was back in less than 10 minutes. A muscular guy, face almost covered up with a hoodie, accompanied him. Ramona was carried downstairs, slumped unceremoniously over his shoulder. Carmen had managed to take off the soiled clothing, wipe her face and wrap a sheet round her. It was just beginning to get light so the men wasted no time outside in bundling her into the boot of the car they arrived in. Within seconds they had driven off.

Carmen collected a laundry basket and cleaning materials from the kitchen before trudging wearily upstairs. She now had the job of cleaning up the evidence that a young Romanian girl spent her first and last night in the city of Manchester, in that room.

Francesca Scilacci

She always found the whole sacrament process harrowing. It was always cold in the church and she tugged at her trouser legs that had ridden up as she knelt down. She could sense the the waves of disapproval seeping through the ornamental lattice work into her side of the stall.

"Forgive me Father for I have sinned." As usual the words do not come easy to Francesca. But it is something that she has come to regard as a useful tool, on any day when a batch of new arrivals were expected. Her motto was get your penitence in beforehand. Nothing wrong with getting the Lord on your side so to speak.

She heard the priest, Father O'Callaghan sigh. Her identity should be an unknown factor but he knew who she was and he would know what was coming. He would also know only too well on which side his bread was buttered. So he would give Francesca the succour she craved. And he was certainly savvy enough not to seek out any answers to the questions that buzzed around like mad flies in his head whenever she paid a visit to his confessional booth.

"What do wish to tell me my child?" He asked with a heavy heart.

"I will be welcoming some friends from across the sea later today Father and however careful and considerate I try to be, at times things can still have a tendency to become unpleasant. I am sure you understand my predicament."

The priest she knew would be cringing and wringing his hands as he stewed in a dilemma of his own device. He was in no position to deny Francesca, not with the evidence Dom and Kinkaid held on his sordid secret one to one sessions with some of the more vulnerable young boys in the choir of St Mary's.

"Ten Hail Mary's."

Francesca smiled. She pulled back the curtain and left the booth. She walked up the aisle without looking back she knew the ten crisp fifty pound notes would already be out of sight under Father O'Callaghan's cassock.

*

Francesca looked keenly at the twelve photographs lying on her desk. The passports had been delivered late last night by Chunky her brother's closest henchman. One image was standing out clearly from the rest. She checked the name, Valeria, she liked the feel of the word and rolled it around her mouth letting it come to rest against her front teeth in a satisfying bump.

Francesca felt this girl was good enough to drop straight into Lena's on Sparkle Street. Their showpiece brothel deserved only the best that Eastern Europe could offer. Of course before that could happen, the girl would require to learn some obedience, which of course she would, once the procedure had been carried out. Instinctively she glanced across at the open fire and saw the steel poker glowing red, right up the shaft, almost reaching the glass handle.

*

The girl's eyes had the glazed over, the dead look, peculiar to people new to enforced heroin addiction. Sometimes the instant drug dependency may have been enough but Francesca always applied a belt and braces approach to be entirely certain of a girl's continued loyalty. Even Dominic had been known to wince sometimes at her primitive methods but Francesca knew that he could not argue with the results.

"Come in Valeria, come and warm your bones by the fire. You've had a long journey and this coupled with your weakness has left you confused. Here in England we like our girls to be happy in their work but sometimes the clash of our different lifestyles can be misleading, and acts kindness can be easily mistaken for cruelty."

The girl was shaking now. An unpleasant mixture of withdrawal symptoms and fear. Francesca turned to her smiling. "Roll up your sleeves, Valeria it is rare to see such a lovely skin tone at this time of year." She watched as the girl tentatively exposed her forearms. The screams that followed, as the air in the room filled with a malign tinge of burnt flesh, would not elicit any sympathy to her situation. Francesca looked again, the girl had passed out but she now knew that any resistance had now been snuffed out by the hot steel signature.......

*

The email had worried her. Dominic never conducted any of this side of the business online. Of course the legitimate stuff was there for anyone to paw over. This however was a crude attempt at phishing. It purported to be from Wisley Holdings and was an invitation for the chance to invest in the facilitation of a global work pool that could provide short term labour solutions without the red tape of employment law getting in the way.

Something was nagging at the edges of her awareness. She had been on edge following the death of one of the new girls, Ramona. The girl had suffered an adverse reaction to the intense heroin programme. Of course she would never be found. She had joined a group of unfortunate still-births in the general hospital incinerator. This email and the subject heading was too close to home. She would have to get Techo, Dominic's computer whizz to check it out…

*

Techo was unusually quiet. Normally he would accompany the whirring of his fingers with constant chitter-chatter. Today nothing. He was not even responding to Francesca's prompts for updates.

Finally he looked up shaking his head.

"I can't de-steam the vapour trail."

Francesca knew Techno meant the electronic path that all interactions online left behind. This was not just unusual for Tech, it was unheard of.

"It must lead somewhere?" She screamed, her latent aggression never far below the surface.

"It leads somewhere alright. All the way back to your inbox." He shook his head again. "In ten years at this game I have never come across it before. Someone is very serious indeed about shaking your tree. Of course you could always consider investing in Wisley Holdings. The money trail would give us the opportunity to flush them out…"

*

After discussing the rogue email with Dominic, who thought she was overreacting, they had hatched a plan. They agreed to invest a hundred thousand pounds in Wisley Holdings, which Techo transferred immediately. They also showed an interest in using the global work pool their money would help to finance.

Techo had replied to the original email from his duplicate computer, assuring Francesca it would be impossible for the recipient to know that this was the case. He also reassured her that the money was completely safe and would never leave her account. The response was instant. The laptop pinging the arrival of the incoming email. Techo opened it remotely. It looked innocent a simple thank you message and an attachment waiting at the bottom.

"Well? Do we open it?" Francesca was eager. Techo signalled for calm by patting the air. His fingers once more became a blur over the keyboard before he clicked it open. The attachment box immediately started to glow red before vanishing, this was quickly followed by the missive itself. "What's happened?" She shouted, panicked by the blank inbox...

Kerry Blazer

They call it liquid concussion. Two yellow labelled bottles of it stood on Kerry's kitchen unit. Rohypnol. Next to it was a roll of tape, two burner phones, night vision binoculars, a canvas drawstring bag holding a change of clothes, a black Lycra ski mask, a rolled up nylon ladder and a hard leather case. It was time. Kerry was ready to strip off the veneer and crank up the tension a notch on Dominic Scilacci. She picked up the kit and dialled for a cab using one of the burner phones. She then destroyed it, giving it two pings in the microwave just to make sure.

She left her flat on Blackfriars Street and walked along Market Street before turning onto Corporation Street. Once there the Arndale Centre stood before her. The taxi arrived at the front of the main entrance two minutes later. A conservatively dressed young lady smiling as she climbed into the back of the cab thanked the driver for holding the door open and settled down for the fifty minute journey.

Scilacci lived in leafy Cheshire, an old manor house that sits in seclusion on the outskirts of civilisation protected on all sides by a ten feet high brick wall. Kerry was in a small copse over three hundred yards from the main drive, looking through night vision binoculars. She had compromised the alarm system in the first month of her CCTV vigil.

The property would hold no unwanted surprises. It was not Kerry's first visit. The layout firmly burnt as an imprint in her mind. She had even stayed over when the Scilacci family were on vacation in Florida. Her target tonight, Millie Scilacci, a poisonous brat that could do no wrong in the eyes of her father, occupied a large south facing bedroom filled with the latest technology. Tonight she would be having a visitor.

Kerry watched as the electronic gates slid smoothly open. The BMW 6 series surged out onto the road, quickly eating up the tarmac. The gates eased shut immediately behind. Kerry, now dressed all in black, gave it fifteen minutes then approached the perimeter walls from a small water meadow at the rear of the property. She checked her mobile signal, five bars. She retrieved the small hard leather case from inside her coat and took out a small rectangular block. It had a yellow label with a logo of black batwings, underneath was the legend Kill Wings. The device was no more than six inches in length and three inches wide. It had eight plastic coated antenna sprouting out of the top giving it a range of two hundred and fifty yards. It was not infallible but should be ample for tonight's operation. She flicked it on and a small red light began squinting at her in the darkness, she looked back at the burner phone screen again and smiled, it showed no signal bars.

A house this size carried with it the corresponding security. The nylon ladder had made brief work of the perimeter wall, now came the tricky part. The methods she would normally use on suburban doors was the traditional flexible friend. But her American Express card would not be any use here. There were at least four deadbolts and it would take far too long to be picking locks of this strength tonight. Kerry switched off the Kill Wings and took out her iPhone, the signal bars reappeared. She clicked on the Let's Get Talking icon.

*

Millie Scilacci picked up her phone as the text message bleeped in. She scowled as she read it. It was from her father informing her that he had forgotten to tell her that Janine would be calling in the next fifteen minutes to drop off some urgent paperwork, so be sure to have the front door unlocked ready.

Cursing to herself as she went downstairs she disarmed the alarm and deactivated the locks. As the last deadbolt clicked home the door exploded in Millie's face. The shock quickly gave way to terror. An intruder wearing a full ski mask was on her instantly. She felt a sharp jab in her arm and then the world became fuzzy. The last thing she remembered was her head hitting every step as she was dragged back upstairs…….

Valeria

Valeria awoke with a start. She lay very still in the darkness waiting to hear the sound of her father stumbling through the door drunk but all she heard was the gentle snoring of the girl in the next room. And then she remembered. She had escaped from her unhappy life in Moldova and been transported to a new world which was a hundred times more miserable. How could she have been so stupid? Her dream of living and working in England had turned into a nightmare. She rubbed her eyes in an attempt to clear her foggy brain. How long had she been here? The days had blurred into each other. She could not remember. Was she losing her memory? She tried to picture her mother's face. It had become more difficult over the years since she had walked out of their lives.

The face of her mother quickly faded and was replaced by a dear, familiar little face. Bright blue eyes and rosy red lips framed by long blond hair which was really strands of yellow wool. Strange that the face of her old rag doll should be clearer than that of the woman she had called Mama. She had loved that doll more than anything in the world. It was the only present she had received on her fourth birthday given to her by an old neighbour who loved children but had never had any of her own. She had named her beloved doll Patsy and had shared all her secrets with her. How she wished

Patsy were here with her now to comfort her.

What had happened to Patsy? Her last memory was of her two older brothers throwing the poor doll backwards and forwards to each other while she screamed and cried "Give me back my doll." Like their father, they had always enjoyed teasing her and making her cry. She had cried when they left and that was partly because she would miss them but mostly because she would have to look after the drunken good for nothing that was their father. She had lost her mother, she had lost her brothers, she had lost her doll and she had lost her best friend Ramona. She had no idea where any of them were and wondered if it could be all her fault.

Ramona must have escaped but how could she? The doors were always locked and the keys were never visible. She had tried herself to open the windows but it was not possible. It may be a house but it felt more like a prison. 'Worse than a prison ' she thought as the cotton sheet brushed against her arm causing the angry burn to sting.

Ramona had been a wonderful friend, just like the sister she never had. It was incredible that she would have deserted her. They had done everything together until they had arrived here and been forced into different rooms.

Before going back to sleep Valeria silently said a prayer, "Please God give me the strength to find Ramona and escape from this place."

Scarlett

It was a thirty minute drive from the International Casino near Warrington. Lee was her regular taxi driver and so Scarlett settled down in the back seat of the taxi knowing she was in safe hands. The world always felt a better place after one of her girls' nights out, as she liked to call them. Friendships had to be bought nowadays, all of her former friends had deserted her and visits to her family in North Wales had become rare events. Two or three times a week Lee drove her to the International, the Grosvenor at Chester or a family run casino she particularly enjoyed visiting on the Wirral. Never, ever the casinos in Manchester, she preferred to keep out of her husband's domain. She had learnt never to ask about his businesses or where the money came from, she just concentrated on spending it.

Champagne flowed constantly in these establishments and she had got into the habit of never refusing a glass. Her dependency on alcohol had been a gradual addiction over the years of her marriage. She knew Dom did not approve, it reminded him too much of how it had increased his father's violence. Sadly Dom also had a violent streak. Although he had never laid a finger on her or their daughter, she had witnessed it several times. Dom was a dangerous man if he did not get his own way. She had considered divorce but had to accept it was not an option. Dom would never let her live freely in the big, wide world, she knew too much, her life would be in danger.

At the beginning of their relationship he had loved her, she was sure of that. She had been a personal trainer at the David Lloyd gym in Chester. Her toned, slim body and gorgeous red hair had attracted many admiring glances from the men as they pounded away on the fitness machines. But Dom had been more persistent, impressing her with meals in top-class restaurants, flashy cars, expensive gifts. He called her his 'fiery Welsh dragon'. People around him seemed to treat him with respect and so, when she became pregnant with Millie, marriage seemed the right thing to do. Scarlett Scilacci. It had an exotic sound to it. The name had rolled off her tongue.

After the birth of Millie, she saw Dom in a different light. It did not take her long to see it was not respect his employees showed towards him, it was fear. There was no way she would be a working wife, he also had a jealous streak and expected ultimate control over her. She had to settle for being 'Mrs. Scilacci' but she made sure she would not get pregnant again.

*

It was almost 1.00 am when the taxi drew up outside the Scilacci residence. Being one of their trusted drivers, Lee had the code to open the imposing, ironwork gates which in turn switched on security lights. The taxi scrunched along the gravel drive and stopped directly in front of the wide, paved porch area. Although he was paid on account, she stuffed two £50 notes into his hand. It had been a good night on the gambling tables.

With Smart key ready to deactivate the latest hi-tec security system, she opened the front door. The new system had taken out the worry of tapping in wrong numbers and cause alarms and floodlights to go off. Fortunately there were not any neighbours near to disturb but it was an inconvenience she could do without.

"Good night, Mrs Scilacci," called out Lee. She did not turn round to acknowledge, she had to concentrate on getting to the front door without falling flat on her face. Safely inside she shut the door and walked across the spacious hallway to the kitchen. The house was large enough to get lost in. Separate bedrooms, separate bathrooms, separate lives when it suited them.

Coffee was what she needed she thought. Ignoring the latest deluxe espresso machine standing prominently on the counter, she filled the kettle and took out a jar of instant. Slumped over the counter as she waited for it to boil, she looked and felt every bit of her forty one years. Tomorrow she would make her weekly visit to the beauty parlour. The pampering and attention she received there always lifted her spirits. Another pleasurable distraction was her personal masseur who visited her here, at the house. Remembering his last visit brought a coy smile to her face.

The kettle had switched off making the house unusually silent. Millie must be asleep upstairs she thought. She made her coffee, strong and black, no need to worry about caffeine keeping her awake tonight. Now she was aware of a tapping sound. She went to the front door and reset the security system making sure the bolts were across the door. Dom was always telling her there were bad people about. Well, he should know.

*

As she headed back to the kitchen she stumbled on the tiled floor and landed with a bump. Her hand touched something red and sticky. Blood, her blood? It would not be the first time. She checked herself over, relieved to find she was intact. Then she heard the tapping sound again and realised it was coming from upstairs. Looking up the gallery style staircase she saw a few spots of blood staining the light-oak woodwork.

"Millie, Millie," she called out as she struggled to get up from the hall floor. "Are you up there? Are you all right?" Straining her ears she could hear nothing.

Now more alert, she clambered upstairs as fast as she could, mostly on hands and knees. A few more drops of blood stained the cream coloured carpet on the landing in the direction of Millie's room. Scarlett switched on the light and let out a cry of anguish when she saw the back of Millie's head crudely bound with duct tape making her dark auburn hair stick out at angles. Her arms were behind her back tightly strapped to the desk chair. The chair had swivelled slightly off balance and Millie's leg was tapping against the leg of the desk.

All sign of drunkenness gone now, Scarlett ran over and began to gently remove the tape. "Oh my darling, my darling, my poor baby. Who did this to you? Tell me, where are you hurt?"

Millie did not answer, she appeared to be in a daze. Scarlett shook her slightly until her eyes opened. Immediately she began to shake with terror.

"It's me, it's Mum. Everything will be all right now my darling. I'm here to look after you."

She looked into Millie's bleary, blood-shot eyes, noticed her sweater pulled off on one side. "Did he try to....try to?" She could not say the word she feared. Millie shook her head, tears silently streaming down her face.

Scarlett could not loosen the straps binding Millie to the chair. Frantically she searched for some scissors in the huge bedroom. She could not believe it, all the latest technology devices and not a pair of scissors to be seen. She ran into her room then into the bathroom and snatched up her nail scissors then back to Millie to hack her way through the straps. Millie was now beginning to shake and sob uncontrollably.

"Keep still my darling, I'll soon have you free," she said, trying to keep a calmness in her voice. She helped Millie to the bed and began rubbing her arms to bring some circulation back into them. "Lie down, you must lie down and rest."

"It wasn't my fault, it wasn't my fault," Millie sobbed weakly before she passed out again.

"Of course it wasn't your fault. Nobody will say it was your fault."

Scarlett looked at Millie's tear-stained, pale face and saw that her whole body was trembling. There was a small cut on her forehead which needed attention and what looked like a needle puncture on her arm. Oh my God, she said to herself has she been drugged?

"Shush, my darling, you've had a huge shock and I must get some help. Lie down and try to rest."

Scilaccis do not usually invite the Police into their lives but this was an emergency. She ran downstairs to call 999 from her mobile, then she called their private doctor always willing to make a house call for an extortionate fee. Then she called Dom.

Buchan

The nightmare had returned, once again he had seen his mother's pleading eyes and heard her screams and now he lay in bed soaked in sweat. His left leg was twitching as if it had a life of its own. He knew what had caused it, it was the frustration of knowing that his observations and evidence gathering had achieved nothing. The Stretford Star had published stills of his recordings with the faces blurred and stridently demanded action. The police had taken action, but too late. By the time the brothel was raided the birds had flown. The police Chief Superintendent had passed the buck and blamed the Star for publishing before the police were ready to act. Following this the Star had not used any of his videos of drug dealers working openly in the area.

Buchan was back to square one, he swung his legs out of the bed and decided he would move on to phase two and take positive action. But first he would have to obtain some lethal, and highly illegal, firepower. He had heard rumours and thought he knew where he could obtain it.

*

By nine o'clock he was on the road heading south, M6, M5 and then main roads across Salisbury Plain and finally catching sight of Poole Harbour spread before him as he drove down into the town. He knew some of the SBS men he'd worked with in Iraq and Afghanistan would sooner or later wander into the Red Lion in Hamworthy, hopefully they would be able to point him in the right direction, he parked outside.

As soon as he walked into the pub he saw a familiar face, Barry Harrison, he looked as if he had left the service now and put on some weight. Buchan saw he was drinking alone and reading the Sun newspaper. He ordered two pints and placed one in front of Harrison, "Hello Bazza, fancy bumping into you, and here of all places."

Bazza picked up the pint and tasted it, he looked at Buchan with one eyebrow raised "Bloody hell Greenie what are you doing here? Don't try and tell me you just happened to wander in by chance."

Buchan smiled, Greenie was what the SBS and SAS troops used to call him, it was short for Green Slime, the army's nickname for members of the Intelligence Corps. They chatted for a few minutes, Harrison now worked delivering boats from along the south coast to wherever the owners wanted them taken. Buchan told Harrison about the murder of his parents, the lack of a police response and his determination to find out who killed them.

After commiserating Harrison looked Buchan directly in the eye, "Now tell me why are you really here, what is it you want? You know we'll do anything we can."

"I'm trying to get in touch with Wayne Dixon, do you know where I can find him?"

Wayne Dixon and two other marines had used their Special Boat skills to smuggle cigarettes and rich migrants into the UK and landing them in the small inlets along the South Coast. The three had been caught and only sentenced to one year in prison and were all out within six months. Buchan put the light sentences down to recognition of their service in war zones or perhaps it was to keep them quiet about some of the more dubious operations they had been involved with in the middle east.

"Dixon, he works on the dark side, he lost everything when he was in jail and knew he would never get work with any decent company, not being straight out of jail. He has his own business, if you can call it that, and I don't want my name being linked with his." He paused "I'm only doing this because I know you and what happened to your folks. Dixon's name's poison round here, officially that is, but I'm just suggesting you go into the Portsmouth Hoy on the quay any evening, you might find him there if he's in town."

Buchan knew the Portsmouth Hoy and walked into the bar at nine that night. Sure enough in a window seat was Wayne Dixon with two other men who had that indefinable, ex-service look about them.

He approached the three men, "Hello Dixie, I thought it was you when I walked in, it's been a while."

*

Dixon was typical of many special forces soldiers, not the big Jack Reacher types of fiction, but of moderate height and build and carrying with him an air of fitness, efficiency and confidence. His grey eyes carried out a cool appraisal, "Hello Greenie, I read about what happened to your folks, you must be gutted."

Buchan grimaced, "I am and that is why I'm here, can I have a word?"

Dixon jerked his head to indicate outside. They both walked out onto the quay and stared across the water at the millionaire gin palaces being constructed in the Sunseeker boatyard. A trickle of cars moved over the old lifting bridge to their right and couples walked by admiring boats they would never be able to afford.

"Right Greenie, I know you haven't come down here just to seek me out for old time's sake, what are you after?"

"I've heard rumours about your new line of business, if I heard wrong just tell me to bugger off and you won't see me again."

"You heard right, but I'm surprised, you never struck me as the type to step outside the law."

"I never expected to, but my parents were killed to stop my mother giving evidence against the same bastards who did it. They even have the detective who's investigating in their pocket. One way or another I'm going to make them pay."

"I take it you want firearms. These are the rules. When you've placed your order I want cash, small notes, no fifties. I'll want fifty per cent up front and the rest on delivery. When I have the deposit, I'll contact you on a secure phone and tell you where and when you can collect the goods. We'll use burner phones that are to be destroyed as soon as the deal is done. Next a bit of advice, if you do use any of the weapons, deep six them straight away, otherwise they're likely to come back and haunt you. Right what do you want?"

Buchan took a deep breath, "You seem well organised."

"I am and I'm not going back inside again, so what do you want?"

"Nine mil pistol, snub nose back up gun and if possible, a full automatic, a scorpion or something similar, plus a good supply of ammo."

Dixon laughed, "Bloody hell are you going to start a war? You really are going to make them pay aren't you, and I can't say I blame you. But your order presents me with a bit of a problem. I can get you a full automatic but I'm taking a chance and if you start an all-out shooting war up north, the law will pull out all the stops. If you're going to do that I have to make sure you're not in a position to lead them back to me."

"I've had the same training as you, I know how to keep my mouth shut."

"I know that, but I need to be sure and you've come along at exactly the right time to help me out of a hole. The police, the coast guards and customs all know me and my mates faces too well and they've spread our mug shots all along the south coast. I've got a job that'll make me a lot of money. If you help me out with it I'll get you what you want at a very special price. Are you in?"

Buchan knew where Dixon was coming from. If Buchan did what Dixon wanted he would be involved in the crime and would be in no position to tell the police or anyone else anything. He thought for a moment, "What's the job?"

Dixon smiled, knowing the message had been received and understood.

"I want you to hire a fast rigid inflatable and pick up a rich Iranian and his family from a ship in mid channel. I'll work on the details while you see about hiring the boat. Still interested?"

"I'm interested, but I want to get my hands on the guns as soon as I can? When do you want it done?"

"It will obviously be a night time job and it will be next week, probably Tuesday or

Wednesday. I'll give you the when and where when I know. It will be up to you to hire a RIB in your own name, the boatyard will want ID, details of your experience and a damage deposit. Can you handle that? You'll get more than enough off the price for the guns to cover it."

Dixon handed Buchan a mobile phone, "Use this to contact me, my number's already in it. Any questions?"

"If I'm hiring a boat I'll need to know how many I'm picking up."

"It'll be three adults, four children and possibly some luggage. As I said, these people are wealthy Iranians, I think they've upset the regime, so they'll have no problem getting asylum. Not like the poor buggers who try to row over the channel."

"What do you think I'll need?"

"Get charts for the Solent and a GPS. Arrange the boat so you have a couple of nights to practice night navigation and boat handling in good time. I'll meet up with you when I have full timing and location details."

Buchan needed to know more, "Yes but we'll need a meet and have a full briefing close to the night. I don't want to be left with a boatful of illegals and not knowing where to land them. I'll want them out and away before anyone sees them or the boat."

*

As Buchan walked away he knew he was risking everything. The boat hire company would have his full ID and bank details. If the police got their hands on the boat he would have no hiding place and go to prison for a long time.

His next job was to arrange the boat hire. He googled RIB boat hire and found that Solent Boat Hire in Southampton had a DNS Rigid Inflatable Boat able to carry up to twelve passengers. The RIB was fitted with a powerful 250 horse power Suzuki outboard engine. It seemed perfect for the task in hand. He contacted the company by phone and arranged to visit the boatyard the following morning.

When he arrived at Solent Boat Hire he was directed to see the assistant manager, a tall fair haired man who again had that ex-military look about him. He introduced himself as David Macintosh. Buchan explained that his family would be travelling down to the south coast on Saturday and he wanted to surprise them by hiring a boat for the week, it was the children's half term holiday.

Mackintosh questioned him closely about his experience and seemed interested when he said he had used RIBs when in the services. Mackintoshes face broke into a smile, "In the services, what were you in?"

"I was in the Intelligence Corp." He knew all too well what would follow.

"Intelligence Corp, I thought all you lot drove was a desk, a desk well away from any fighting."

Buchan was not offended, he knew it was no more than standard service banter, "Don't tell me, I bet you're one of the web footed lot from Poole, I did some ops with them."

Macintosh looked at him with new respect and, as is usual with ex-servicemen, they swapped names of those they knew. Buchan was careful not to mention Wayne Dixon.

Having established a rapport, Macintosh took Buchan out into Southampton Water and watched as he demonstrated that he could be trusted to use the boat. Buchan produced his identification, paid for five days hire in advance, including a £1000 damage deposit and the two men parted with a friendly handshake. Buchan would pick up the RIB at ten on Saturday morning.

Francesca Scilacci

Francesca dropped the handset back in its cradle her ears still throbbing. Unsurprisingly Dom was incandescent. The family had never been subjected to such a sustained attack before. She instinctively knew that these things were linked, the computer crap that they were experiencing and the lowlife attack on Millie. Her blood boiled at the thought of the terror the young girl would have gone through.

Techo had still failed to come up with anything substantial. It was incredible to believe anyone would dare to infiltrate their systems and in Dom's case his home. According to Dom the CCTV had given them absolutely nothing. Kinkaid was also proving to be worse than useless.

Why had nothing shown on the CCTV? The system had not been disconnected and if the police forensic team were to be believed, not tampered with either. She picked up her iPhone and hit Techo's name. He answered almost immediately.

"Well?"

Techo took his time. "I think we're asking the wrong questions. We need to come at this from a different angle."

Francesca waited. Unlike her brother she knew the value of silence when the occasion required it.

"The police checked the perimeter wall's CCTV and found nothing. Ditto the external and internal cameras at the house. But we know for a fact the outer wall and the house were breached. So we have to assume the system is hacked. We also know that Millie swears a text came in from Dom's cell. So again we must work on the theory that whoever is responsible has taken remote control of Dom's mobile.

"This leads us straight back to that WISLEY HOLDINGS email. Put the two together and there's your link. The message is crystal clear. This is all about the girls. Someone has a healthy hatred of the business we trade in."

"So what can we do about it?"

Techo looked at her in admiration. This woman never fell back on sentiment. She retained the steely glare and ice cool nerves that always come through to win in the end.

"Come on there must be something we can do."

And then Techo saw and heard sign of weakness in her last words. He did nothing to allay her fears with his reply. "What do we do? We start searching for the invisible man. That is what we do."

"Or invisible woman," she said raising a well tweezered eyebrow into a forbidding arch

Buchan

Buchan received his instructions on the Sunday morning in a WhatsApp message from Wayne Dixon. "Meet fishing boat at Open Sea Map ref 50.35 x 1.30 2200 Tuesday. Bring package to landing stage at OS ref 99.3 x 90.2. Use route to the south of the big island. Buchan shook his head, so much for the detailed briefing he wanted.

But, although brief, he had to admit the text told him everything he needed to know. He would meet a fishing boat at a point off the Isle of Wight and take the Iranian family to a landing stage in the Hamworthy area of Poole Harbour. Once he had collected the 'package 'and returned to the harbour he would use a discreet route to the south of Brownsea Island to reach the landing stage. At first Buchan thought Dixon was taking a chance by operating almost next door to the Special Forces camp. But then he thought again, Dixon was very well connected in the camp and would no doubt pay some of his old comrades to keep experienced eyes on the area for any police or customs movement close by.

Like all well trained military operators Buchan was a believer in repeated practice before an operation. First he drove to the landing stage and observed the lie of the land and was again surprised when he saw just how close it was to military craft that were moored inside a small floating harbour. There were others pulled up onto the hard standing that was separated with nothing more than a substantial fence from the public waterfront. There would obviously be armed guards on duty, all day every day. He shook his head reflecting, "Dixon must have half the camp on his pay role." The landing stage was an old wooden jetty about two hundred yards from the military fence.

*

Buchan had moored the RIB in the Poole Quay boat haven and made himself known to other boat users and the officials on the quay. He used the RIB several times a day and spoke of exploring the coast line down as far as Seaton. He practised the route from the harbour entrance and round the south of Brownsea Island in the dark. It was not difficult if he kept the speed down. He checked the tide chart and saw the tide would be at its highest point at exactly the right time, no doubt all part of the Dixon plan.

Buchan slept in late on Tuesday, there had been no further communication from Dixon so he had to assume all was well. He knew it would take under an hour to reach the pick-up point and started the Suzuki engine at 9pm and prepared to leave. He slowly left the sheltered haven before increasing his speed to get the RIB skimming across the surface of the water. There was a blustery wind blowing and he hoped and prayed it would not increase too much outside the harbour, the last thing he wanted was a difficult combination of wind and waves. Inside the enclosed harbour there was no movement of boats, they had all appeared to have been secured for the night. He knew the Cherbourg ferry would be arriving at about 11:00pm. If his timing was right he might be able to use it to shield him from the view of watchers on the populated shore.

He increased the speed as he reached the harbour mouth and spray was flying up from the bow and blowing over him. As he headed out to the open sea the height of the waves increased and more spray was being thrown up as the bow smashed into the oncoming waves. He could see the lights of Bournemouth to his left and the Needles Lighthouse ahead. He knew the course he needed and kept on it by constant glances at his compass. After forty minutes he switched on the GPS and saw a red dot on the coordinate he had programmed into the device. He adjusted his course and aimed for it and as he inched closer he started to scan the darkness for any sign of the fishing boat.

A light flashed ahead of him and he aimed for it hoping it was not the border control vessel that patrolled this coast. He saw a solid black shadow ahead and slowed down. It was the expected fishing boat. The skipper had thankfully positioned it facing into the oncoming waves and wind. Buchan prepared to come alongside, there was a three or four foot gap between the crest and trough of each wave, he knew it was going to be difficult and dangerous to transfer people who were untrained and unfit from the deck of the fishing boat into his RIB.

He positioned himself close alongside the fishing boat, it was rolling in the waves and the RIB was rising and falling as it crashed against the larger boat. A man on the upper deck threw a rope to him which Buchan attached to his craft. The RIB was jumping and bucking and spray was cascading over him.

On the deck Buchan could see a huddled group of people. A deckhand was waving them forward. As the first arrived he could see it was a small figure, obviously one of the children. The man held one arm and heaved the figure towards Buchan, he grabbed it and fell back into the RIB. He could see it was a girl of about twelve. She looked up at him with terror in her eyes. He signalled the deckhand to send the second one over and another girl was safely lowered into the RIB in the same manner. Buchan looked up and another smaller bundle was ready but this one was fighting and struggling in the deckhands arms. His grip slipped, and the child, a boy, fell into the sea with a cry.

Buchan never hesitated, he didn't even have to think, he threw himself into the sea after him. He hit the icy water and spitting out seawater looked round frantically. He could see the small figure rising and falling in the waves and being swept away from the boats. The boy was obviously wearing a life jacket but was still in danger of disappearing into the darkness or freezing to death. He struck out with powerful strokes keeping the him in view. Gradually he overhauled him, but the boy grabbed him round the head, while screaming. Buchan needed to calm him down. He ducked him under the water to shock him. As he surfaced shouted in his ear, "Relax, lay back I'll help you." The child must have understood and lay still, or more probably was terrified into silence.

Buchan tried towing him back towards the two tethered craft but was making no headway, in fact he was being swept further away. He could already feel the cold gnawing at his bones and knew the boy must be in a worse state. The fishing boat engine rumbled into life and moved towards him and the child. As the boats moved closer Buchan thanked God for a switched on skipper. When the Rib was manoeuvred to a position where he could reach it, he was able to grasp one of the rope handles and with a superhuman effort pushed the child into the boat. He hung on the side for a moment exhausted and then, assisted by a rising wave, hauled himself back into the boat.

*

He lay gasping for breath for a moment and then signalled for the next migrant to come forward. Three adults followed, two women who both fell screaming into the boat as they crossed over. The first one immediately took her coat off and wrapped the smallest child in it. Finally a bearded man clambered down and joined them. As soon as the man was in the RIB he grasped Buchan in his arms shouting, "Thank you, thank you." The women and weeping children clung together crying and laughing and cuddling each other at the same time.

Buchan pushed the man away and pointed to the seats signalling him to be seated and belted into the safety harness. He watched as suitcases were thrown from the deck into the RIB and when he was assured all passengers were in their seats and secure he cast the line off and headed for Poole Harbour.

The RIB was now running with the waves and wind and there was little spray entering the boat. Ahead of him he saw a huge ship that dwarfed his frail craft. It was showing hundreds of lights that lit up the night sky as it headed towards the harbour entrance. He increased his speed catching it and placed the RIB behind and to the left of the ship, this was obviously the Cherbourg ferry. As the ferry passed through the harbour entrance it took a course swinging right to stay in the main channel and Buchan veered left and aimed for the route to the south of Brownsea Island. He slowed down and followed the marker posts and continued round the island in total darkness. Before long he was clear of the island and on a course speeding over the water towards the landing stage at Hamworthy.

He knew this was when everything could go wrong, he would be caught, the migrants would not receive favourable treatment and he would go to jail instead of avenging his family. He anxiously scanned the dark shore he had already resolved to spin the RIB round and make a run for it if the police were waiting.

Even more slowly he approached the landing stage with the engine just ticking over, a light flashed, and he headed towards it, two men were waiting. As he eased alongside one grabbed the bow rope and pulled him close in.

"Let's have them all out, we'll see to the cases," the second man jumped lightly into the RIB and started hefting the cases onto the jetty.

The children were first to be passed up followed by the women, one of the women picked the boy up and held him closely. The bearded man approached Buchan and gripped his arm, "Sir, I must reward you, you have saved the life of my only son. I will pay money. I will give you anything, what is your wish?"

Buchan gently pulled the hand away from his arm, "You owe me nothing, I would do the same for any child. My reward is to see your son safe and well."

The man was crying, tears streaming down his cheeks and into his beard.

One of the men on the jetty was whispering urgently telling them to hurry and Buchan said, "You need to go, please go."

The bearded man shook his head, "No, I will reward you, please, please take this."

He removed a watch from his wrist and forced it into Buchan's hand. "I shall be offended if you try to return it."

Buchan nodded and the man climbed onto the jetty and in a minute the area was clear, there was nothing left but darkness and silence. Buchan pushed the watch into his pocket and thought nothing more of it.

*

When he returned to his hotel he stripped off his soaking clothing and stood for ten minutes in a steaming shower before crawling into his bed. He did not know if he was unconscious or asleep, but it was mid-morning before he came to.

As soon as he had a coffee in his hand he sent Dixon a text, "Job done, when can I collect my goods?"

He received an immediate response, "You did a good job, me and my client are well pleased, he told me he rewarded you for saving his son, you're a lucky man. I'll text you with an RV for the handover."

Buchan was puzzled, Dixon had forgotten to tell him how much extra cash he would need. Then he thought, 'Why am I a lucky man?" He picked up the watch. It was a gold Rolex Submariner and it looked genuine. He googled 'Gold Rolex Submariner 'and found an identical one.

He nearly dropped his phone, the watch he was holding was advertised for £23,000 and some change, and that was the second hand price. If he kept the watch would last him a lifetime and still be worth a fortune for any children he passed it on to. In a happier frame of mind he spent the rest of the day cleaning and tidying the RIB. It did not appear to have suffered any damage during its night time adventures.

*

Buchan decided to stay in Poole until he took delivery and two days later received a text message that consisted of a six-figure map reference and a time, 0600. He checked the local Ordnance Survey map and found the location to be a car park in the Wareham Forest. He knew the area, but not well.

Setting out as dawn was breaking the following morning, he drove to the Wareham forest and found the car park, it was empty. He waited and aware he was ten minutes early, got out of his car and looked around. On the far side of the road he could see heathland stretching into the shadows, behind him was unbroken pine forest, dark and brooding. The wind carried flurries of rain that only added to the gloom.

A voice spoke behind him, "Hello Greenie, what are you doing, waiting for a bus?"

Buchan had not heard him approach, "Bloody hell Dixie, you trying to give me a heart attack?"

Dixon laughed, "I've got the guns you wanted and the ammo. The pistol's an automatic, itis a Russian Makarov nine mil with two magazines. For a back-up I've got hold of a Beretta 3020, a thirty-two, lovely little hideaway gun I was tempted to keep it for myself. I've also got the Scorpion you wanted with two mags. If you don't use it, I'll be happy to buy it back. They've been used but they're all in good nick. Then there's 100 rounds of nine mil ammo and a dozen thirty twos for the Beretta. I've also been holding on to a couple of M75 grenades for a while and I don't dare let my usual clients get their hands on them. So I'll throw them in as well."

Buchan knew the M67 was a very powerful grenade that could be ignited using Wi-Fi or a mobile phone.

"Thanks Dixie, but if I need to use them you'll know I'm really in trouble. The down payment was me paying for the RIB, so how much else do I owe you?"

"Nothing else to pay, the client was more than generous and well impressed by you. If you find yourself at a loose end come and see me again, I can always use a man who can think for himself and be relied on."

Buchan shook his head, "Thanks, but I've got other plans."

Dixon shrugged, "Oh well I tried, best of luck and if you get to use any of those things, give them one for me."

They shook hands and Dixon faded silently into the darkness of the forest.

*

Buchan picked up the black holdall that Dixon had placed near his car and put it in the boot. He knew if he were stopped and searched he would spend at least ten years in jail. He drove carefully back to the hotel and parked. His next job was to return the RIB to Solent Boat Hire and leave Poole as soon as possible, every day the guns remained in his car increased his risk of exposure.

He took the RIB back to the owners and explained that he had been called away on business. He ordered a private hire taxi back to Poole and was ready to travel north. Buchan drove carefully away from Poole and returned, without stopping, to his flat in Market Drayton. He didn't want to get pulled over for speeding or anything else and was careful not to draw attention to himself by driving too cautiously.

He gave a sigh of relief as he closed his door behind him and emptied the contents of the holdall onto a table. As Dixon had promised the weapons were in a used well maintained condition and on first inspection, they all appeared to be in good working order.

Buchan muttered to himself, "If I get caught with this lot I'm definitely going down for life."

He knew he would have to find somewhere secure to store them, but for now they could stay at the flat.

*

He visited his local country sports shop and bought gun oil, a pull through and four by two for cleaning the guns. All the while he was thinking someone would challenge him, but this was a farming area and the staff barely looked at him.

That evening his mobile rang, it was Maria Ross.

"Hi Paul, I haven't seen you for a few days, have you been away?"

"Yes, I just wanted to get away for a while, I should have kept in touch."

"Not at all, that's my job, I do have some news for you, and I don't think you are going to like it. The Crown Prosecution Service have dropped the charges against Wayne Osman, they say the Judge would have to warn the Jury about the danger of relying on the evidence of a deceased witness because that witness can't be cross examined by the defence lawyers. They say it particularly applies in cases where the witness claims to recognise the defendant and the identification has never been tested. They also say we simply don't have enough other evidence, so, I'm sorry but that's their decision. I can let you have a copy of the advice we have had from them. The charge is being dropped and Osman will be released tomorrow morning."

"Thanks Maria, it's what I expected. I'll come back up tomorrow, perhaps we can meet, I'll read what the CPS have to say then."

"Yes of course, It'll be good to see you again."

Buchan hung up and hurled his phone onto the bed. Scilacci and company might have won this round, but they did not know about him and would did not know about him, but he would be in the shadows watching and pulling the strings, they would feel the force of his anger.

Annie Gray

In an effort to reduce her heavy workload, generated by the Stretford fire, Annie got to her desk at 8am, one hour earlier than her normal start time. She switched on her HP Pavilion and dropped into the inbox. At a glance she could tell which emails to discard. She was skilled in sniffing out the commercial pitches wanting free advertising against those with a real story to tell. Annie was not opposed to advertising in itself, her objection lay with companies making a pitch look like a story when in fact it was a veiled advertisement.

She had a grudging respect for the Star's advertising staff, knowing the newspaper could not exist without the revenue raised from its adverts. A rift occasionally existed, however, when advertisements encroached too much into editorial space.

Annie cruised through her emails and paused when a heading in bold type caught her eye. It stated, "PERVERT PROFITS FROM GIRLS TRICKED INTO PROSTITUTION." This drew her into the body of the email, which told her the sender had proof that a man known as Dominic Scilacci had invested in a company linked to human trafficking and the Star should check him out.

It said also that he was running immoral businesses using young girls as though they were pieces of meat. And, if Annie wanted to do something about it, she should go to the Aurora restaurant in The Avenue, which was frequented by Scilacci. The email went on to say that he could be recognised by his swarthy looks and the vulgar diamond stud he wore in one of his ears.

Annie carefully considered the email before replying, when she asked for more information and a contact number. Immediately she pressed the send button her mobile rang. There had been no time for Annie to say even "hello" before a cool, female voice announced,

"You don't know me. I sent the email regarding Scilacci. Please listen to what I have to say. Scilacci pays people to source vulnerable girls to use in his brothels. I can categorically tell you that he invested £100,000 in Wisley Holdings, believing it was linked to people trafficking. The company was set up to trap him and I'm asking you, a journalist, to *challenge him about the deal. He is a violent man, the dregs of Manchester's low life. His tyranny is touching the very people of Stretford that you say in your newspaper you are trying to help. Well Annie, here's your chance. Every bit of this information is true, what you do with it is up to you. Goodbye."*

*

At no point during the call had Annie been given the opportunity to speak. Stunned by the anonymous revelations she was at a loss to know what to think. She was certain, though, that her editor would not contemplate Annie getting involved with this man, especially as there was no concrete evidence of any wrong doing.

If the caller had proof of a crime, why was it that she herself had not done anything about it, wondered Annie. Unless she too was on the wrong side of the law and maybe had a grudge against this man. It all sounded a bit dodgy. Annie went back to her inbox but inexplicably there was no trace of the email and there was no evidence of the perplexing call on her iPhone.

She had scribbled the name Scilacci in her notebook and decided to check out the restaurant she knew was in Manchester's city centre. She realised the job would have to be done in her own time. Annie reckoned the restaurant was around fifteen minutes' drive from the Star's office and decided to check it out during her lunch break. She resolved to repeat the journey twice only and, if there had not been any action, she would forget about the whole idea.

*

Having managed to get through a decent amount of work Annie left the office at noon and got to the city in just under fifteen minutes. She parked her car in a multi storey car park and walked along The Avenue to the Aurora. She passed several metal tables and chairs that had been set out on the pavement in front of the restaurant and went inside.

The Aurora had a distinctive Italian feel. Wooden tables and chairs were surrounded by walls of wine and clear jars of pasta with decorative vines woven between them. Rustic baskets of eggs, tomatoes and mushrooms were displayed on tables near the entrance, giving an atmosphere of warmth and friendliness.

Most of the tables had been taken by office girls and boys, older couples, women who met for lunch and young mothers with babies in their pushchairs. Annie could tell by their chatter the mothers were from Eastern Europe.

Customers were being served by pretty, young waitresses with foreign accents. An older, serious looking woman supervised the waitresses from the business side of the counter, on which stood a notice stating that cash only would be accepted. Annie thought it quite strange to have an obviously lucrative, city business that would not accept credit cards. Her tendency to be suspicious led to her wondering if the restaurant could be a hub for money laundering.

She had a good look round and as far as she could tell there was no one fitting the description of the Scilacci she had in her mind's eye so she made her way to the outside seating area. There were no other customers taking advantage of the fine day, apart from a group of three heavily set, bruisers of men, who were deep in conversation. Annie could hear they also spoke with an Eastern European tongue.

One of the men wore a shirt that revealed some of his muscular chest and Annie noticed he had a thick, gold chain round his bulbous neck. Another boasted gold rings on his fingers, through which he wound a small row of beads on a chain. Not, thought Annie, the sort she would wish to meet on a dark night.

One of the waitresses eventually came outside and took Annie's order for a panini and a cappuccino, after which one of the men picked up his glass and sternly motioned to the waitress that he wanted a refill. She seemed to know him and nodded her head in acknowledgement. Annie did not think he looked like a regular customer and again wondered if there were some hidden, unhealthy aspects to the business.

She told herself to close her over active, sceptical mind and concentrate on the job in hand. She had not come to get embroiled in any more dubious goings on, especially as she did not have any proof, it was all just a feeling. However, she believed herself to be quite perceptive.

Annie was half way through her panini when one of the three men jumped up and held out his arms to greet a man who was walking towards them. The two hugged and jovially shook each other's shoulders in an act of camaraderie. Annie noticed the diamond stud in the ear of the newcomer and, if she needed further proof of who he was, he shook hands with the other two men at the table, one of whom called out his name, Scilacci.

Looking sharp in a grey, silk suit Scilacci gestured to a girl who was following him and introduced her to the men as his daughter, Millie. Two chairs were pulled from an adjacent table so that the five could sit together. The girl looked to be in her teens and was expensively dressed in a designer jacket and skin-tight jeans. She was quickly followed by a powerfully built man, who Scilacci told to sit at the table next to them and to get in some drinks. Annie guessed he must be a minder.

Trying to look casual, she occasionally glanced at the group and grew a little nervous. Annie had not thought through how she was going to approach Scilacci, not expecting to see him on her first visit. She pushed aside her half eaten lunch and walked into the restaurant.

She paid her bill then found the ladies toilet, where she put on some lip gloss, combed her hair and took several deep breaths before leaving. The heavy restaurant door slowly closed behind her as she approached Scilacci, who raised his head to look up at her. Simultaneously the "minder" threw his chair out of the way as he shot to his feet. He towered over Annie. She promptly thought of her father, who she had often heard say, "When you are in a tight corner, come out fighting".

She gathered herself together and stood as tall as her five feet two inches would allow and said, "Annie Gray, Stretford Star Mr Scilacci. It's come to our notice that you have an interest in a company called Wisley Holdings, which is believed to have links to people trafficking. Is it true?"

Scilacci banged his hands on the metal table as he leapt to his feet. His face was crimson with rage and Annie could see the white of his knuckles as he fought to keep his clenched fists down by his sides.

She wanted to run away but her leaden feet held her to the ground. The "minder" grabbed her arm and pulled her away from Scilacci before marching her from the restaurant. Scilacci called after him saying, "Drop the bitch. There's too many people around and I don't want any of this in front of Millie. We know who the hack is and what rag she works for. We'll deal with the slut later, then she will see firsthand what I have links to."

Annie ran to her car and made for home en route to the office so that she could recover from her ordeal. She was still shaking as she pulled up to the house. She opened the front door, fell into the hall and burst into tears.

Through her tears she loudly blamed herself for being so stupid and reckless to have challenged a man like Scilacci, and without a modicum of proof. Anything could have happened, she told herself, and no one from the office would have known. She was filled with remorse.

She calmed down after having a mug of coffee and pulled herself enough together to return to the office, where she reflected on her foolhardy assignment. Annie realised she had demeaned Scilacci in front of his friends and his daughter, which she was not sorry about. However, she may have opened a can of worms and made matters worse for herself. As she mulled over what had transpired Scilacci's threat rang in her ears.

Maria

"Damn." Maria also threw down her phone. She could hear the disappointment in his voice, did he think she had let him down? Telling him about Wayne Osman's release had been playing on her mind all day but she knew it had to be done. As his Family Liaison Officer it was her duty to keep him informed. She wanted so much to impress this man but was it purely from a professional point of view? Truthfully, she was not sure. Even in his immediate grief her heart had gone out to him. His brown flecked hazel eyes had looked so troubled. It had been a natural instinct to put her arm around him. As he had bent his head towards her she had so wanted to touch his neatly cut, dark hair. And he hadn't pulled back had he? "Stop it," Marie she said sternly out loud, "he's probably got lots of girlfriends. Get to bed." It was going to be a busy day tomorrow she surmised. It was always a busy day in the criminal world of Greater Manchester.

She made a hot drink in preparation for retiring to bed. Her mind wandered to Paul, it had a habit of doing that these days. If he had a regular girlfriend why wasn't she there to comfort him in his hour of need? "Stop it, stop it," she chided herself again. At least now with Osman off the hook the double funeral could take place. Maybe that would bring some comfort to him.

First thing tomorrow she would make it a priority to delve into the reasons the CPS were releasing Osman. If she spotted anything in the least bit suspicious, she could share it with Paul. She had trusted him with her suspicions on Kinkaid, there was no going back now.

He had said maybe they could meet up tomorrow with just that slight hint of a Manchester accent which made her tingle. For goodness sake, he was just being polite she told herself. Why then was she taking extra care in choosing her work clothes for the morning?

Kerry Blazer

The photographs and word documents in the file came from various sources. Newspaper articles, police reports, tax returns, obituary notices, town council planning meeting minutes, Crown and Magistrates court's agendas. Kerry checked this file on a weekly basis. She did not want to miss any new activity concerning Scilacci. Twice now she had successfully blocked proposed business set ups.

The latest police reports showed that aggravated house burglaries were on the rise highlighting a particularly nasty break-in on the Lancashire/Cheshire border. A twenty year old girl had been found bound to a chair in her bedroom, semi-conscious and in a state of undress. A medical examination and detailed interviews to determine whether or not she had been sexually assaulted had proven to be inconclusive. The only things stolen during the raid were the girl's mobile phone and two laptops.

Kerry thought back to that night. Millie's distress was unfortunate, collateral damage that Kerry had battled with in her own mind. Scilacci was of course incandescent with rage. His own daughter attacked in his house. A house with the very latest security technology breached and both the police and his daughter had been unable to tell him how.

What the report did not mention of course was the new infrared surveillance system now installed in Scilacci's office. Already this had paid dividends, supplying Kerry with new names and business fronts to begin work on. She also now knew that she had followed a false trail on Rawls and Ross. It appeared they were both clean.

As she scanned through the obituary notices in the Tribune, the name Buchan cropped up. Kerry read the funeral details of the double deaths. She had earlier been scanning through editions coming across reports into the tragic deaths following a house fire that had subsequently turned out to be arson. The thing standing out to Kerry was the name of one of the investigating officers, Detective Constable Maria Ross.......

*

They sat in the window of a coffee shop on the High Street. Ross had her back to the street and Kerry. The man opposite to Ross, who Kerry could see clearly, appeared nervous and edgy. Kerry clicked a button and the Nikon D850 high resolution camera fizzed into life. It whirred constantly taking image after image. She pressed an icon and the Snapbridge connectivity linked instantly with her Lenovo Thinkpad. The screen on the Nikon now showed the homepage of the laptop. She opened the facial recognition software. In less than twenty seconds it had provided her with a name, Paul Buchan.

*

It had to be connected. Her background checks on Buchan had proved enlightening. A career military man who had recently given up his position with the Army, why? The death of his parents in such tragic circumstances whilst being tragic, should still not be enough to precipitate the end of a career. That meant Buchan had other reasons and it was not too much of a stretch to deduce that he was no longer operating within the law. His parents had been subjected to a violent, unwarranted death, which could easily drive someone over the edge.

Kerry was unsure if any of this fed back to Scilacci but she decided to add Buchan to her ever expanding surveillance programme. She would run a more detailed check on him later. The link he still had with Ross was puzzling Kerry. Usually any continued dealings with a victim of crime would take place with a trained victim support officer and not in the window of a high street coffee shop.

The man had arrived in a blue Ford Mondeo ST. The vehicle was double parked on the corner opposite the Starbucks coffee shop. Kerry left the vantage point of her own car and placed a micro magnetic Enforcer tracking device under the near side wing. The device used smart charge-saving technology which is activated when the vehicle is in motion. The live GPS coupled with cellular and satellite connection is a huge advantage and the reason she always used this model.

*

The low intermittent beeping had now stopped for more than two minutes, which almost certainly meant that the vehicle was now parked. After a further minute an IDEO marker pinned the location. Kerry looked up to the bank of screens on her apartment wall. The image on screen twelve showed her that the high tech tracker had been worth the purchase price. The blue Mondeo was parked up two blocks from Scilacci's showpiece brothel on Sparkle Street…

Buchan

Buchan called Ross and arranged to meet at her flat. She was going to need careful handling and he did not want to do it in public.

When she answered the door, he stood back and admired her, she was wearing slim jeans and a bright red silky blouse that perfectly suited the colour of her skin. He had originally thought of her as black but had quickly realised she was in fact a rich mellow brown and her clear unblemished skin glowed with vitality. She looked more desirable than ever, he was not looking forward to doing what he now had to do.

"Come on in Paul the coffee's on, make yourself at home and I'll bring it through."

He made his way into the sitting room and sat down on the settee. Maria soon walked in with two mugs of coffee, she was smiling.

"You sounded serious. What is it you want to talk about?"

Buchan took a breath, he knew what he had to do." Look Maria, I really appreciate everything you've done for me. I don't know how I would have got through the last few weeks without your support but I think it's time for me to move on and stand on my own two feet."

She stared at him, her mouth slightly open and tears glistened in her eyes, "But Paul, even with Kinkaid in charge there will be reviews, the force may take the investigation off him, anything could happen, surely I can still keep in touch."

"I think we both know that Kinkaid has made sure my parents' murders will never be truly investigated. It was never going to be easy even with somebody else in charge. I told you once before I would go my own way if the police failed to find the killer and that's what I intend to do and I don't want you or your career put at risk."

She was angry now." I told you I would help you and I will. I've already done enough to get dismissed. I'm an adult, you don't have to treat me like some helpless woman who needs protecting from the realities of life."

"It's not that, things are going to get violent now, it's not me just trying to protect you or your job, you could end up in prison. What sort of sentence would a serving police officer get if she were found to be helping me? You would go down for years."

"I've told you, I know the risk. I joined this job to protect decent people like your parents not to stand by while people like Scilacci and Kinkaid are flooding the city with drugs and prostituting young girls. I want to hurt them and I don't care how I do it."

They were both standing now. Buchan took a step forward, put his hands on her shoulder and stared deeply into her eyes.

"Can't you see it? I've come to think the world of you and the last thing I'm going to do is anything that may harm you. I don't want you suffering because I've dragged you into my personal crusade. Please let me deal with this my way, you deserve better."

"I've already told you, I'm old enough to make my own decisions." She put her arms round him and stared into his eyes, "You bloody fool? I've been in love with you since the first time I saw you in the interview room looking so sad and so vulnerable."

He crushed her to his chest, "I just don't want to see you getting hurt, I want to protect you from that." She pulled him into a deep emotional kiss. He broke away, "Sit down, you don't know half the story yet, you may change your mind." He told her where he had been for the last three days and how he had obtained the firearms. "Is that enough to make you change your mind? It's going to get serious now."

"I've already told you," she hugged him, "You're stuck with me through thick and thin. We'll do this together and, by the way, you don't have to stay in that horrible hotel any more, you can stay here with me, we need to get to know each other better."

They kissed again and she led him through to the bedroom. They never got round to drinking the coffee.

Adriana

It was not yet ten o'clock. Adriana looked at her mobile phone for the tenth time that morning. It was two days since taking the girls to the local job centre. She had cheerfully waved to her daughter and the girl from Moldova even though her heart was breaking. She had wanted Ramona to have a better life in the UK but now she was uncertain and just wanted to hear her voice.

Nothing, not even a brief message to say they had arrived. No news is good news she tried to reassure herself. They were obviously excited and too busy to think about her. She would wait until this evening and if she had heard nothing she would call.

*

Fifteen minutes later she was opening the popular hardware shop she owned in the centre of Zalau. There was always a need for household goods. She sold curtain rails, light bulbs, nuts and bolts, paint, brushes and other everyday things. After a day of serving customers, tidying shelves and ordering stock she returned home determined to speak to her daughter. On the third attempt, being told once again that the phone she was calling was not available, she began to feel uneasy.

Taking her coffee into the small room which she used as her office she booted up her computer. 19.00 hours… The first English Language School listed in Manchester closed at 6:00pm. The second one was open until 8.30 pm so she quickly made the call, took a deep breath and said slowly and carefully. "My daughter is here? Her name Romana Radu." After a slight pause an English voice responded, "you think your daughter is a student at this school? Just a moment I'll look at the register. The name is?" She heard the pages of a book being turned and then the voice said. "I'm sorry there is no student here with that name."

Surprised at how many Language Schools there were in Manchester she phoned all those still open and having had no success she made a note of the names and numbers of the others. She would try them in the morning.

Before going to bed she tried Ramona's mobile again thinking she could have been in an interview with her phone switched off.

No luck. It was to be a long sleepless night.

*

Adriana was emotionally exhausted after making six phone calls and being given the same reply. "We have no student with that name."

Before opening her shop she went to the Agenția Locală Pentru Ocuparea Forței de Muncă where the girls had read the advert. The woman behind the counter listened and nodded thoughtfully. Yes she remembered the young girls but she had no idea of their final destination, only that it was England. After arranging their transport there was no need for the agency to be involved. No, she did not have the name of the Language School and no, she didn't have contact details of the person who had posted the ad. "But I'm sure they'll be fine. They'll have a much better life. They'll forget all about you, you'll probably never see them again," she said. "That's kids for you these days."

Adriana wasted no time arguing. She was annoyed with herself for not checking the details before they left.

*

That evening, back at her computer, she found that Jet 2 were flying from Budapest to Manchester at 14.20 the day after tomorrow. The 378 km drive to the airport meant she would have to leave at 7 o'clock in the morning and would arrive at 16.20 in Manchester, giving her plenty of time to find a hotel. She would make further plans during the journey.

It was not the first time she had travelled by plane. She would have enjoyed it had she not been so preoccupied but she was not prepared for the number of people milling about at Manchester Airport. Heading straight for the Information Desk she decided she could do with some help. An efficient young man soon had a taxi organised to take her to the MacDonald which he assured her was the cheapest hotel in the centre of Manchester.

Once there she had a small meal, a long hot bath and went to bed. Her nerves jangled and sleep evaded her. Everything felt so strange and foreign. She wished she had taken the trouble to learn English properly when she was younger. She knew it would not be easy to find her daughter in this enormous, noisy and busy city with her poor command of the language.

Creep

Arrivals: Manchester Airport

It had been a typically busy day at Manchester Airport. Creep Evans was looking forward to the end of his shift. The nick-name suited him well. As an official porter, he had the perfect opportunity of helping folk find what they needed. Like, for instance, those who might be wanting a 'special massage'. They were given direction to Lena's Massage Parlour with a 'tell them Charlie sent you'.

Then there were the ones who were desperate for a much needed 'fix'. Creep could easily spot those. Too risky to do any business himself, he directed them to unlit corners and back streets where their cravings would be attended to. These locations changed daily due to constantly altering circumstances. He was informed of these via a coded message on the phone which miraculously appeared in his locker the day after he started here. In fact, getting the job in the first place was an amazing feat considering his background.

Of course, these little acts of 'helpfulness 'had to be done discreetly away from the ever expanding reach of security cameras which were the curse of his life. 'No bloody privacy anywhere 'was his constant moan. Having done a stint inside for dealing he did not intend to go back there again. Any little packages he got by way of a 'perk 'were traded with extreme caution around his own patch. As long as he did not get in the way of the top man's dealers, he was safe. No names were ever mentioned, nor did he want them to be but he had his suspicions.

He had just taken a trolley of matching suitcases to the taxi rank followed by a smart couple wearing designer clothes. To impress he had helped load the luggage into the taxi but still only received a meagre tip. As he slipped the coin into his pocket he thought how predictable it was, the ones who had the most dosh, tipped the least. Oh well, it would help to fund his gambling costs. He was running up a bit of a debt.

Going back into Arrivals, his bulbous, blood-shot eyes scanned the crowd coming through. A flight from Budapest had landed about half an hour ago. He had frequently 'helped 'passengers from Eastern Europe. An attractive lady, possibly Romanian he thought, caught his attention. As she wheeled her small suitcase through the barrier, she looked like a frightened rabbit. She paused, looked around in total confusion and then spotted the Information Desk. He made his way towards her, following behind, trying to make it not look too obvious. She was now in conversation with one of the smarmy young assistants at the desk. He knew they regarded him with distaste but his luck was in, this one beckoned him over. There would be no tip forthcoming, he was sure of that but it would not hurt to help her anyway.

"The taxis are this way," he said leading her to the exit. "First time in Manchester?"

"Yes," said the woman getting more anxious as she looked around. "It's very busy."

"Holiday or business?"

"Not holiday, I come to find my daughter and her friend. They are at Language School but I don't know which one."

Creep's ears were fully alerted.

"Where shall I tell the driver to take you to?" he asked, trying to look only partly interested.

"The McDonald hotel, please. The man at the desk said it is very nice."

"It is and I hope you find your daughter," said Creep.

With that interesting information, Creep decided it was time to take a smoke break. He went via his locker, managed to send a short text and headed for the smoking area. Maybe he would get his tip after all. The message got picked up instantly by Chunky who just as quickly messaged Scilacci.

A couple of hours later, Creep was clearing the conveyor belt of unclaimed items, his last job of the day. He was aware of someone watching him. Turning casually and slowly, he saw a security guard standing in one of the few blind corners of the baggage area. There was the slightest nod of the head, only apparent to someone looking for it. Creep knew it was worth his while to check out his shabby shed on the run down allotments down by the canal, well away from airport sniffer dogs.

Adriana

Next morning while the kettle was boiling for her coffee she looked through the local brochures advertising places not to be missed in Manchester. Amongst them was a city map. Manchester is a far bigger place than she had expected! Some of the words meant nothing to her but spotting Greater Manchester Police Headquarters she understood and an idea began to formulate.

She would walk there after breakfast. "Can I help you?" Asked the man at Reception seeing her with a map. She put the map on the counter and showed him. "I walk here." He shook his head "no" and picking up a pencil illustrated. "A two minute walk to Travis Street, catch a 203 bus for three stops." He drew three leaps and with each one said "ding ding." Another three minute walk," demonstrated with his fingers "to Oldham Street, stop A for bus 83, this time 12 stops," writing the number and pointing to his three leaps. "Turn right to The Gateway, first exit at the roundabout." more symbols and then the words Police Headquarters. "OK?" How kind. It was quite clear. "Thank you," she said and set off smiling.

"How can I help you?" Asked the young police woman at the desk. Adriana took out her passport showing who she was and where she was from. It was not so easy to explain about Ramona and Valeria but the girl seemed to understand and made some notes. It helped when she remembered she had taken a photograph of the two girls with her phone. "I'll take a copy of your passport and the photograph" said the woman "and I will need your phone number and address of your hotel."

She was not sure what the police could do with the information they had but she felt better for having done something, Getting back to the hotel was not too difficult she followed the receptionist's instructions in reverse.

But what would she do now. She knew it would be like looking for a needle in a haystack but she had to do something. She would go to every shop, bar, restaurant in the area looking for her daughter.

*

After another restless night in the hotel she went out for breakfast and wandered around the area for most of the day stopping to sit down and have a coffee when she was tired.

Lonely and dispirited she started to make her way back to the hotel. She was not concentrating, her mind was drifting as a bus pulled away and she crossed the road.

The screeching of tyres pierced the humdrum sound of the traffic. She froze, unable to run and the car kept coming, throwing her into the air and dropping her into the space where the bus had been.

Witnesses said it all happened so quickly. The bus had driven off slowly and the car had suddenly appeared out of nowhere, hitting the woman and continuing along Oxford Road without stopping. It was thought to be a red Fiat Panda but nobody was sure and there certainly had not been time to note the registration number.

Maria

It had not always been easy for Maria growing up in the Worsley area of Manchester. She had inherited her mother's Caribbean chocolate-brown skin and dark curly hair. As a child she was not thankful of this when she was called names such as 'darky' or 'fuzzy' at school. Her mother had come to England in the eighties to take up a nursing post at the Salford Royal Hospital. Her father, born and bred in England, instantly fell in love with her when she stitched him up after a rugby boot made contact with his eye-brow instead of the ball. He still proudly showed the scar, saying she stitched him up in more ways than one.

Maria was close to her parents and loved them dearly. They had always encouraged her to be proud of her heritage and not let it stop her from achieving her potential. In school she had heeded this, worked hard and obtained good grades in her studies. Initially surprised at her choice of career, they supported her in every step of the way as she rose from Police Officer to Detective Constable. But she knew they were concerned about the violence in the city and called them on a regular basis to allay their fears. When her shifts allowed, she joined them for dinner. Always they would ask 'what case are you working on?' her answer always the same, "you know I can't tell you." Thank goodness they had no idea she was involved with someone using illegal means to fight the law. Not only that, any mention of the name 'Scilacci' would have them casting worried glances at each other.

At eleven years of age, Lower Salford Comprehensive School happily offered her a place, despite her being out of the catchment area. It had an excellent reputation, taking pupils from the more affluent parts of Greater Manchester. A recent article in the local paper had accused the school of being racist. 'Why are the majority of its pupils white?' the headline asked. For the first time in her life, the colour of her skin had been an advantage.

She applied herself well, was considered a model pupil by teachers and was never short of friends. Inheriting an enthusiasm for sport from her father, she became captain of the junior hockey team, adding to her popularity.

When Maria was thirteen, a new pupil joined her class; a girl with all the latest gadgets, designer trainers and a steely look for anyone who challenged her, Fran Scilacci. Maria's two best friends, Jessie and Megan, were soon in awe of Fran's worldly presence and her boasts about life outside school. They followed her around like little puppy dogs, flattering her, offering to do her homework. Excuses were given when Maria suggested meeting up after school as they used to, they were 'revising' or 'having to tidy their bedroom'. At school the next day, Maria would catch them giggling in the cloakroom about what they were really up to, sniggering when Fran's hard stare warned Maria to keep out.

The following school year brought a change in atmosphere to Maria's class. There was a division between those pupils Fran allowed to be in her band of followers and those she scorned. Packages and money began discreetly changing hands in unsupervised corners around the school. 'Raves' in secret locations were hinted at, with drugs and alcohol available. Maria, being a member of the 'scorned' group was never invited, nor did she want to be. She heard about them from Jessie and Megan, deliberately whispering a little too loudly in the cloakroom or waiting for a class to start. Their eyelashes fluttering as they swooned over an older boy; Maria surmised it was Fran's brother. The way he talked was 'sexy', his dark eyes were 'sexy', the way he touched you was 'sexy'.

At the time, she was bereft at being left out; her parents got to hate the name Fran Scilacci, uttered so many times through Maria's sobbing, blaming 'that spiteful Scilacci' for stealing her friends. Maria's school grades suffered, only on the hockey field did she excel that year as she took out her frustrations with her hockey stick.

Then, as they entered the final year of Secondary School, the class was buzzing with news that Megan had almost died due to a drug overdose during the holidays. The whole family had moved away abruptly, Maria never saw them again. In her naivety, she thought it was from choice but is almost certain now they were either paid off or bullied into leaving the neighbourhood. Fran also did not return for the final year, gossip said she had transferred to a private girls' school in Cheshire. School life settled down for Maria, she resumed her friendship with Jessie, although it was never quite the same and her grades improved.

There were no repercussions for the Scilaccis. It seemed that even in those days they could buy their way out of trouble. Maybe these events, at such an impressionable age, led her to think about the Police Force as a career.

*

Last night had been an amazing night with Paul, she had fallen for him in a big way. She had dated a couple of guys before, even had a yearlong relationship with a fellow Police Officer when she first left the Training school in Preston but nothing compared to Paul's tenderness last night. Today she had been absorbed in taking statements from scum-of-the-earth youths involved in a particular violent burglary in the city centre. It had resulted in a middle-aged family man fighting for his life in the Royal Infirmary. During breaks she had checked her mobile, her heart thumping in anticipation, longing for a message from Paul. Had she been rash in offering him a place to stay? It was not like her to act impulsively but there seemed to be a sincere connection between them. Maybe it was when she had seen that look of love and tenderness in his eyes as he identified his parents. It had seemed perfectly natural for him to cling to her for support. Now she had experienced his tenderness what she craved for was to see that look of love in his eyes again but for her only.

And how would she explain that she had had previous dealings with the Scilacci family? She knew she would have to tell him. Maybe she should get it over with tonight? But what if he thought that was why she was so desperate to stay involved? What if he thought he was just being used to get back on a teenage vengeance?

Annie Gray

Annie contacted Manchester Police Media Office every day, including weekends, asking if there were any updates on the Hale Road fire incident. She was getting used to the usual scripted comment. 'At this time we have no further information since the last press release'. She kept up the pressure for new facts, however, knowing investigations surrounding the fire and the Stretford shooting were ongoing. She believed something would eventually be revealed and there was no skin off her nose by just asking. In fact she was developing quite a thick skin as far as put downs by the police media were concerned and, like a knife through butter, she cut past police jargon which tended to confuse rather than make clear.

Officer Will Bush and Annie were now on first name terms and they were beginning to understand each other. He was realising she was not easily fobbed off and Annie felt she could read the spaces between his verbal lines, so to speak. While he did not give way, he became more generous with his time and, when Annie put forward her own ideas of what might be happening behind the scene, he did not agree or disagree, which signalled to Annie there may be something in what she had said. Rightly or wrongly she decided his silence was encouraging.

When Will Bush had said all he needed to say the telephone conversation would normally abruptly end and, if she had any further questions, Annie would have to get in quick before he put down the receiver. Today though he held on, which she thought was another positive sign.

Checking her shorthand notebook, in which she had written bullet point questions, she asked, "Will, can you tell me if there is anything new on the Wayne Osman case? Has a trial date been set?"

There was a pause before he replied, "Actually, Annie, there has been a development, which has just come through and a press release regarding the matter is under way as we speak. Since you are on the line now I'll let you have it." Another positive, thought Annie, who was ready to take down every word in shorthand. She had a certificate to say she had achieved a speed of one hundred words a minute and she had no trouble keeping pace as Will Bush sped through the formal information. In a nut shell the press release informed the Crown Prosecution Service had terminated proceedings against Wayne Osman because of insufficient evidence.

"So Will," said Annie with a critical tone in her voice, "Osman, a known drugs dealer, arrested in relation to the shooting of a rival gang member and taken into custody awaiting trial at Manchester Crown Court, has now, since the death of a witness to the shooting, walked free?" There was no mention of drugs or the murder of a witness in the press release but Will Bush knew where Annie was coming from and his silence confirmed her understanding of the case.

Annie immediately understood the significance of this new development and felt another vox pop coming on, knowing the people of Stretford would be appalled at the news.

Annie said, "Thanks Will, this information is huge and I'm sure your lot will be expecting more trouble from Stretford. She asked him if the police were any closer to finding the arsonist responsible for the deaths of Mr and Mrs Buchan but, reverting to type, he abruptly ended the conversation, having no desire to discuss details.

*

Annie walked straight into the editor's office and told Dave Arden the shocking news about Wayne Osman.

"Well Annie, you were hoping for some developments from that quarter and now you have it, well done," he said.

"How are you going to play it?" she asked.

"Front page. Dig out all the previous we have on Osman. We can bring up some of his criminal past and now there is no trial there's no risk of contempt of court."

"There's nothing new regarding the illusive arsonist," said Annie, adding "The police are saying it was probably a drunken or drugged up lone youth. I could re-hash that story and, to set the cat among the pigeons, I'll try to get some comments regarding the lack of response to the appeal for witnesses to the fire." She continued, "I'd also like to carry out a vox pop. Word gets round, people aren't stupid, I think they'll feel very let down by the police."

"Go ahead with that but be careful," warned the editor, "Don't put words into people's mouths. On this occasion that could be dangerous, not only for them but for you too."

Annie unstuck a mug from her desk and, despite there being several ringed stains in it, filled it with coffee from the machine that stood outside the journalists' office. She then settled herself in the seat of her swivel chair and rolled it up to her laptop where her fingers flew across its keyboard.

She was pleased with the subsequent edition of the Stretford Star, having achieved the lead article on the front page as well as a further half page featuring her vox pop with the expected comments from outraged residents.

*

Annie leafed through the newspaper and took cuttings for her own personal file. There was a technical library of information within the office but Annie liked to clip the stories she knew would be ongoing. She backed up her articles on a memory stick but found hard copy useful for sticking on her news board for immediate reference as she typed.

It was while she was filing her cuttings that a call had been put through to her phone. "Annie Gray," she said in her clipped telephone voice.

"Miss Gray?" asked the voice.

"Yes, this is Annie Gray," she repeated. It was a man who sounded as if he was fit to burst. He began to rant when Annie said, "Just a minute, who am I speaking to?" He refused to give his name saying instead he was sick of what was going on in and around Manchester.

"It's all right for you, whoever you are, to go ranting on but unless you give me your name I'm afraid I don't think I can help you," she explained. He repeated he was absolutely fed up with what was going on in the area and the upshot of his rant was that the police are not doing anything to stop it.

"If you give me your name I might take what you're saying more seriously," said Annie with a little laugh in her voice.

"It's no use Miss Gray, I won't be doing that," he said.

"Your telephone number then?" She asked.

"That's not possible either," he said adding, "Just listen to what I'm telling you."

Annie was intrigued and giving way to him said, "Go ahead then, I'm listening."

He told her he had posted a memory stick for her attention marking it private and confidential. He said the memory stick was evidence that men were going in and out of a brothel at 23 Rosswell Street. He continued saying he was sending an identical memory stick to the police. He put Annie's back up when he added, "I expect you to make sure they don't just put it in a drawer and forget it."

His torrential flow of fury led Annie to imagine the veins on the side of his face must be pulsing with rage.

"Hang on a bit, just let me get this clear," she said. "You ring me up out of the blue telling me you have evidence of a brothel in Manchester and expect me to just go ahead and publish it, presumably attributing it to an aggrieved Mr Anonymous?"

He ignored her sarcasm and in a steady, clear tone he told Annie she would receive more video evidence of crimes being openly committed on the streets of Manchester and he expected the Stretford Star to hold the police to account if they did not take action. With that he ended the call.

*

"You'll never guess what's just happened," Annie said as she closed the door to Dave Arden's office. She plonked herself in the chair opposite him on the other side of his desk and said, "I've just had the most mysterious and alarming telephone call from an unnamed person." She related the nature of the call, to which her editor said, "Have you checked the call log on your phone?"

"That won't do any good. Apparently he was using what he called a burner phone, which I believe is a disposable cell phone and the number can't be traced," she explained.

"Well, we'll look at the so called evidence if it arrives but we can't use it. For all we know he could be some bloody crackpot," said Dave.

"The man sounded hopping mad but I don't think he is a crackpot. He said he will be sending an identical memory stick to the local Chief Superintendent with a note saying that we already have a copy."

Falling back into a relaxed position in his well-worn leather high-backed chair he said, "Let's wait and see what happens. If we receive the memory stick, we'll check it out, give it a day then get in touch with the police. If they admit they have received the memory stick we will have to take our lead from them. If they say we can use it, fine but I'm not going it alone."

"Yes," pleaded Annie, "but after all that's going on surely we can do something, get round it somehow?"

Cutting her short he said, "No Annie," I've said all I'm going to say on the matter for now." He dismissed her with the usual nod of his head in the direction of his office door.

She was almost out of his office when she turned and said, "We won't be telling the police about the telephone call though, will we?"

"No Annie, we won't do that."

The following day a jiffy bag holding a memory stick arrived on Annie's desk. She immediately took it into the editor's office.

"So this is the mystery man's evidence," he said and, as he inserted the memory stick into the USB socket on his laptop he added, "so let's see what's going on in and around Manchester. Before we get started Annie fetch Briggsy, I'd like another opinion on this."

Briggsy was the assistant editor and had been at the Star since leaving grammar school twenty five years ago. His real name was Mitchell Briggs and he was revered by colleagues for his encyclopaedic mind and for having instant recall, a great asset in journalism.

It was 12:15pm, according to the video when two well-dressed Asian men got out of a taxi and were greeted by a woman, who invited them into number 23 Rosswell Street. Dozens of men of different races followed suit throughout the day until well past midnight. They all arrived on foot. The exception was when a man, rolled up during the evening, in a Mercedes which left as he was warmly greeted by the woman who had welcomed the two Asian men seen at the beginning of the video. The Mercedes returned an hour later, the man got in it and the car drove away.

"Whatever his motives are our mystery man knows something about surveillance," said Dave Arden.

"Though he was irate on the phone I thought he spoke with confidence," said Annie, asking, "Who are the sad girls in that brothel? Where do they come from? And who is the vile creature running it?"

"It's more likely being run by more than one person," said Dave Arden. Briggsy interjecting asked, "What about the police? They will have seen the video. Surely they will have to do something about it."

"So what do we do now Briggsy?" Said Dave Arden.

"We've got two days before we go to print. If we haven't heard anything from the police by then I think we should go ahead and publish," replied Briggsy, who went on to advise. "To limit any risk of libel we'll have to obscure everything that could identify the people involved, exactly where it is and the number plate on the Mercedes. Our mystery man is right, the crime rate in Manchester is rocketing, criminals are blatantly flouting the law and here we have a brothel in Rosswell Street. Now you can't tell me that the ordinary law abiding residents living in that street haven't complained to the police, yet it still goes on. Something has to be done. People have the right to know what's going on in their area and they also need to know what the police are doing about it," replied Briggsy, who apologised for his soap box rant saying to Dave Arden, "Well you did ask!"

Annie called the police media office on the following two days and spoke to Will Bush. She casually mentioned there was a rumour about a brothel somewhere around the Rosswell Street area but it fell on deaf ears.

Referring to the police, Dave Arden said to Annie, "They've had two days to give us something, they've said nothing so let's go with it."

In the following edition of the Stretford Star the story of the brothel featuring photographs taken from the video was printed without a byline on the front page.

That day the table turned when Will Bush for the first time telephoned Annie. He asked her where the Star got its information regarding the Rosswell Street brothel.

"Why don't you ask your Chief Superintendent Will? He was sent the same information as us and, cast your mind back, for two days on the trot I mentioned the brothel to you and you said you had no information on this."

"Which was true, Annie and I ask again, where did your information come from?"

"Even if I knew I wouldn't tell you, as you are aware, Will. Your Chief Superintendent was also told that we had been sent the same information yet no one from your side did anything about it."

"We have taken action, the house has been raided but there was nothing found," he explained.

"When did this happen?" asked Annie.

"Last night."

"Too late Will, far too late, but thanks for the follow up," said Annie just before the line died.

Maria

It was just after midnight. Maria was in bed. It had been a hectic day dealing with local scumbags and she had missed three calls from Paul. Why had he not left a message? Had she frightened him off? When her phone rang she could see it was Paul calling and snatched it up quickly.

"Paul," she almost shouted in relief.

"Maria, are you sure about me moving in?"

"Paul, I've never been more sure about anything in my life before."

"Thank goodness," there was a long pause, "I'm outside, with my things."

"What now, you're moving in now?"

"I'm sorry, I shouldn't have, how stupid of me. I'll come back later."

But Maria had already leapt joyfully out of bed and raced to the door to let him in. A passionate embrace followed, then only two journeys to the car by Paul, to unload his few belongings.

When she had calmed herself, Maria made them hot chocolate so she could savour the excitement of the situation.

"Paul, I can hardly believe this is happening. I can't wait to tell my parents tomorrow, I mean later today, when I call round for dinner. They love me very much and I know they'll love you too," she paused, "When you feel ready to meet them that is, there's no rush."

"I would love to meet them, today, tomorrow, whenever you feel it's right."

"Just don't mention the name Scilacci," Maria laughed nervously then stared at the floor.

"What is it?' Paul was nervous now. 'Please tell me. If Scilacci has ever laid a finger on you," he stood up to emphasise it, "I swear his death will be even more painful than the one I've envisaged."

"It's nothing like that Paul," Maria stumbled for the right words. "But I have been involved with the Scilaccis before, years ago when I was at senior school. Please, sit down and I'll tell you about it. I should have told you before."

She added a tot of brandy to their hot drinks and told him about her unhappy teenage years when Francesca had almost driven her to a nervous breakdown.

"Those days are way behind me now Paul but my parents will always remember."

Paul was aghast at the far reaching evils of the Scilaccis. He had been focusing on present day activity. Now he had learnt that for more than a decade they had been destroying the lives of decent hard-working people in ways he had not even considered. He gritted his teeth to contain his anger knowing it was not appropriate to show it now.

"They won't get away with it for any longer," he said, enveloping Maria gently in his arms. "Their time has come."

Francesca Scilacci

"Is it done?" She asked, already looking away from Chunky.

"It's done."

"How?"

"Hit by a car crossing on Oxford Street."

"False plates?"

"Of course." He smiled. "They'll think it's that nosey cow who works on the Stretford Star and Wayne drove off slowly enough for the number to be registered. She's been sniffing about around a friend of ours so she is going to be spending the night down at the Pig Parlour trying to prove her whereabouts."

"You made it difficult for her I hope."

"Oh yes. The stupid mare agreed to come for a meet on foot. We nicked her number plates, so she has no alibi. Of course CCTV will eventually clear her but it will take up her time."

"You've done well Chunky, there'll be a bonus for you this week. Do you want it in money or the usual?"

Chunky said. "You know me too well Franny. I will take an hour with that new girl Valeria."

*

Techo looked edgy. "Anything?" She asked but already knew the answer.

He shook his head. "We are dealing with someone out of the ordinary. I can't get anywhere. I have always said there isn't a computer programme been invented that I can't hack. Well somebody has proved me wrong."

"So what can we do?" Francesca was starting to feel nervous. Who was in their systems and what did they want? As yet they had received no demands and other than the first email offering the investment opportunity there had been no contact. Was it a one off, or would they be back?

Techo said, "The only thing that would ensure we are free from viruses would be a complete new system and that would take time and the cost would be enormous."

"You're telling me that at this minute in time you cannot guarantee we will not suffer another infringement by the lowlife creeping around our electronic airspace?"

Techo simply nodded.

*

The war council consisted of Francesca, her brother Dominic, Techo and DI Mick Kinkaid. Francesca could see Dominic was incandescent. "I will feed them their own kidneys when we get hold of them."

Techo reluctantly spoke. "Whoever is behind this will be almost impossible to trace."

Francesca looked to Kinkaid. "Surely the filth with their computer network must have the logistics and technical support to find out who this is."

Kinkaid was hot, the sweat showing through his tee-shirt. Francesca looked at him and had an idea. "These computer whizzes don't just pop up out of thin air. There must be a trail somewhere in the past where their name has been flagged up. Get Techo a list of any computer geek from the last ten years who has come up on the police computer. Let's flush this slimy bastard out."

Buchan

Buchan had the weapons. He knew the targets and all he needs now, is the means of ensuring he does not get caught.

His first requirements were an anonymous car and a secure lock-up garage in which to keep it and his weapons safely hidden when not being deployed. He did not want to leave any recordable or digital trail, so he scanned the for-sale notices in the newsagent's shop windows scattered round the area. He soon found an advertisement for a garage for hire at £20 a week, he had to laugh, it was on Rosswell Street. He phoned the number and spoke to an elderly sounding lady, she explained that her husband had recently passed away and she did not drive and had no need for the garage now. He arranged to visit the following day.

While perusing the notices he also noted a number of cars being advertised and decided to buy a common, unnoticeable, easily forgettable car, preferably a Ford Fiesta.

*

The following day he returned to Rosswell Street and met a Mrs Adamson the owner of the garage. She explained there were just a chest of drawers and a few shelves left inside and now she had sold her husband's car it's virtually empty. She handed him a key and gave him directions, the garage is one of six to the rear of the even numbered houses.

He checked out the garage and was satisfied. It was not overlooked and was timber with a firm dry earth floor. It was weatherproof and reasonably secure. Returning to Mrs Adamson he paid ten week's rental in advance. Now for a car.

The first two calls are to owners who have already sold. He arranged to view two others when the owners have returned home from work.

The first one was just a short bus ride away and he knew straightaway it was not suitable. The owner, a young man of about nineteen, had adorned it with 'go faster' stripes and Manchester City stickers. He said, "thanks but no thanks" and moved on to a second car. This one was a blue ten year old Ford Fiesta in reasonable condition, the type of car that would not look out of place anywhere. The owner, a man in his sixties, was happy to let him have a test drive.

The car, a 2009 blue Ford Fiesta, was in clean condition and drove well and it had six months left on the test certificate. It was exactly what he wanted. He paid £900 in cash, left a false name and address and drove the car back to his garage. Now he needed to find another old blue Fiesta in order to steal its number plates. The one he had bought would show up on automatic number plate recognition cameras as untaxed and uninsured and was likely to attract the attention of the police.

*

Later that night he drove to Chester in his own car and soon found a suitable blue Fiesta. As he removed the number plates. He felt sorry for the owner who would have to replace them, he shrugged but it had to be done.

He reviewed his progress, he had secure storage for his illegal items but not left any paper or digital trail. He would keep the Beretta nearby and stash the other two guns and ammunition in a hole he would dig and board over under the chest of drawers in the garage.

His campaign would start as soon as the pit had been dug and the weapons hidden.

*

Two days later the time had arrived for him to make his first open move against the Scilacci organisation. He dressed in dark clothing with his face partially concealed with a black scarf. The Beretta he tucked into his trousers in the small of his back. In his coat pocket was a cosh of ancient design, a sock packed with wet sand. Crude but murderously effective.

He drove the Fiesta towards Manchester and parked in Scilacci territory to the south of the city centre and walked to an area where he had seen the drug dealers at work. For a target he selected a tall thin youth walking jerkily up and down the pavement, he only stopped to look hopefully at cars that slowed down, one driver stopped and there was a swift exchange through the driver's window and the car moved on. Buchan looked round, there was nobody else about and he walked towards the dealer.

"What have you got mate?"

"What do you want? I got weed, spice and Charlie and if you want anything else, I can get it."

Buchan whipped the sand filled cosh out of his pocket and with a round-house swing smashed it against the side of the dealers head. The dealer fell onto the pavement, tried to regain his feet but fell back again.

Buchan stood over him, "Give me your drugs and money, come on quick." He reached down and swiftly emptied the dealers pockets onto the ground.

"Are you crazy?" He spluttered. "Scilacci's gonna have you killed."

"Tell Scilacci his times up. He's out of business."

He then emptied all the drug packets into a drain in the view of the dealer.

"What are you doing?"

"I'm removing filth from the streets of Manchester. Tell Scilacci he's next."

Buchan walked away and returned to his car. He had expected to feel elated but instead felt guilty. The dealer was not yet out of his teens and the pale scared face that looked up at Buchan had given him no sense of triumph. He knew the youth would be roughly handled by the Scilacci gang who would suspect him of stealing his own stock of drugs and cash. The only way to support the scared young dealer was to rob several dealers to prove there was a pattern. That way Scilacci would know the young man and others were telling the truth and understand that somebody was attacking him and his organisation.

He moved a few streets away where he found a second dealer who was busier. Buchan noticed that some buyers would stand almost out of sight in an alleyway, give a discreet wave and the dealer would go to them. Perfect, he would have cover from view in the dark shadows. He walked into the alleyway from the far end and observed. The wind was cold and nobody was hanging around in the area except the dealer. Non-buying members of the public walked quickly by. Knowing what was going on and not wanting to be involved. This dealer, stocky and alert, looked more capable of defending himself than the previous one. He glanced into the alley and Buchan waved him over.

The dealer strode over, confident and apparently unworried about the police or anyone else.

"What's your fancy mate? Haven't seen you before."

As before Buchan caught him by surprise hitting him hard on the side of his head. The dealer staggered back and Buchan followed up by punching him hard in the centre of his face. He felt the dealer's nose scrunch and he went down. He still struggled trying to and get up but stayed down when Buchan kicked him powerfully in the ribs.

"Money and drugs now." Buchan had to drag cash and packets of drugs out of his pockets and found this dealer also had a kitchen knife in his pocket. Once again he showed the dealer how he disposed of the drugs down the drain.

"Tell Scilacci he's finished. He's on my territory now and he's out of business."

*

He went back to the fiesta, parked it in his new garage, picked up his regular car and went home to Maria.

He told her what he had done and she looked at him frowning with lips pursed.

"You've really wound them up now. They will take precautions and you won't find it this easy again, just be careful."

Buchan nodded "I will. I doubt Scilacci will send any more dealers out on their own until he's found out who's behind it."

"You're right but it won't be just the Scilaccis you have to worry about. He'll spread the word to Kinkaid and he'll let the lads on the shifts know what's going on. He'll tell them this could turn into a gang war and they will be looking to stop it spreading."

"Why would the police be concerned about some dealers getting robbed?"

"They won't give a damn what happens to the dealers, they just don't want mayhem on the streets, they have to pick up the pieces."

"Are you having second thoughts? It's not too late for you to drop out now you know if you're worried."

She grabbed him and kissed him, "You don't get rid of me that easy."

*

The following nights Buchan saw just how right Maria had been. Every dealer had somebody loitering nearby and others signalled a helper to bring the drugs in, one at a time. After a few quiet days the gang seemed to have relaxed, perhaps thinking they had scared him away, so he went back to work.

He waited until past midnight and parked once again on the edge of Scilacci territory and started walking. Tonight he was carrying the 9mm Makarov tucked in the front of his jeans. He only had to reach under the front of his waist length jacket to draw it, he hoped he would not have cause to use it. The dealers were once again operating alone but they were making a point of being out in open view rather than skulking up alleys or in deep shadow. As he walked, he planned, he was sure he could stick the gun in the ribs of a dealer and get him out of view to rob. In Ferry Street he had noticed one who was not far from an alley. He carefully examined the area round the dealer. There was a fried chicken shop quite near at the end of the road with a few customers wandering in and out but nobody who appeared to be covering the dealer. The night was clear and all the street lights were working. He would have preferred a shabby street with plenty of shadows.

He made his approach from the back of the dealer and walked at a normal pace. The dealer gave him a casual glance and looked away. Buchan grabbed him round the shoulders and hurled him into the nearby alley. The dealer fell stumbling trying to retain his footing with Buchan following closely behind cosh in hand. He struck the dealer hard in the lower back and then on the back of his head. He lay groaning on the ground but Buchan could hear excited voices and rushed back to the mouth of the alley. A short youth, no more than about fourteen, was pointing and shouting. "There he is Wayne. He's the one, he just jumped Jezza, I saw him."

He was calling to a far more formidable figure, a powerfully built man in his mid-twenties. He had virtually no hair and was wearing a black leather jacket. He was pulling something from his pocket as he ran towards Buchan who soon realised it was a knife and it was in his hand.

"Got you, you bastard. You don't rob Scilacci and get away with it, you're gonna die."

He was closing fast and Buchan could see he meant business. He held the knife out in front. The blade looked about a foot long and glittered in the street lights. His eyes were glaring and wide and his teeth bared. He was ready to fight and he intended to make Buchan pay.

Buchan had eased the Makarov out from his jeans and was holding it close to his right leg. He dropped to one knee and pulled the gun forward holding it in a two-handed grip. He pointed it at the centre mass of Wayne's body and then, thinking he did not want to kill him, dropped his aim and fired. There was a bright flash and the sound of the shot echoed in the alleyway. He breathed in the familiar smell of burnt propellent. Wayne had been hit in the right thigh. He screamed and dropped to the ground grasping his thigh. The knife skittered away into the road. Buchan pointed the gun at the youth who had raised the alarm." Run." The youngster turned and ran for his life.

Buchan stepped quickly forward," So you're Wayne, Wayne Osman?"

"Just get me an ambulance you prick."

"Not so brave now Wayne, hurts doesn't it? Now you know how it feels."

Buchan could hear sirens in the distance and ran through the back-street route he had planned in advance and was soon in his Fiesta and quickly left the area. He knew he had changed the rules of combat, not only for himself but for Scilacci and the police.

*

As he drove home in his own car with hands shaking on the steering wheel, he knew he would have to steal the number plates from another blue Ford Fiesta. If his current plates had been caught on ANPR or CCTV a routine enquiry in Chester would soon reveal the false trail. He knew he needed to take a break now before resuming hostilities.

He let himself into the flat and Maria gave him one swift alarmed look.

"What have you done now?"

He breathed deeply, "I've just shot Wayne Osman, he was coming at me with a knife."

She put her hand to her mouth," Did you kill him?"

"No, I could have done but I shot low and hit him in the thigh."

"Did anyone see you?"

"Not close up but I think I need to keep my head down for a while."

"You know what's going to happen now. The police will be all over it and the media will be stirring everyone up demanding to know what they are doing about the 'guns on our streets'. We can't stop the papers printing what they want but Kinkaid is taking a close interest in you. He called me into his office today and asked if it was true that I'm living with you. I played it cool and said we did have something going but nothing too serious. He turned on me then and said it was unprofessional and I needed to keep my distance. He kept on at me, where did you go? Who did you see? Had you said anything about getting your own back? I looked at him as if I was puzzled and he let something slip. He asked me if I knew you had worked with special forces in Iraq and Afghanistan. He must have been making enquiries through the military.

"They will just confirm basic facts, they won't go into details about operations."

"Don't make the mistake of thinking Kinkaid doesn't matter. I've told you before, he may be a crook but he's also a bloody good detective. He's got his eye on you now and if he finds anything he won't let it go and it won't be the police who come calling."

Buchan nodded, "I need to distance myself from you, publicly at least, I can't have you getting hurt. I'll rent something out of town and operate away from this area. We need to rethink. All I'm doing at present is grabbing some low growing fruit. I need to attack the organisation where it hurts, at the moment I'm little more than a nuisance."

They clung to each other, both in tears knowing their idyll was over. Now it was getting serious.

Kerry Blazer

Hereward the Wake lying in quiet repose filled the screen of the Lenovo Thinkpad. Kerry held down the cursor over his eyes and slowly dragged each lid open. A new window opened and Hereward was replaced by the floor plan of Francesca Scilacci's penthouse flat.

Kerry swapped to the Voodoo Envy. She hit the lens icon and was granted immediate access to the Belvedere Court CCTV pictures. Every floor was covered by the cameras that Kerry now controlled. Francesca lived on the highest level, the twelfth storey. Kerry had also remotely installed some new software that gave her full control of the system. The software also triggered an alarm which flagged up on Kerry's iPhone whenever the door to the penthouse flat opened. Her mobile had indicated that an opportunity may just have opened.

She checked the alarm time against the CCTV images which saved her the endless scrolling of dead images. Francesca had left the flat at 6:15pm almost certainly headed for Sparkle Street, so it gave Kerry a window of at least five hours.

*

Belvedere Court was a swish apartment block overlooking the River Irwell. Its residents would have no fears of a Grenfell Towers type tragedy happening there. She returned her attention to the Lenovo Thinkpad. The floor plan of Francesca's penthouse had been obtained by hacking into the town hall planning office. It showed the penthouse was fully equipped with the latest safety technology currently available.

Kerry pushed on a brush icon and the floor plan changed to the whole of Belvedere Court. She was interested in one particular aspect, the sprinkler system. Her problem quickly became apparent. The building was fitted with a deluge system, meaning the whole network was linked. These system types use latch valves and because the standing pipes remain free of water, which only becomes live if activated as the sprinkler heads are open at all times. The downside of this system is, whilst it is undoubtedly cutting edge, it wraps the whole building in a water blanket not just the source of fire.

Kerry had to isolate the penthouse flat from the rest of the building without compromising the safety of the other residents of Belvedere Court. The pipe layout crisscrossed the floors competing with the underfloor heating and high fibre cables that were supplying her with the surveillance images. Kerry zoomed in on the plans, although the pipe work was interlinked she reasoned there must be a way of isolating each flat for maintenance purposes alone.

Kerry used the Lenovo's super zoom facility and there they were. Gate valves electronically connected to the fibre optics. She was in. Using a drop-shot trojan she set a silent alarm to prime the system with water and then she deployed the gate valves controlling the sprinkler heads to off, except one.

*

On the Voodoo Envy Kerry watched as the penthouse flat began to fill with water. It did not take long. She made sure the place was uninhabitable before draining the system and returning everything to how it was. It was just before midnight when an alarm pinged on Kerry's iPhone, the penthouse door was being accessed. She fired up the laptop . She did not want to miss this.

Annie Gray

The urge to check out the brothel at 23 Rosswell Street was too much for Annie to ignore so she persuaded Briggsy it was worth a follow up story and took a run out in her Fiat Panda. She arrived at the semi-detached house to find the windows and doors boarded up. It had also been cordoned off with police tape warning people not to cross it.

Annie wanted to know what the neighbours thought about the goings on at number twenty three and, noticing a car on the drive of the house attached to the brothel, she

walked up to the front door and rang the bell. The door was immediately flung open causing Annie to stumble backwards as she faced a middle-aged looking woman wearing a nurse's uniform.

"I'm sorry," said the woman, "did I frighten you?"

"I wasn't expecting the door to be opened so quickly, it startled me," said Annie, who explained who she was and why she was in the area.

"Well I'm just off to work now and I don't have much time but I'm happy to speak to you if you'll excuse me as I talk while I put my bags in the car," said the woman.

"Please carry on, I don't want to hold you up. I would just like to have your thoughts on what has been going on here," said Annie.

The woman said her name was Kathy Kitchin and she worked at the Royal Salford Hospital. As she got into the driving seat of her car she whizzed down the window and in a calm assured way told Annie, "I've seen my fill of the results from criminal activities that are rife in and around Manchester. Wounds from knives and guns can be patched up but when it comes to drugs, exploitation and young girls trafficked for prostitution, it's nigh on impossible to come back from that unscathed. That is what I'm sure has been going on next door."

Annie asked if she had seen or heard anything from the brothel.

"Yes," she replied. "From time to time I've seen girls getting out of a transit van and last week as I came home from being on nights I saw a girl running down the street with a brute of a man chasing her. When he caught her he hauled her into the Mercedes that was following them." Through tight lips she continued, "The obvious signs of what's been going on though, are that men blatantly come and go all day long and the curtains are always closed."

"Did you do anything about what you saw happen to the girl?" Asked Annie.

"I contacted the police and told them everything I've told you." she said and, with a look of sorrow in her eyes, she despairingly shook her head saying. "They took my name and address but no one came to see me. I didn't hear another thing about it and living among such people, you have to be careful so I didn't pursue it any further. I'm sorry I really have to go now," She said as she closed her car window and drove off.

*

Annie was hearing too many times about the police being aware of crimes committed under their noses and appearing to be reluctant to act quickly, if at all. She had enough information for a follow up on the brothel story and decided when she got back to the office she would tackle Will Bush on the constantly ignored complaints.

While she was out and about she took a turn towards Stretford to call on Robbie George whom she knew would not be at work until after one o clock. She wanted to ask if he could help her contact Paul Buchan. Annie hoped that as a little time had passed since the death of his parents he would be able to talk about them and their lives.

She did not think he would wish to talk with her after seeing and hearing him speak at a press conference. Annie surmised he did not look the sort that would fall for the idea of a story featuring his stalwart parents to help bring hope to a saddened, demoralised community. She resolved to give it a try in any case.

Though Annie was on a mission to do what she could for the people of Stretford her search to glean from every angle all she could from a story may be seen by some as cynical. In truth she thought she could not argue against that.

Annie got to Stretford just before midday and was glad to catch Robbie George before he went off to work. He would not give her Paul Buchan's telephone number but said he would contact him and ask him to get in touch with Annie if that is what he wanted to do.

Annie thanked Robbie and asked how the Hope Lunch Club was going.

"It's going really well at the moment. We have quite a few more volunteers who walk home with the residents because they still feel a bit unsure about walking the streets alone," he said and added, "The vicar and one or two helpers actually pick up some of the regulars. So all's well at the moment."

"That's great news, Robbie. Now you know where I am if you need me," she said as she was about to leave his doorstep.

"Actually Annie we're holding a tea dance in a few weeks and would love some publicity."

"Just let me know when and where Robbie and I'll be there," she said as she waved goodbye.

*

She grabbed a ham salad baguette from a corner shop and ate it as she drove back to the office where she was told by Briggsy that she had just one hour to put together all she had.

She quickly rang the police media office. "Hi Will, it's Annie Gray. Have you got anything new on the Rosswell Street brothel?" she asked.

"No, Annie, I already told you we've been and found no trace of the occupants and," Annie knew what was coming next as he reeled off, "At this time we have no further information since the last press release."

As she was pushed for time Annie decided to cut short the call, especially as Briggsy was yelling at her across the office, "I need five hundred words and I want them now. And here's the headline, Police Ignore Brothel Complaints. Annie's fingers were already flying as Briggsy warned. "You've got twenty minutes before we put the paper to bed!"

Kerry Blazer

The alarms went off in sync. Kerry watched the bank of screens in readiness for the mass evacuations. The first sign of activity was on the fire escape at the rear of the brothel on Sparkle Street. Bodies scurrying like insects in a bid to flee the unknown. Before long every entrance at six brothels across town were bustling with anxious punters keen to be away before the emergency services arrived, particularly the police.

She watched as Scilacci's money disappeared down the warren-like backstreets of Manchester. She accessed the master computer of their brothel trade and did a quick audit of their recent finances. Through the direct interference of Kerry in numerous guises, the business had suffered a ninety percent decrease in profits.

She had enjoyed unbridled success but it was not enough. Kerry was convinced that the Scilacci empire was responsible for a large part of the crimewave that had engulfed the city in recent years. Whilst working in isolation, Kerry knew that she remained invisible to even the best hackers on the planet. But she felt that the time had come to branch out. She had been considering several possible candidates as a partner; a reporter from the Stretford Star Annie Gray, ex-serviceman Paul Buchan, who had lost his parents to a suspicious house fire and police officers Maria Ross and Judith Rawls.

After an even more detailed online search into the possible candidates for a partner and deliberating about losing her anonymity, she settled on Maria Ross who she was aware was in a relationship of some description with Buchan. Kerry had yet to decide how best to make contact, it would be simplicity to hack the detective's mobile but she did not want to begin any future relationship with a breach of trust on her behalf.

*

In the end Kerry abandoned her occupation of the ether world and simply waited in the favoured coffee shop of Ross's. She turned up an hour later ordering her usual skinny latte and retiring to a booth at the rear of the cafe. Kerry gave her a few seconds before introducing herself. She approached the booth and offered her hand.

"Hello, my name is Kerry Blazer and I'm the reason Dominic Scilacci is having sleepless nights..."

Buchan

Buchan felt his burner phone vibrating, it was Maria Ross.

"Hi Maria, what's up, missing me already?"

"Not in the least but I am with someone you have to meet."

"Sounds serious, who is it?"

"I'm not going to use her name on the phone but I can say she's on our side and she's been giving our mutual friend sleepless nights. I'm satisfied she is on our side."

"OK, let's meet in the saloon bar of the pub where we ate the night before last. When does your friend want to do it?"

"She says now would be a good time."

Buchan disconnected. He was close to the pub and would have time to get there in advance of Maria and the mystery woman.

*

He was soon positioned out of sight and over the road from the Lord Nelson. He saw Maria and another woman arrive and enter the pub. He waited, watching to see if they had been followed and when satisfied they were in the clear, he followed them inside.

The woman with Maria was slim, pale faced, with dark makeup and short spiky dark hair. She was wearing tight leggings, Doc Martin boots, a red anorak and carrying a black laptop bag. Her eyes picked him up as soon as he walked in but they did not meet his, they were carefully watching the doorway behind him and glancing round the bar.

Maria intervened, "You two go and sit down, there's a table in the corner, I'll get the drinks, usual Paul?"

He nodded and led the way to the corner table. The woman hesitated and then followed behind him. Buchan sat down and the woman joined him, sitting on the edge of the chair and looking back at Maria.

Buchan thought it was time to break the ice, "Well you know who I am, what shall I call you?"

She gave one last glance around the bar, "You can call me Kerry. Let's wait until Maria joins us and she can tell you what I've done and what I can do to help you."

Maria brought their drinks over and joined them. Buchan noted that Kerry appeared to be drinking tonic water.

Maria took a sip of her drink and started talking, "Paul, I was in Starbucks today and Kerry introduced herself, she traced me and you through the internet. She's a grey hacker, that's one who can do good by using her IT skills. She tells me she's been hacking into Scilacci's accounts and is stealing his money even faster than he's making it. That's not all, she's been in his house in the sticks and left an infer-red surveillance system in his office, a system she can access at any time using her mobile phone or computer. She suggests we have a look at what's going on in his office now to prove she can do what she claims."

"Suits me, let's see what you've got Kerry".

Without answering Kerry placed her laptop on the table and following a blur of high-speed typing, turned the screen round for him to see. It showed a well-appointed, comfortable looking office. A young woman was removing books from shelves that covered one wall of the office. They watched as she dusted the empty section of shelving and replaced the books.

Buchan smiled, "That's impressive, I presume you get audio as well?"

Kerry nodded, "I've hacked into most of his systems. The only way he can escape from me now is to install a completely new system. I don't think he'll do that, too much expense and bother. No, he'll come looking for us and he's got that crooked cop Kinkaid on his payroll to help him."

Buchan decided to trust her, "I've been making my own moves against Scilacci and his gang and I even had to shoot one of them the other day but I want to hit him harder. What I'm planning should really stir them up, although depriving them of their ill-gotten gains the way you do will probably hurt them even more."

Kerry stared unblinking into his eyes, Buchan felt as if she were exploring deep into his soul, he knew that if he told a lie this woman would sense it and he would get no further help from her.

"I want to get those poor girls out of his grip but while we do it we can have some fun frustrating Scilacci. I'm looking forward to it".

"OK Kerry, you have his office under surveillance and you're ripping him off, what else can you do?"

Kerry grinned and visibly relaxed, the first emotion he had noticed, "I can get through all the alarms at his house and Maria tells me you are looking to hire a place a little out of town to lie low between operations, I can arrange that without using your name."

"That will be great, not too far out but far enough to be away from the prying eyes of Scilacci and his goons in the city."

Maria banged her glass down on the table with some force, "You two are getting very comfortable and enjoying yourselves and having a laugh but I need to remind you both, we are not dealing with idiots. For a start Kinkaid has already made it clear he suspects you Paul of being behind the trouble his dealers are having. He has a legitimate reason to go to a magistrate and take out a warrant to search your flat in Shropshire. He can, again legitimately, get a trace put on your phone and it wouldn't't surprise me if he put one on mine as well. So, let's grow up, it's not a lark, remember it'll be deadly serious if we're found out."

Paul leaned back, "You're right of course, what do you suggest?"

"For a start Paul, you need to switch your own phone off permanently unless you are in town and have legitimate calls to make, then switch it off again immediately afterwards. You need to hide it well away from anywhere you stay or where we may meet. Find somewhere outside to store it, away from anywhere we are likely to be operating. We only communicate using burner phones and never when you have your own phone with you. Kerry you are an IT expert and know better than me how to avoid being traced but don't assume Scilacci doesn't have somebody as equally skilled in his crew."

Kerry Blazer did not respond and sat unmoving, Maria could not tell how her comments had been received.

Maria Ross turned back to Paul, "Right Paul, now I've got that off my chest, what's your next move?"

"I'm going to get the police into one of the brothels in large numbers and in circumstances where they have to get the girls out and question them. It will be on such a scale so that Kinkaid won't be able to hush things up and it might get a bit messy. Kerry if you can text me on the burner when you have an address for me, I'll get to work."

He walked from the pub suitably chastened by Maria's comments, he had become over enthusiastic and lost his professional detachment, it would not happen again.

Maria

Maria, taking a much needed break, stared into her coffee and marvelled at how much her life had changed since meeting Paul Buchan. She had never before felt so happy and yet so afraid of the future. Suddenly she became aware of a conversation nearby.

"You know that hit and run case? The foreign woman?" the young officer asked thoughtfully.

"Yes, I heard about it." replied her colleague, lifting his eyes from the headline he was reading.

"Well, I spoke to her!"

"Where? When?"

"The day before yesterday when I was on the front desk she came here. She didn't speak English very well but I understood she was looking for her daughter. The daughter had come to Manchester with another girl from Moldova to learn English at a school, hoping to find jobs here. The woman was obviously very worried because she hadn't heard anything from them and the daughter wasn't answering her phone. I felt sorry for her. I copied her passport and a picture she had of the two girls. I didn't know what else to do!"

"Poor woman. A lot of accidents happen because foreigners look in the wrong direction when crossing the roads. They're not used to vehicles being on the left hand side. Where was she from?"

"Romania."

Maria stood up but, before leaving the canteen, she stopped at the next table.

"I couldn't help overhearing what you've just said Susan. I'm actually on my way now to visit the woman in the hospital. You should come with me, you'd be a face she'd recognise. Maybe she could tell us something about what happened."

They arrived at the Royal Infirmary to be told the woman was unconscious and in a critical condition. Witnesses at the scene had been of little help. Everything had happened so quickly. The red car had appeared out of nowhere and vanished into thin air as if by magic. They sat at Adriana's bedside for a little while wondering how to continue with their enquiries.

"I don't suppose the hotel would know anything?" offered Susan. "She was staying at the Macdonald."

"It's worth a try, well remembered!" Maria smiled.

*

The man behind reception at the hotel was very happy to talk about the foreign woman. She had arrived by taxi two days ago. She was looking for her daughter he told them and explained how he had helped her with directions to the Police Station. Yesterday she had spoken to him as she left the hotel. She had not told him where she was going but he thought she would probably just wander around Manchester in the hope she would see her daughter and her friend. "A bit like looking for a needle in a haystack!" he added shaking his head.

*

"There's one more thing you could do for me" said Maria as they went their separate ways.

"See if you can locate the woman's next of kin. The name, hopefully not her daughter's, will be in her passport."

Maria liked Susan, her enthusiasm was a breath of fresh air and she used her initiative. She had found two names in the passport, one was Ramona Radu who she knew was the daughter and the other was Anka Bratu, presumably a relative. She had phoned the Romanian Embassy in London, explained what had happened, sent a photo copy of Adriana's passport and asked them to contact Anka Bratu. They would report back.

This case was proving to be very difficult with no leads at all. Back at the station however there was a ripple of excitement. The red car had been identified as the little Fiat driven by Annie Gray, the journalist from the Stretford Star. She was to be brought in for questioning. No doubt on her way to some news breaking situation and did not want to miss a scoop, people were speculating. Not good, the spotlight would now be on her.

Annie Gray

Letters responding to the Star's incendiary narrative, highlighting the police's lack of action in dealing with Manchester's street crime, swelled Annie's in box. The correspondence criticised the authority and dominated the 'Letters to the Editor's' page.

Some of the letters were from people not wanting their name and address published and were signed as, 'Outraged, Distressed and Sick and Tired of Stretford'. These were concluded with the newspaper's standard, 'name and address supplied'.

Annie was pleased the campaign to be a voice for law-abiding citizens was sparking comment and hoped it may be the beginning of the end of apathy on all sides.

Having dealt with the latest batch of letters, Annie was trying to make up for lost time following a lead that did not materialise. She had received a call requesting publicity for a group of runners. They were all said to be aged at least eighty two years old, which was the key to the story. At 3:30pm Annie was to meet a Mr Smith near one of the four benches that were centred on each side of the bowling green at the Stretford side of Longford Park.

*

The sun came out just as Annie arrived at the green but there was no one to be seen. While waiting for Mr Smith she stretched out her legs and relaxed on one of the benches and, closing her eyes, she lifted her face to savour the golden warmth of the sun. She waited for around half an hour before leaving and smiled as she realised she was in a park to meet a man and had been stood up.

She made the most of the fine weather and slowly meandered along the path that edged the park's manicured lawns, wondering if she had correctly taken down Mr Smith's information. She immediately dismissed the thought, knowing it was second nature for her to double check names, times and places.

The nearest car park to the bowling green was a ten minute walk which Annie had enjoyed. She spent far too much time indoors and relished the slight breeze lifting her hair as she strolled back to her car.

She passed a notice board. Posted on it was a list advertising activities that were to be carried out in the park. Not being one to miss an opportunity Annie made a note of the name and telephone number of the organiser of a charity fun-run soon to take place and was happy to have turned a negative into a positive. This brought to mind another of her father's sayings; 'Any time you suffer a setback or disappointment put your head down and plough ahead.'

*

When she returned to the office she began gathering the details for the fun-run. It was a pleasant change from the heavy disturbing stories she had lately covered.

When her colleagues suggested going to the gym for a spot of spinning and then on to the pub Annie was content her working day had ended well. She invited the group of six back to her place and on the way they picked up Chinese takeaways and pizzas.

The party broke up in the early hours of the morning when Annie began to clear away the used food trays and a copious amount of empty lager cans and wine bottles. She grinned as she realised any calories lost during the spinning session had very quickly been replaced.

She was dropping the debris into a plastic carrier bag when she heard the doorbell continuously ringing. Thinking one of her friends had forgotten something she opened the door wearing a wry smile and was about to say something sarcastic. However was taken aback to find a serious looking man and woman standing on the doorstep. She quickly half closed the door, jamming her left foot and leg behind it as leverage, so that if she needed to she could quickly shut it.

"Miss Annie Gray?" said the man.

"Yes, what do you want?" she asked, keeping the door between them.

"We're police officers. I'm Detective Sergeant Havers and this is Detective Constable Ross of Manchester Police. We would like to talk to you," he said, as the two of them flashed identity cards.

"What about?" asked Annie, looking puzzled.

"It would be better if we did this inside, Miss." he said, gesturing towards the door. Nervously she held the door open and ushered them into the front room.

The woman was black and taller than the Detective Sergeant. He stood with both hands in the pockets of his three quarter length coat which was turned up at the collar. The Detective Constable was muffled against the night air in a wide, woollen scarf, which was wrapped several times round her neck.

"What's this all about, then?" said Annie. "Has something happened?"

"We want to talk to you and would like you to voluntarily come with us to the police station to be interviewed." said DC Ross, giving the room a once over.

Baffled, Annie asked. "Why, what for, I mean, what is going on?"

"It will be better all round Miss Gray if you come with us to the station, that way anything that is said will be on record and, if you wish, you can have the services of the duty solicitor who is completely independent of the police."

Annie could not believe what she was hearing, "Yes but I haven't done anything wrong. Why should I come with you?" It was perplexing, she felt as if she was in the middle of a weird dream.

DS Havers remained tight-lipped at the side of DC Ross who suggested again it would be better if Annie voluntarily went with them. Annie agreed to go not knowing what else to do. Feeling fazed she put on her coat and grabbed her keys from the hall table and threw a bag over her shoulder. As she stepped outside she saw next to the police car a flat-bed tow truck, onto which her car was being chained.

"What's going on?" Asked Annie horrified at the scene. The dream was turning into a nightmare. "Why are they taking my car?"

"As we have said, Miss Gray, we will explain when we get to the station," said DC Ross.

They drove in silence, though the atmosphere could have been cut with a knife. The car sped through the almost deserted streets quickly arriving at Manchester Police Station.

*

Annie was taken to a small, gloomy looking room and was asked if she would like to have a solicitor present during the interview. She had no idea why she should need one but decided to err on the side of caution and nodded her head.

The room smelt musty and was in need of fresh air. The only window in the room was mirrored. Annie guessed it was a one-way mirror and imagined police officers standing on the other side of it watching her every move.

She sat fidgeting on an upright chair at the side of a wooden table. Her mouth was very dry and she was frightened, wondering if, without knowing, she may have done something wrong.

Annie could not remember when she felt so desolate. She spread her forearms on the table and rested her head on them. She was so tired. Checking her watch Annie worked out she had been waiting for half an hour before the door was opened by the duty solicitor, who introduced herself as Truly Sully.

"Do you know why I am here?" Asked Annie.

"The police have reason to believe you are involved in a hit and run."

"That's ridiculous. They are terribly mistaken. Now I know I am having a nightmare. This cannot be happening." cried Annie, who stood up and walked round the room, ringing her hands in anguish.

*

Truly Sully calmed Annie and after a few minutes they sat down. The solicitor then advised Annie of her rights and discussed what she should say or not say during the interview. Annie felt a little easier now that she had next to her someone who appeared to be on her side.

The two detectives entered the room and sat opposite Annie and the solicitor. DS Havers placed two discs into a recording machine placed at the end of the table before asking Annie what was her name and date of birth. He then explained she was not under arrest and that she was going to be cautioned, after which he reeled off the mandatory warning.

Annie knew she would not be able to cope with the intrigue and resolved to answer the questions as straight as possible, hoping it would quickly bring an end to the ordeal. She was asked where she was at around four o'clock yesterday. She had lost track of time now that it was in the middle of the night and it took a few moments for her to remember that she had been at that time sitting in Longford Park waiting for Mr Smith.

"Can anyone verify that?" asked the sergeant. To which Annie responded with a shrug of her shoulders, saying "he didn't turn up and there was no one else around."

She explained what happened, relating the story from beginning to end. The officers allowed Annie to speak without interrupting her. When she finished another police officer came into the room and whispered something to DS Havers then glanced at Annie, who was beginning to feel preyed upon. She could not understand how this could be happening to an innocent person.

DS Havers scribbled something down in a notebook and asked Annie to repeat her story. She stated, as close as possible, the time she left the office and the time she returned, after which DS Havers asked if anyone could verify any of it. Annie replied that her boss at the Stretford Star knew where she was going and with whom she was to meet.

"This so called Mr Smith, according to you, did not arrive, so there is no one to verify where you were at around four o'clock yesterday afternoon, is there?" quizzed DS Havers, who added, "the fact that you told your boss you were going is not proof that you actually went to the park."

He then asked, "Do you know Adriana Radu?"

"No, I've never heard of her, why?" asked Annie.

"She was the victim in the hit and run car accident yesterday afternoon."

"I was at the park at four o'clock and this car accident has nothing to do with me," said Annie, realising her back was against the wall. She managed to summon up enough courage to ask the sergeant, "What proof do you have that I was anywhere near the scene of the accident?"

DS Havers ignored her question and asked instead, "Why did you agree to meet a man you don't know in a lonely spot in a park?"

"It's my job," exclaimed Annie, raising her eyebrows and holding out both hands in confirmation. "And I ask again, what proof do you have that I was anywhere near the scene of the accident?"

"Your car was captured on an Automatic Number Plate Recognition Camera hitting a woman before speeding away in Oxford Street ."

"There must be some mistake. My car was parked in the car park at the Stretford side of Longford Park, where I got into it at about four forty five and drove back to the office. Is that why my car was taken away?" Asked Annie defiantly.

"Your car is currently undergoing a forensic examination," replied DS Havers, who then left the room, which was recorded by DC Ross, who took over the questioning.

"Does anyone else have access to your car?"

"No, no one since my father died has driven the car but me."

"Where did you take the call from Mr Smith?" The tone of questioning softened and Annie got the impression that DC Ross almost believed her.

"It came straight through to my mobile," replied Annie.

"Show me," said DC Ross, holding out her hand for Annie's phone.

"I don't understand," cried Annie, "I can't seem to find the number. Maybe it came through as private caller, I can't remember now."

*

For all the world Annie could not figure out what or why this was happening to her. She did not have an alibi for the time of the accident and there was no telephone number from Mr Smith registered on her mobile. Her new found strength was diminishing to the point she just wanted to cry.

DS Havers returned to the room, which again was recorded. He asked Annie, "What have you done with your number plates?"

"What do you mean," asked Annie, her voice now much weaker.

"They are not on your car."

"I have no idea, I had not noticed they had gone."

DS Havers quietly said something to DC Ross and left the room. Truly Sully was about to say that, unless Annie was going to be charged, she should be allowed to go. At this point DC Ross recorded that the interview was terminated at 3.30am.

There was a hint of sympathy in the eyes of DC Ross as she told Annie she could go.

"What happens now?" Asked Annie.

"The investigation is ongoing but there will be no further action involving you."

"And my car?"

"It will be returned to you in due course."

Annie supposed the forensic examination had proved her innocence, though she could not understand what had happened to her number plates.

Truly Sully drove Annie home and gave her a contact number in case she wanted to get in touch with the solicitor.

Annie closed the front door, wearily climbed the stairs to her bedroom and, kicking off her shoes, she fell exhausted into bed, where she sobbed into her pillow calling for her mum.

Buchan

Only three days after the meeting at the Lord Nelson Kerry Blazer messaged Buchan. "Your new home is Apricot Cottage in the village of Rostherne, it's furnished and the rent is paid for six months. You can pick the keys up from the agents, Scarman's in Stretford , use the name Alec Roberts, enjoy." Buchan replied with a smiley.

He checked Rostherne online and found it was in East Cheshire, south of Manchester and still within easy travelling distance. It looked perfect and within two hours he had picked up the keys from the agency. He realised for the second time how fortunate he and Maria had been when Kerry had decided to take an interest in them and support their activities.

 The cottage was situated on the edge of the village of Rostherne not far from Rostherne Mere, it appeared to be an oasis of calm well away from the frantic bustle of Manchester. Buchan thought it was probably an old farm worker's tied cottage, the worker no doubt replaced by machinery. There were two bedrooms, as well as the usual, bathroom, sitting room, kitchen, shed and a gravel driveway, a farmhouse was visible across the fields.

With his experience of multiple moves in the army, Buchan had become accustomed to laying his head down wherever he happened to be and he was soon settled.

*

Now he had to plan his next move, this would involve him attacking one of Scilacci's brothels, without injuring any of the girls and ensuring the police responded in sufficient numbers to make sure Kinkaid would not be able to minimise the incident and sweep it under the carpet. First, he needed to observe likely targets and plan, not only his attack but also to be sure he would be able to escape unhindered, it was no small task. Maria had supplied him with four addresses and, using street view on Google maps, he quickly identified the Anson Hotel as the one most suited to his plans. The location gave him a wide choice of roads heading south that would enable a quick getaway and after the attack he could and should, be many miles away before the police were able to respond in sufficient numbers to present a problem.

He made a start by visiting the area the following morning. He drove to the edge of the neighbourhood in his, yet again renumbered, Ford Fiesta and, without driving directly past the Anson, explored the roads in the locality and the best routes leading to the main roads heading south. After this he parked up and walked, criss-crossing and familiarising himself with the paths and alleyways he could use to approach and escape on foot. Conscious of the possibility of CCTV, he wore a peaked cap pulled down over his face and a scarf covering his chin. He saw the Anson Hotel was a three-story yellow brick building, probably built in the nineteen twenties or thirties. It had obviously seen better days and carried an air of neglect with dark curtains pulled carelessly across the front facing windows.

Having completed daylight observations, he repeated the exercise in darkness, he remembered again the old military adage, 'time spent on reconnaissance is rarely wasted'. He dressed in dark clothing and black training shoes, his loose-fitting top had pockets in which he could keep his gloves, woollen hat and black scarf to disguise his pale face, he knew nothing is more recognisable to the casual observer than a pale oval face set against a dark background. The hotel still gave no indication of wanting to attract custom and busy road traffic was driving past, Buchan suspected brothel customers were directed to park a short distance away. His intention for the night was to gain access to the roof of a building opposite the hotel, it had the appearance of having once been a bank and had a fancy pillared balustrade edging the roof. This would give Buchan an unobstructed view of the front of the hotel and provide him with cover from view.

*

He parked up and approached what he now thought of as 'the bank'. There was an overgrown garden to one side, an old abandoned wooden gate and some broken fencing was leaning against the wall toward the back of the building next to a pile of building rubble. He entered the garden from a shadowed section of pavement and saw the rear of the 'bank' was less impressive than the front. He was able to lean the gate against the lowest part of the structure and paused while listening and waiting. When he was sure nobody had seen him enter, he was able to clamber up the gate and scramble over the guttering onto the roof. Ensuring he was still in the shadowed area, he crawled over the roof and down to the balustraded frontage. The elevated position gave him a clear view along the road in both directions and the front of the Anson Hotel, traffic was quieter now.

He settled down to watch but after an hour became increasingly concerned when he saw there had been no movement at the front of the building, the front door remained closed and in darkness. He wondered, had the gang moved on again?

He climbed down from the roof and reconnoitred on foot. There was a narrow alleyway at the side of the hotel, as he watched he saw a brief glimmer of light at the far end. Moving cautiously, he circled round the hotel and approached from the rear, it soon became clear that somebody had given a great deal of thought to getting customers in and out of the building unnoticed. A heavy black screen curtain had been strung across the alleyway between the door and the main road. He watched as two men approached having walked along a footpath at the rear of the building. When they had been allowed inside and the door was closed Buchan followed the footpath and found it led to a small fenced car park, a man stood at the entrance, he was obviously a lookout and presumably checked those arriving. This was not going to be an easy operation, Scilacci's gang had taken sensible precautions and he would have to find a way past their defences.

*

As he drove back to the farm cottage an idea came to him but he would need Kerry's help again. He sent her a text. "Are you able to order and pay for smoke grenades? They are legal but you may have to convince the company you order them from that you have a valid reason, such as filming or other entertainment, before they let you place the order. I want, 6x MIL-X smoke grenades, these operate the same way as military ones with a handle that flies off and last 60-90 seconds, also 6x CM 75 smoke grenades, these will produce huge volumes of smoke for three minutes and have a simple top pull operation. You can order them to be delivered to the farm cottage. Thanks."

Kerry replied using just four words." Leave it to me."

Buchan thought he would be able to create sufficient noise and disorder to attract huge numbers of police and the fire service, with the plan that was maturing in his head.

The smoke grenades arrived the following day, Kerry had obviously paid for express delivery. Now he was ready for the operation, he checked the stores he needed for it to be successful.

His clothing would, as usual, be dark and unobtrusive. He would take the smoke grenades in his backpack. He would carry the Makarov pistol with a full magazine of eight rounds, this would be tucked into his trousers and the spare magazine in his pocket. The Berretta would be in the small of his back as back-up. He packed a hammer and, from the piles of old newspapers in the shed of the farm cottage, he had a black bin bag full of loosely crumpled newspaper. He had plans for how he could make use of that.

*

He waited until it was fully dark and loaded the Fiesta, he longed for a more powerful car but knew it was more important to remain inconspicuous. He drove into Manchester and parked in a quiet street, one he had selected earlier in his reconnaissance of the area, he knew he would be able to reach it quickly after the operation.

First, he removed the black bin bag and carried it to the pathway between the car park and the rear of the Anson and pushed it into bushes. He checked and found the car park lookout was in place and eight cars were parked, mainly Mercedes and BMWs, with one Lexus, he smiled, they would make a satisfactorily expensive fire. He knew that igniting petrol that had been poured over cars to set them on fire was less effective than simply smashing a window and setting fire to newspaper on a rear passenger seat. It also presented far less danger to the him when he was setting the fire. He knew he would have been at risk of burning himself if he leaned into a vehicle to ignite anything giving off a vapour such as petrol or any other accelerant and singed eyebrows are a giveaway to any curious police officer on the lookout for an arsonist.

Now for the risky bit, he admitted to himself that he was scared, he could feel a nervous weakness in his legs and he knew his hands might shake before he made his attack. This was normal, in his early days attached to Special Forces, a Sergeant had asked him." Are you scared? Because if you're not you should be, face up to it, fear will keep you alert, don't try and be the big man, only a fool or liar can claim they don't feel afraid before action, learn how to handle it, control it and you'll be alright."

Buchan had never forgotten that advice.

He ran through a mental check list once again, gloves, back pack, pistol, spare magazine, back-up weapon, camping fire lighter, hammer, lower part of face covered and wearing black hat.

*

Breathing deeply, he braced himself, he was ready to go. He circled round to the front of the building and observed from across the road, still no sign of movement. He went to the pile of rubble, selected a brick and quickly crossed the road through the passing traffic and approached the Anson hotel. He climbed the steps to the front door and using the brick smashed the glazed section of the door and threw in a MIL-X smoke grenade, he heard the spring click as it operated and knew smoke would be pouring into the building, he reinforced the effect by dropping in two CM75s to provide another three minutes of thick smoke. He could hear raised male voices inside and it sounded as if they were panicking.

He drew his Makarov pistol and moved into the alleyway at the side of the hotel, forced his way past the thick curtain and reached the door he had seen being used by customers. It flew open and a man staggered out coughing, Buchan grabbed him by the scruff of the neck and pushed him back inside. Buchan followed him, forcing him further inside and screamed." Stay inside, anyone who tries to get out will get shot." He raised Makarov and fired two shots into the ceiling shouting. "Move, get moving" He fired another shot, smoke was pouring from the front of the building. Buchan ignited two further CM75 smoke bombs and fired another shot, he could hear a voice shouting." Get the front door open, get everybody out, come on get it open." There was banging and crashing as somebody was obviously trying to force the front door open. He was starting to enjoy himself but turned and ran back out of the door, he noticed how smoke was being drawn into the upper parts of the building and could hear people running down the stairs and the sound of female screams.

*

Now for stage two, he ran from the hotel along the footpath, picked up the bin bag with the newspaper and entered the car park, the lookout came running at him, moving fast. What's happening?"

"You're needed at the hotel, now move." Buchan pointed the Makarov at the man's face screaming "move, run," and as the man ran, he loosed another shot into the air.

Next was the cars, hammer in hand he smashed a rear passenger window on each car and the alarms immediately sounded blending into a shrieking wall of noise, he threw an armful of paper into each car setting fire to them all. Buchan stood back and looked, the fires had taken hold, the car alarms were blaring, orange car indicator lights were flashing and in the street lights he could see smoke pouring into the sky from the upstairs windows of the Hotel.

He then put a shot through the driver's door of three of the cars, he wanted to make sure the police would know a firearm had been used, they would not be able to downplay the evidence especially when they saw the ejected bullet cases. Two men ran from the back of the hotel into the car park and skidded to a halt twenty yards from him, Buchan fired one round in their direction and the man nearest him fell, scrambled to his feet and limped away, the second man just turned and ran without looking back, it was the lookout, both men disappeared back in the direction of the hotel.

Buchan cursed and then felt relieved, he'd just committed a cardinal sin, he'd heard the 'dead man's click', the sound you get when the magazine is empty and the working parts of the gun fly forward, without a bullet to pick up and load into the breech. He had failed to count his shots, he quickly changed the empty magazine for the full one, he would not allow that to happen again, it was amateur, unprofessional. He knew he had been lucky, if the lookout had been closer to him when it happened, he could have been overpowered by the two men.

But the job was done and he could hear sirens sounding in the distance, it was time to go. He reached the fiesta and dropped inside, he realised he was sweating and wiped a hand across his face, he could feel his heart pounding. Slow down he thought, just slow down. Only slightly faster than normal he pulled away from the kerb and headed for the route south. When he reached the edge of town he pulled into the side of the road and stopped, his heart still pounding but not as fast or loud as before. He quickly sent a text to Maria on her burner. "On my way home, job done."

*

Back at the farm cottage he stripped and cleaned the Makarov, reloaded the empty magazine, and stored the remaining smoke bombs in the shed, now he needed a shower and a drink.

Seated on the settee later he sipped a whiskey and water and switched the television on, selecting Sky news. He whooped, he had made a big splash on the news, Sky was showing the scene outside the Anson Hotel, there were police cars, fire engines and what appeared to be scores of flashing blue lights. A young blonde female reporter gasping with excitement was about to interview a senior police officer with silver braid on the peak of his cap.

"Chief Superintendent, what can you tell me about what happened here tonight, have there been any arrests, is it correct firearms have been discharged, why was the hotel attacked?"

The Chief Superintendent looked at her with weary disdain. "What I can tell you is that we are aware of one person who has been injured and yes a firearm has been discharged but not by my officers."

"Have you made any arrests?"

"We have detained a number of foreign nationals and will be interviewing them to establish their status in this country, we are in the early stages of the investigation and will make a further statement when the situation has been clarified." He then went on to make the usual appeal for witnesses to come forward.

Buchan was delighted, even though he had said little, the Chief Superintendent had said enough for Buchan to know the girls had been removed from the Anson and were, for the moment at least, safe in the hands of the police and there was no way Kinkaid could keep this quiet.

Annie Gray

Annie awoke with ringing in her ears. She was disoriented and lay in bed staring at the ceiling trying to restore her equilibrium. It was a few minutes before she realised the ringing was coming from her doorbell. Haltingly she slid her legs from under the duvet and sat on the edge of the bed. It was one o'clock in the afternoon, she had slept for ten hours.

She was rank. Her clothes were sweaty and crumpled and catching sight of herself in the dressing table mirror she saw her father pointing his finger saying as he often had. "You look as if you have been dragged through a hedge backwards."

Sadness engulfed her as she thought of her parents who she mourned but never more than at this moment. Walking to the bedroom window she looked down and saw DC Ross standing on the doorstep.

*

"What now?" thought Annie, who was tempted to ignore the call but had second thoughts, wondering if it was news about her car. She held on to the banister rail as she slowly walked downstairs and opened the front door.

"Good morning Annie," said DC Ross. I hope you don't mind me calling you Annie."

Annie did not say anything but opened the door wider, indicating an invitation to enter.

"What do you want this time?" said Annie in a voice devoid of emotion.

"I came to see if you are okay."

"No thanks to you or your lot if I am," said Annie, who walked along the passage to the kitchen, leaving DC Ross to close the front door.

Annie went to put on the kettle for coffee but the detective constable took it from her saying, "Here sit down let me do that for you."

DC Ross placed two mugs of coffee on the kitchen table and sat opposite Annie, who looked pale and listless. The detective felt sorry for her and gently said, "My name is

Maria Ross. I knew who you were, Annie, the moment I set eyes on you. I read your stuff with interest and that is partly why I'm here."

"Tell me first of all, when will my car be returned to me?"

"In due course."

"How long will that be?"

"I can't say at the moment but it is held in a safe compound and the only thing wrong with it is that the number plates are missing. When you returned to your car after your failed meeting with Mr Smith did you really not notice your number plates were not in place?"

"I really didn't. I was busy making notes as I walked along and just jumped in the car and left. I wish I knew what was going on, it's driving me mad."

"Well that's what I came to tell you. We have CCTV footage showing your car in the vicinity of the park with your number plates intact and a while later your car was captured on the same camera but going in the opposite direction with your number plates missing. We think they were stolen while you were waiting for Mr Smith, who we believe does not exist. The number plates were found at the scene of a burnt out Fiat Panda, the one we think was used in the hit and run."

"But why, I mean, surely it would eventually become obvious that I am innocent."

"We believe the people implicating you in this crime wanted to put the frighteners on you. It's a warning. Don't forget some of the things the Star has written, not to mention the photos you've published, were very incriminating."

"Well, they have succeeded in frightening me but if they keep committing crimes on our streets and the Star finds out about them it will be reported. It's unavoidable, I mean, your own press office is duty bound to inform the public about what's going on. Not that they are very forth coming unless it suits them," said Annie, biting back.

"Look, I commend you and the newspaper for keeping Stretford in the news. I think it makes the people who live there feel a bit safer but you must be aware that you are now on the criminals' radar, so please be careful."

"So what are you lot doing about all this then?" asked Annie.

"The investigation is ongoing," was all DC Ross was prepared to say. She stood up to leave. "I have to go now but if you want to contact me you can do so on this number. It's my personal number so please and I must stress this, don't let anyone else have it."

As they said goodbye they had a mutual, though unstated, understanding. Annie made herself two slices of cheese on toast before going upstairs to enjoy a long, hot shower, after which she rang Dave Arden and explained everything to him. He was concerned about her welfare and told her to take the rest of the day off and to ring him if she needed anything.

*

In the early hours of the following morning she was disturbed by the ring tone of her mobile. She recognised the voice on the end of the phone as that of the mystery man, who advised her get over to the Anson Hotel if she wanted another good story.

In the absence of a car Annie telephoned her taxi driver friend, George Sparrow, who said he could be with her in ten minutes. Annie was back in the saddle.

Kinkaid

Detective Inspector Mick Kinkaid was an angry man, who the hell had authorised a raid on the Skipton Street brothel and why hadn't he been informed. He suspected somebody had deliberately kept him out of the loop, and he felt vulnerable. He paused for a moment to collect himself and pushed open the door to the uniformed Inspectors office and when inside slammed it shut. There were two people in the office, Inspector Ahmed Khan and WPC Sharon Drake, they both looked up startled.

Ahmed Khan glared, "What the hell are you doing bursting in here like that, don't you know how to knock?"

Kinkaid slammed the file he had been holding down on the desk and shouted, "Who authorised this? I'm in charge of crime investigations in this station, why wasn't I informed?"

"There wasn't time and you weren't on duty. Before you start shouting again, just remember we hold the same rank. Being a detective doesn't make you senior and give you the right to charge in here shouting your mouth off. Sharon, can you leave us please."

Sharon Drake jumped up from her seat and fled, closing the door behind her.

Kinkaid realised Khan was not going to be bullied, "OK, I'm sorry but I've had my eye on that place for a few weeks now and I wanted to trace whoever's behind it. Why did you take it upon yourself to raid the place?"

Khan smiled enjoying the moment. "You can thank young Sharon for that she keeps her eyes open and came to see me and said she had spotted something and wasn't sure what to do about it."

"Spotted something, what did she mean, she's only got five minutes in the job. What the hell does she know."

"She's a sharp girl, we've all heard the rumours about that house in Skipton Street, so she decided to keep an eye on it when she's passing. It's as well she did we pulled a couple of very young Romanian girls out before they were, what you might call, inducted into the trade. One of them is only fifteen. They thought they were going to a language school and would have a well-paid job when their English improved."

Inspector Khan looked Kinkaid in the eye. "So tell me, why are you so angry? We got two young girls out of the clutches of a gang of pimps and got two good arrests out of it. What did we do wrong?"

Kinkaid was thinking hard, he knew he had to tread carefully. "You're right of course but what did Sharon see that made her so suspicious."

"She saw the girls being taken from a car to the front door, they looked scared and one of them was obviously very young. She knew she had to do something, so she contacted me and raised the alarm. I made an emergency application for a warrant and the lads were ready to go and waiting while I swore it out. We acted fast and it worked out perfectly. We have rescued two girls and have locked up the scum who had them. The gaffer spoke to me earlier this morning and said we had done a great job."

Kinkaid knew he was taking a chance but still spoke, "You were lucky this time, I prefer careful preparation before a raid."

Ahmed smiled, "One of the lads told me it is the first raid he's been on where they weren't expecting us. We have a leak in this station and I'm going to do my best to track down where it is and plug it. If it's one of our own I'll make sure they go down for a very long time.

Kinkaid was sweating now but had to show support, "I'll pass on any info my team gets, you're right we've got to find the leak if there is one."

Khan continued "Remember, if we hadn't acted quickly it would have been too late for the girls and the scum who had them would never have been arrested."

Kinkaid thought it best to mollify Khan, he had enough enemies in the job already without making another one. "I'm sorry Ahmed, I suppose I took it personally. But can you give me an assurance that you'll give me a heads up if anything like this comes up again, even if I am off duty. After all we have to work together don't we?"

"Of course I will Mick," Khan lied. "By the way, I'm putting Sharon up for a commendation and I hope I can rely on you to back me up on it."

*

Kinkaid did not reply and walked back to his own office a worried man. He hadn't been there many minutes before he felt his mobile phone vibrate, the one he used when he needed to talk to Scilacci, and he didn't want to answer it. He knew what Scilacci would say and what he wanted, but he was trapped. He swiped his finger across the screen.

"Hello Dom, can we make this quick I'm in a meeting and just nipped out for a slash."

Scilacci's deep gravelly Scottish accent boomed in his ear, "Get your arse down here Kinkaid, you can't hide from me, I know what your game is and now it's time to pay your dues. If you're not here in one hour, I'll come looking."

"No need for that Dom, I'll get to you as soon as I can," but he was talking to a dialling tone.

He knew he would have to go and face Scilacci sooner or later. Scilacci had been raving since the attacks on his dealers, bloody Annie Gray and her stories and Wayne Leeson getting shot. There was fiasco at the Anson Hotel, and now this. Scilacci was after blood and he wasn't going to take no for an answer.

He put his jacket on, straightened his tie and walked into the CID office. He tapped Detective Sergeant Ellen Smithson on the shoulder, "I've got to nip out, one of my snouts wants to see me and it sounded urgent."

He quickly left the station and drove towards the Sparkle Street building, making sure he parked two streets away, you never know who's watching. When he first got in with Scilacci it had seemed like a win-win situation. Scilacci paid him well, gave him the choice of the girls and tips about other gangs. It helped Kinkaid's career no end, and he got an impressive list of arrests to his name. All Kinkaid had to do in return was tip Scilacci off when he heard about any planned raids or anything else he thought Scilacci should know. He also had to run interference when the Scilacci organisation was being investigated.

Now he knew better, Scilacci wanted him to find out who was behind the attacks on his dealers and the Anson Hotel. Kinkaid thought he knew but hadn't dared tell Scilacci, he was worried and thought it was all getting out of hand. He didn't want to come under the spotlight if it ended up with Scilacci murdering someone. He would go down for life if that happened and as an ex detective he would serve a very rough sentence.

He entered the building through the rear entrance, the 'tradesman's entrance 'as Francesca Scilacci called it. One of Scilacci's heavies pointed to a door, he was smirking.

Kinkaid walked in, Scilacci was waiting and without speaking punched him hard in the solar plexus. Kinkaid fell to the floor and stared up at Scilacci wheezing and gasping for air, he felt sick and faint, it was so unexpected. Scilacci was not a big man but he was broad, with wide shoulders and powerful arms.

"Get up you big girl and listen."

Kinkaid staggered to his feet and Scilacci grabbing him by the throat and smashed him back against the wall, holding up him there with one hand while he shouted into his face.

"Do you take me for an idiot, do you, do you think I don't know what your game is?"

Kinkaid struggled for breath, "There's no need for this Dom, I'm doing what I can."

Scilacci threw him across the room, Kinkaid bounced off a chair and was once again back on the floor. Scilacci stood over him, "You have been taking my money and screwing my girls and if you don't get out there and find out who's been ripping me off and shooting my friends, the whole world will know what you get up to down here I've got it all on video. What do you have to say you worthless piece of shit, well?"

"I was going to tell you Dom honest, I just wanted to be sure."

Much calmer, "Tell me now."

"You know the soldier, the one who's parents were killed in the fire, I think it's him. He's ex special forces, but I've got no idea where he is, he's just gone to ground."

"Then you'd better tell me how I can find him I don't have to use your methods and I have my own ways of making people talk."

"That DS, the black girl, Maria Ross. He was living with her and she tried to tell me they'd finished but I don't believe her. Yesterday I heard they've been seen together again, she'll know how to get hold of him, she's bound to."

Scilacci leaned over speaking softly, "Now why couldn't't you have told me that before?" He patted Kinkaid softly on the cheek and then pulled his hand back and slapped him hard across the face knocking him back to the floor.

"Just remember, I own you, you get no more girls or money until I have him, I want to see him bleeding, I want to hear him screaming and then I want to see him dead, and his tart."

Scilacci stormed from the room while Kinkaid lay shaking on the floor once again gasping for air. He knew he had no choice, he had to back Scilacci all the way or he was doomed.

Valeria

It was five days since the burning incident, although Valeria herself was not able to keep track of the number, being kept in a drug-induced, groggy state. The wound had begun to heal even though she had only been given a dinghy-looking bandage to cover it with. She asked Carmen every day where Ramona was. "She's sick, in hospital." Carmen replied, without making eye-contact.

In her more cohesive moments, Valeria remembered Ramona's mother, her concerned face, telling them to text as soon as they reached England. Valeria could not be sure when they were told to hand the phone over but she knew she would never see it again.

*

At some point during the day, she was escorted to the bathroom by Carmen or another girl who spoke in a language which she could not understand. After showering and washing her hair she dressed in whatever clothes had been left for her, usually tight leggings and a gaudy top.

For the past two days, she had then been taken down to the kitchen and offered bread and cheese or a dish of pasta with a tasteless sauce. Yesterday another girl had been sitting at the counter half-heartedly eating a bowl of breakfast cereal, her teeth crunching slowly on the flakes. She acknowledged Valeria with a quick nod then moved in silence to a tiny table positioned against the wall.

Today, the outfit left in the bathroom for Valeria was a strapless, red Lycra dress. Hanging on the door handle was a set of matching lacy lingerie, also red. When she got downstairs, Carmen pointed to a pair of black high heeled shoes to complete the outfit. Valeria was conscious of the wound which was now without a dressing. Carmen handed her a short jacket of imitation leopard fur which Valeria put on, glad to have a covering over the ugly mark.

"You look very nice," said Carmen, without making eye contact.

The girl she had met in the kitchen stood silently in the hallway, dressed in a similar fashion. A shortish man with dark features held a bunch of car keys. He looked Valeria up and down and smiled smugly to himself.

He opened the front door and led the way to the Mercedes parked outside on the street. Valeria felt self-conscious in the skimpy dress, it was not an outfit she would ever have chosen. The shoes pinched her toes and she almost cockled over. The girl caught her and helped her into the back seat, then sat beside her. Carmen sat in the front passenger seat.

"Do you know where we're going?" Valeria asked the girl, in English. The girl nodded and turned to look out of the window.

*

After ten minutes or so, the car drew up in front of a semi-detached house. At first, Valeria thought no-one was home but inside she froze with horror when she recognised the woman who had administered the poker.

"Come along dear," Francesca crooned smoothly, as she pulled off the jacket and glanced at the red scar, "I think it was a lesson well learnt." She nodded to Carmen to take Valeria upstairs; the other girl was already out-of-sight.

Valeria was taken into a room dimly lit by two bed-side lamps. The king-sized bed had a purple satin sheet draped over it and an assortment of beaded cushions. The curtains were tightly drawn. Valeria stood facing the closed door; she had not heard a key turn but had no strength to make an escape. She heard a deep, male voice booming a greeting downstairs and then heavy footsteps. Her heart thumped rapidly as she stood watching the door. An Asian man, older than her father, entered the room.

He threw off his jacket and stood in front of Valeria. As he slipped the straps off her shoulders, she shuddered at his touch and looked down at the floor.

*

"Oh you want it rough do you?" He laughed pinning her arms up behind her as he pressed his body onto hers. Valeria fell back onto the bed, the action making her shoes fall off with a clunk on the thin carpet.

He pulled off Valeria's dress, leaving her slim body exposed in the lacy underwear. She tried to cover herself with her arms, which were now free and he noticed the burn.

"Looks like Francesca's work," he said, keeping his eyes on Valeria's face as he removed his trousers and underwear.

Valeria felt his heavy body on top of hers and his hands pull off her underwear. His unkempt beard was scratching her face, she could hardly breathe never mind fight back. Agonising pain seared through her whole body as he entered her with force, she wanted to scream out loud but somehow, she sensed that was what he wanted. Then… nothing as she managed to turn her face towards the smooth sheet and transpose her thoughts and emotions to a place outside her body, telling herself she was still travelling through Austria and everything would be all right.

*

She was aware that the frantic up and down movement had stopped and relieved when his body slid off hers, allowing her to breathe more easily. The man dressed quickly. "Very nice," he said as he left the room.

She wanted to cry, she wanted to curl herself into a ball but she just lay there and then slowly, slowly she began to whimper as the smell of the man's sweat and semen reached her nostrils.

The door opened, this time it was Carmen, she held a towelling gown out to Valeria and swooped up the clothes and shoes.

"Come with me," she said.

Valeria stood up, the pain still searing through her body, a trickle of blood ran down the inside of her legs. She could barely walk to the adjacent bathroom. From downstairs, she heard the easy, relaxed laugh of the man who had just raped her but, even more frightening, was the sound of Francesca's high pitched response.

"You have five minutes," said Carmen, standing in the doorway of the bathroom, "your work here is not yet done."

Valeria cleaned herself up as best she could, aware that she had not been allowed any privacy.

"Drink this," said Carmen, offering Valeria what looked like an innocent fruit drink. After a few sips, Valeria almost reeled over but Carmen caught her arm and led her into another bedroom. As the door opened, Valeria saw several naked bodies intertwined on a massive bed. She looked away, not wanting to register what she saw.

*

She felt hands touching her in intimate places as she was laid across bodies in the middle of the bed. Her own hands and arms felt leaden, she was powerless to prevent her clothes being removed again. The sensation of sweaty, hairy bodies rubbing over her breasts caused her to cry out, her vision impaired as she drifted in and out of consciousness. Each time she was raped, burning pain racked through her body, she lost count after five or six violations.

Men's faces, girls' faces came briefly into focus, then blurred together in the smoky haze of the room. Voices called out commands over her, emitting stale cigarette and alcohol breath. Her brain could not make sense of the groaning and panting sounds around her.

Valeria was unaware of the room emptying and silence descending as she had completely blacked out. She was unaware of Carmen throwing the fake fur jacket over her and ordering Slim and the driver to carry her downstairs and bundle her at speed into the car. Back in her shabby room, still unconscious, she was also unaware of the money she had earned for Scilacci that day.

Kerry Blazer

It was unlike her but she had almost missed the anomaly. She let the cursor hover over Gittens & Son and there it was. Carlylink@justonly. Gittens & Son had supplied the leasing agreement for a six month term for Apricot Cottage. She checked the official website for the estate agents letting the cursor hover once more.
Gittens_1927@rostherne.uk

She was not mistaken and unfortunately knew the consequences of what the discrepancy in the web address meant. She took the cellophane wrapping from a new disposable mobile dialled the burner phones A B C and D, nothing. A quick search of google maps deluxe told her the best she could hope for was forty two minutes.

*

She managed it in twenty five minutes but it made no difference. The door to the cottage was open, flapping wildly in the wind. Kerry tentatively pushed it fully open. She entered the narrow hallway and went into the sitting room, there was evidence of a skirmish, chairs were upturned and a coffee cup was smashed on the floor. The signs which were worrying, became terrifying when she saw an S smeared in blood on the wall in a sickening signature. The vehicle for smearing the bloody message on the wall was lying on the carpet. Kerry almost retched when she realised she was looking at the severed ear of Maria Ross.

She urgently dialled burner phones A and B again, both went straight to answer phone. The next call was the obligatory 999. She asked for the police but declined the call operative's offer of an ambulance, for that they would require someone to work on. Would Buchan blame her? She did not know but somehow the house letting arrangement had become a compromised operation and it may have cost Maria her life. This was not the time to take on any vows of vengeance. It was a time for careful and meticulous planning, there was no one better placed than Kerry to supply that.

*

The vertical list of names ran for over forty thousand pages but Kerry was certain among those names was the owner of Carlylink@justonly. Given time, no one could stay hidden from Kerry but time was a luxury item she did not have.

The call from Buchan came five minutes later.

"It's Maria." Was all he got out.

Kerry opened up a tracer software package and sixty seconds later had the coordinates for burner phone A.

"I'm on my way." Said Kerry but he was not listening.

*

This time the journey was twenty two minutes. Buchan was in the Top Cat wine bar on Sparkle Street slumped over a pine table. The half empty Scotch bottle he clasped in his right hand had rendered him unable to converse.

A relieved barman helped get his limp frame into her Porsche Boxter and Kerry offered up a prayer to whoever that he was not sick in the vehicle or even worse foul the plush leather seat. When they arrived back at her Blackfriars Street apartment she called the night porter Ernie to assist her. Once in the apartment she left him to sleep it off on the huge six seater sofa. Tomorrow would bring the recriminations.

Carmen

It was 11.00 am on the morning after Valeria's ordeal. Carmen had checked in on her several times, a little concerned that she had not woken up yet. She took hold of Valeria's hand and sat on the edge of the bed, careful not to touch her body, she knew from experience that it would be sore and covered in bruises.

Carmen stared at Valeria's face, already it looked older than when she had arrived only a few weeks ago. How had she managed to get herself trapped here? Red blotches had formed across her forehead, the skin on the rest of her face pale in comparison. Both lips were swollen, she'll have difficulty eating for a few days thought Carmen. Her hair, bright and shining when she had arrived, lay dank on the pillow. Carmen noticed the new skin on the burn wound had been broken, perhaps she could find some ointment to stop it getting infected?

She allowed herself to remember a time when she had been in Scilacci's evil world for about six months. It had been confirmed that she was pregnant although she hardly knew herself what was happening to her body. Scilacci was not pleased and told her it would have to be 'got rid of'. In her still comparative innocence, she had asked Scilacci if she could keep the baby, she'd always wanted a baby. The force of the smack across the face she received in reply, almost knocked her over. The gold ring he wore on his little finger had caught her in the eye. For a few days the severe swelling caused temporary blindness. She was relieved when her sight fully returned but as the months passed, she realised the damage to her eye-lid was not healing, the disfigurement was permanent.

*

It was the most terrifying time of her life. The pain of the abortion, pain even more excruciating than the first time she was raped but this time performed by a woman in a house that smelt of death. Francesca and Scilacci repeatedly muttering about all the money it was costing, telling the abortionist she had better make sure there would not be another pregnancy. There was blood, so much blood for days, then as soon as her body showed some recovery, Scilacci told her it was time to get back to work, there were bills to cover, unless she wanted her sister to take her place.

Carmen sponged Valeria's face, forcing the memories back into a secret place, she knew it was dangerous to have emotions in any of Scilacci's brothels. The slam of the front door alerted her to Scilacci's presence, only he slammed it with such force. She went downstairs to the kitchen. Scilacci was looking disapprovingly at a girl eating a bowl of cereal at the small table. She eyed Scilacci warily, yesterday's make-up encrusted on her face.

"Make sure she's presentable for 1.30, she's got a busy afternoon," he growled at Carmen.

"And she," nodding upwards, "needs to be ready for work tomorrow."

Carmen nodded submissively and without looking at Scilacci asked quietly,

"My father? My passport?"

Scilacci pushed roughly past her. 'You have your orders, 'he said, 'get on with them. 'He did not see Carmen's clenched fists or feel the hatred and revenge emanating from every bone in her body, willing him to drop dead on the spot. The front door slammed again and he was gone.

*

One of Scilacci's men was always 'on guard 'in the house, day and night. They changed constantly but Carmen knew that today's minder had an obsession for burgers and pornographic movies. He also had a habit of leaving his keys lying around in the kitchen.

"Ana, get ready now," she said to the girl. Ana slurped down the rest of her cereal, put the bowl in the sink and went upstairs sullenly.

The minder took his Big Mac out of the brown paper bag and went into the room next to the kitchen. He inserted a disc into the TV and slumped in front of it.

Carmen looked behind the McDonald's bag, her heart started to thump as she saw his keys. She knew which key opened the back door and which one opened the padlock on the side gate. For many years she had imagined this scenario but her courage had always failed her. Now was the time, she must do it! Her life was of no consequence, her passport long out-of-date, there was no chance of seeing her family again but she would get help for Valeria.

She checked on today's minder, he was engrossed in naked figures cavorting on the screen, adding to their exaggerated moaning as he stuffed his face with the greasy burger, his other hand inside his trousers.

No time to waste, she quietly unlocked the back door, slid outside and relocked the door. She thought her heart would burst out of her body as the padlock easily gave way with the small key. Now she was out in the alleyway. She could not run in her flimsy indoor flip-flops so she discarded them and ran as fast as she could to the end of the alley and turned into the street behind the house. All those years she had lived there and yet she had no idea which way to go. A young woman was pushing a buggy towards her, talking softly to her baby inside. She stopped abruptly at the sudden appearance of Carmen.

"Which way police?" Carmen asked the woman.

"Let me get them for you." She said, her phone already in her hand. "Why don't you wait down there?" She pointed to a gap between two houses. Wasting no time, she called the emergency services, keeping her eyes on the entrance to the alleyway. She looked relieved when, in less than a minute, police sirens could be heard.

Carmen did as instructed, she crouched by the wall trying to catch her breath. Her legs gave way at the sound of the sirens, she was now slumped on the floor, there was no going back now even if she wanted to. The young woman lifted her baby out of the buggy, making soothing sounds as his face puckered ready to cry.

The sirens went silent as the police car pulled up.

"She's down there." The woman pointed to the passageway. One of the Officers gently helped Carmen to her feet and into the car.

"You'll be safe now," said the woman. "They'll look after you."

"But you don't know what I did," said Carmen "You don't know what I did."

*

Carmen sat motionless in the back seat of the police car. The Officer next to her spoke kindly, 'I'm PC Hughes, this is PC Taylor. Can you tell us your name?' Carmen began to tremble.

"Who are you running away from?" Continued PC Hughes.

The implication of what she had done suddenly hit Carmen and her whole body shook with anxiety.

"I not important. We have to get Valeria. She in danger. Hurry, go quick!"

She frantically waved her arms forward as if this action would make the car move.

"Where is Valeria?" asked PC Hughes

Carmen turned to the street on the left, still waving her arms. "Over there, number 75, upstairs. We must go! Go now, please! No waste time, she might die."

"Bridgewater Street? Is that where she is?" asked PC Taylor

"Yes, yes, we have to go! Go now! We have to get her before Scilacci comes."

PC Taylor sat up sharply at the mention of Scilacci, the name was cropping up on a daily basis. He radioed Headquarters.

"A woman at 75 Bridgewater Street is in danger." He looked at Carmen, 'there may be other women there too?' Carmen nodded. "And there are other women. Our informer Miss....what did you say your name is?"

"Carmen, Carmen Albescu," she answered, a little pride creeping into her voice.

"Miss Albescu informs us that Scilacci may be there."

Carmen could not remember the last time anyone had used her second name, she was stunned for a few seconds then panic returned and she tried to open the door.

"Where are you going Miss Albescu?"

"I have to see that Valeria is safe."

"We'll drive round and check out what's happening, please stay with us, we want to help you."

PC Taylor drove slowly round to Bridgewater Street and parked at the top. A police car was already outside number 75. As they watched two more came into view. Several uniformed Officers stormed the front door and disappeared inside.

Carmen cried out as Ana was escorted out of the house and into one of the cars. Her skimpy 'work-clothes' were a sharp contrast to the Police uniforms. She looked around her in confusion; Carmen knew she would be terrified.

Two Police Officers held firmly onto the obnoxious minder-of-the-day, as they led him to another car. He squirmed, trying to break free but with hands cuffed behind him, he did not stand a chance. Even from the safety of the car, Carmen shook as he looked around him and was obviously shouting abuse to the small group of onlookers gathered on the pavement. If she had been nearer she would have heard his threat to *'get the fucking bitch who locked him in.'*

Carmen could just make out the colour of Valeria's hair over the top of a bed cover as another two Officers helped her out of the house. She collapsed against one of them and had to be lifted into the third car. Carmen's cries of anguish choked in her throat as she watched it speed away, lights flashing.

"Your friend is safe as well now, they will do all they can to make her strong again." said PC Taylor.

"She won't think of me as her friend," said Carmen, "I did bad things."

"But you risked your life to save her, Carmen, that was very brave. Now we would like you to come to the Police Station with us. You're not under arrest but you can help us catch the wicked people who made you do whatever you did. After that you will be taken to a safe house. You will never have to come back here again. Do you understand?"

Carmen did not feel brave and she did not really understand why she was being treated with respect. For years now she had been led to believe that if she made contact with the Police, they would consider her 'scum' and lock her up. Her anguished wails filled the car as she began to realise the full extent of the evil intentions of the Scilaccis.

Valeria

Regaining consciousness Valeria sensed that she was travelling in a vehicle. Slowly opening her eyes she found she was in the back of a car being driven by a young man in uniform. Beside her a pretty police woman was gently holding her hand. Before she could find her voice the police woman spoke softly. "It's OK. We're taking you to the hospital for a check-up. Don't worry, we'll soon be there."

After being examined thoroughly by an efficient middle-aged female doctor she was given some strong pain killers and a glass of water.

"You'll survive," smiled the doctor.

"Take these now and you should soon start to feel better."

She nodded silently and tried to return the smile. Her legs still felt wobbly. The police woman took her arm and led her slowly back to the car.

*

She was surprised and relieved not to be returned to the house but became anxious when they pulled up outside the police station. Why had they brought her here? Had she done something wrong?

She was lead inside, down a long corridor where a door opened to reveal Carmen and the girl from upstairs. They were sitting at a table with hot drinks and a plate of sandwiches. Carmen jumped up and came over. Grasping her hands and looking into her eyes she pleaded "Sorry, sorry, OK? Sorry!"

Valeria thought she must be dreaming. This could not be real.

A little later the table was cleared and two police officers with pens and paper sat down.

"OK, if we are going to help you we need to hear everything you can tell us."

Carmen seemed happy to tell them the whole story starting with how she herself was brought to England by Scalacci and his gang and forced into prostitution. The two girls stared open mouthed when they heard about the abortion she was forced to have and the way Scalacci had disfigured her face in an outburst of rage. They had not realised that she too had been a victim! Finally, exhausted, Carmen put her head in her hands and sobbed. Valeria stood up and put her arms around her gently rocking her backwards and forwards.

All three were taken to a nearby B & B run by an old matronly woman whose husband was a retired policeman. They would be safe here until other arrangements could be made.

*

When they sat down for breakfast the next morning there was a newspaper on the table. It was the Stretford Star. Valeria picked it up, gasped and what little colour there was drained from her face.

Looking out of the front cover was the face of Adriana, Ramona's mother. Why? Ramona's mother was in Romania, what was she doing on the front of an English newspaper?

When the landlady came in with a tray of food and drinks Valeria was still staring at the paper.

"Alright my dear?" asked the woman curiously.

"No! No! This is the mother of my friend from Romania. I do not understand, why?"

The woman took the newspaper and, after reading silently for a little while, she explained.

"There has been a terrible accident."

Using the salt pot and the sugar bowl she demonstrated. "The car hit her and drove away. It did not stop. She is critical in hospital."

"But where is my friend, Ramona?" Valeria asked desperately.

Carmen did not speak. She was looking at the floor.

"You know?" challenged Valeria, lifting Carmen's chin and looking pleadingly into her eyes.

"OK, OK. I tell the police now," sighed Carmen.

Very little was eaten and Carmen was still sobbing when a police officer arrived. Only then did Valeria learn what had happened to Ramona.

If we had been in the same room that night I could have saved her.

In her distraught state she wished it had been her who had died then she would never have been put through the terrible abuse she had suffered.

Annie Gray

Dave Arden called Annie into his office and asked her how she had handled the follow up article on the Anson Hotel. "See for yourself," she said as she dropped a copy of the The Stretford Star's front page onto his desk. The editor picked it up and read:

Death of Hit and Run Victim triggers Murder Inquiry
City hotel used as a brothel
By Annie Gray

A murder investigation is under way following information received during inquiries on an incident at a Manchester city hotel that was being used as a brothel.

Young women forced into prostitution were found by police at the Anson Hotel, which had been hit by a device causing the building to become filled with smoke. At the same time Manchester Fire Fighters fought to extinguish cars that had been set alight in a nearby car park. Police believe the two incidents are connected and say the smoke device was set to cause chaos but not a fire and was placed by someone who knew what they were doing.

The detained females are foreign nationals and cannot be named for legal reasons. They believed they were being recruited to study and to do honest work in England but cruel deceit led to them being trafficked and transported into sexual exploitation and slavery. The police and appropriate support agencies are working together on the victims' behalf.

Inquiries into the incident revealed one of the females detained by police was very concerned about her friend, who went missing shortly after arriving in Manchester. It then transpired the missing girl's mother, Mrs Adriana Radu, came to England from Romania and contacted Manchester Police asking them for help as she was concerned she had not heard from her daughter. Now Mrs Radu has died of injuries sustained in a hit and run car incident.

The search is now on for the driver of a red Fiat Panda and for the traffickers, who are a well organised gang and very dangerous, according to a statement from the Manchester Police Press Office.

Manchester streets are crippled with corruption and, according to an anonymous source, who it appears sees himself as an anti-crime crusader, says the police are dragging their heels. This newspaper, along with the police, has been tipped off about attacks to not only expose and disrupt criminal activities but also to show the weakness in police response. The latest tip off was about the incident at the Anson Hotel.

Police say they are closer to tracing the identity of our crusader, who they believe is a man who has professional knowledge of firearms and who may have personal reasons for wreaking retribution in a volley of vengeance.

Investigating officer, Detective Inspector Mick Kinkaid, was unavailable for comment.

Buchan

Buchan groaned as a bolt of lightning sliced through his brain, he swallowed, tasting the sour mixture of stale beer and alcohol, he breathed in and could sense an odour, rather like that of the proverbial gorilla's armpit, that drifted up to his nostrils from under the duvet. He tried to roll over but someone was shaking him and then he remembered, he'd had the nightmare again. Hearing the crackling sound of burning and screams, feeling the heat scorching his face and seeing the pleading eyes. This time is was not the young Iraqi and it was not his mother. It was Maria, with blood running down one side of her face and one ear missing, pleading and holding out a hand that he could never grasp. Can she possibly still be alive? If she was, he swore he would willingly sacrifice himself to bring her back to safety.

Kerry Blazer, was shaking him and shouting, "Wake up, come on you've got work to do, I know where she is."

He lay back." Is she alive? Please tell me she's alive?"

"Yes she is and you haven't helped by getting pissed out of your mind, for Christs sake do you even understand what I'm saying?"

"Just tell me where she is, how do you know she's alive?"

"She's at Scilacci's house in the sticks, I saw her, she was being dragged past the door of the office, the one I showed you at the pub, remember?"

Buchan, leaping from the bed, "I'm going out there now and I'll storm the place if I have to, I'll get her out or die trying."

Kerry stared at him. "Take a look at yourself and try thinking for a change, it was you who told me about the six Ps, preparation and planning prevents, piss, poor, performance, remember and in the state you're in now, if you go in with no plan, you'll both end up dead. Scilacci wants you to contact him, so do that, ring Maria's phone. Tell him you left the country after the attack on the Anson Hotel and you're in Spain. You'll need time to book a flight back. That will give you a day to sober up and prepare. God! men, why are you all so bloody predictable?"

Buchan did not argue, "You're right, I've endangered the mission, I'll get a shower now and ring him, he'll obviously be making demands and I'll deal with the six Ps when I know what he's after."

*

An hour later, his head still thumping, Buchan made the call.

A male voice with a gravelly Scottish accent answered.

"Maria's phone, who am I speaking to?"

"I think you know who this is, I'm not going to speak about what you have already done to Maria, I just want her back and then I'll leave you alone."

"Oh no Mr Buchan, it doesn't work like that, I have the woman and I'll kill her and send you a video of me cutting her up, one piece at a time. I want you to meet two of my colleagues in one hour, if you don't come, she dies painfully, very painfully. For every ten minutes delay I take one piece of her, I start with her toes, one at a time, then her hands, one finger at a time then her feet and hands. I don't suppose she'll be able to take much more than that."

"Don't waste your time threatening me, I will meet your so-called colleagues but I can't do it in one hour, I'm in Spain. I came out here to get out of the way and stay out of sight for a while after the Anson Hotel, I know Kinkaid's been looking for me, I'll book a flight as soon as I can."

"I hope you're not playing me for a fool Buchan, I want you here, we need to have a serious talk."

"I know that and I know what you are capable of doing but I have two conditions."

"Conditions, who the hell do you think you're talking to?" Scilacci was shouting now. "I make the conditions, you don't make conditions, I do."

"I understand that but you must understand, I'm not meeting anyone until I know Maria is still alive, I need to speak to her, now."

Buchan could hear Scilacci faintly, he had obviously moved back from the phone. He was shouting again. "Fetch the bitch, it's what I expected, he wants to make sure she's alive."

The sound of movement came from the phone and then a voice, it was Maria.

A sob and then." Paul, is that you?"

"Yes, I'm here." He said, trying not to cry out.

Scilacci was back on the phone." Right you've heard her and she's OK but she won't be if you don't do exactly as I say. You will text me from Spain when you have a flight number and I'll have you met outside the airport by two of my men. When they have you, I'll release the woman, if anything goes wrong, she dies."

"I understand that Scilacci but I'll warn you. You know who I am and you know what I'm capable of. If Maria comes to any further harm, I'll dedicate the rest of my life to tracking you down and killing you."

"I understand you perfectly but you don't have to take that attitude. I can always make use of a man with your experience and skills, nobody has to die and you could make a great deal of money. But remember, if you put a foot wrong you can kiss goodbye to the lovely Maria. You won't even have a body to bury, I'll feed her to the dogs."

*

The phone went dead and Buchan slumped back. "I've got a lot of work to do."

Kerry, business like as ever nodded, "They are bound to have the ability to check passenger lists, so I'll get online and book you an overnight flight from Malaga for tomorrow night. You will have to be all set up and ready to attack before the time the plane is due to land."

Buchan got to work, Scilacci's house was outside the city in the countryside to the east of Lymm. The building was called, Great Oak Farm, a gentrified farmhouse with six bedrooms, all en-suite, a separate quadruple garage, a large kitchen, three reception rooms and an indoor swimming pool. There was also a wine cellar.

Kerry printed off some maps of the area and Buchan drove to the Rosswell Street garage where he busied himself checking his weapons, he would take all of them on this job, he knew he might need everything.

He would wear camouflaged military clothing and carry a back pack. The Spider sub machine gun, his ammunition and the grenades would be in the backpack. The Makarov he would carry in his right-hand pocket until he approached the house and then it would stay in his hand. As usual the Beretta would nestle in the small of his back. He knew he had to make a quick start to get into the area and start his reconnaissance before it got dark. He would have to see the house and it's surrounds in daylight and in the dark, then he would make his final plan.

His burner mobile vibrated, it was a text from Kerry, you are booked on flight LS894 from Malaga tomorrow, taking off at 2150 and landing in Manchester at 0005, make sure you bring her back and good luck. Buchan texted the details Scilacci.

He would have time to scout the area in his car to get the lie of the land and reach Great Oak Farm in time for a daylight reconnaissance before moving in for a night recce.

*

His drive around the neighbourhood of the house revealed little, the farmhouse was situated in a flat area of mixed woodland and fields and all he was able to see was a driveway with closed double metal gates across the entrance. He would have to walk in using the cover of the woods, for the recce he would only carry the Makarov and the Berretta. He parked in a quiet street on the edge of Lymm and started walking, at first following footpaths and then moving through the woods. He found there was a small rise in the otherwise flat countryside about four hundred metres from the farmhouse. He settled down to watch and stayed watching as the daylight faded. There were few lights showing in the windows and all curtains were closed, three men were patrolling round the grounds close to the house, they did not appear to be alert and were not displaying any firearms. Keeping low he moved closer, following the hedge line and using it as cover from view. As he got closer it started to rain, at first a few drops and then continuous light rain. It was then he saw that the sentries were now congregated and standing under partial cover, within a couple of minutes two had started smoking. He smiled and prayed there would be rain tomorrow, these men were obviously not soldiers and seemed to lack any sense of discipline, he could deal with them.

Buchan eased his way back to his observation point and continued watching. He felt his burner phone vibrating in his pocket and walked back into the woods to check the phone, it was Kerry. He rang her back speaking softly and keeping watch in the direction of the farmhouse.

"Buchan, I've just heard the Scilacci half of a call between him and Kinkaid. As far as I can make out Scilacci made a big mistake when he cut Maria's ear off. Her DNA is kept on the police data base, most police officers are, they knew within a couple of hours of going to Apricot Cottage that it was hers. There is a hell of an uproar at Manchester police HQ and police raiding parties are already kicking down the doors of half the criminals in Manchester and that includes Scilacci's brothels, he's talking about making a run for it, he wants you but says he may be forced to kill Maria and run before tomorrow night."

"That means I have to go in tonight, I'll just have to fetch the rest of my gear from the car, it will be in about an hour."

"I think you're right it has to be tonight. I can see where you're parked on the tracker, I'll meet you there and I'll help in any way I can. And Buchan, we have to just make sure we fetch that girl out of there, don't worry about revenge now, that can come later. Just bring her home."

*

Kerry was waiting for Buchan when he returned to his car, she was walking quickly up and down past her car and his, with her arms tightly folded across her breasts.

She stopped and glared, "How are you going to do it, it's impossible, they'll be ready for you and then you'll both be killed."

"I'm not going to go charging up to the front door, I have to find a way to distract them, to attract them to the front of the house while I get in through the back, I'll have to improvise when I get there."

"That's stupid and you know it, I can distract them, just tell me how."

They argued, back and forth with Kerry adamant that she would come with him to the house, with or without his permission.

Buchan gave in, "OK, you can distract them and I know how but you might not like it."

He reached into his back pack and brought the two grenades out.

"Do you know what these are?"

"Bombs or something I suppose but what do you want me to do with them?"

"They are grenades and what I want you to do is roll these under the two cars parked at the front of the house, when they explode they should set fire to the cars and attract the guards and hopefully Scilacci to the front. Meanwhile I'll be round the back and getting in. When I'm in I want you well out of the way, I don't want to have to worry about you while I'm inside."

Kerry nodded, "So, how do these things work?"

Buchan held up one grenade. "I've already prepared them, you will have to pull these pins out and I want you to throw them underarm so that they come to rest, close to or under the cars at the front of the house. The lever on the side of the grenade will fly off when you throw them and the grenade will wait for a signal from a mobile phone before it explodes. These are very powerful grenades and you will have to be at least two hundred metres away and behind cover before you explode them. Do not be tempted to watch the explosions or your night vision will be ruined. The best place for you to do this is over the wall at the front of the house or behind a tree with a big solid trunk. Now I want you to check that your phone is picking up the signals."

Kerry activated her phone and nodded, "I've got the two signals, there's no problem, it's straightforward."

Buchan continued, "When we walk in I'll show you where to wait afterwards, it's a little hillock about four hundred meters from the house, do you understand all of that?"

Kerry looked at the grenades wide eyed.

Buchan touched her arm, "Are you sure you want to do this, just say if you don't, I can manage without you?"

Thin lipped Kerry replied, "I'll do it."

"Do you remember what I've told you?"

Kerry did not disappoint, she recited his instructions word perfect.

"Don't interfere with the alarms, I want as much noise and confusion as I can get and it's possible the shock wave from the explosions will set them off."

Kerry did not respond.

Buchan checked his equipment; Spider sub machine gun complete with full magazine and another in his back pack. Makarov pistol in his right-hand jacket pocket fitted with a full magazine. Berretta pistol in the small of his back, also fully loaded. He pulled his gloves on, he'd never touched his weapons without wearing them. Removing the wheel brace from the boot of his car he thought it would be useful for smashing his way through windows if he had to. He thought for a moment and retrieved the Berretta from his back and offered it to Kerry.

"Do you want to take this you might need it?"

Kerry shook her head, "No, I've never even held a gun, you keep it."

Buchan looked her up and down. She was wearing a black anorak, black jeans and a backpack containing the grenades, on her feet were a pair of black walking shoes but she was also wearing a bright red scarf round her neck. He nodded, "You'll do but leave the scarf in your car and use some black make-up on your cheeks, nose and forehead, to break up the white of your face"

Kerry did as she was told and re-joined him, "I suppose this is it?"

Buchan started walking, "For better or worse, let's do it, keep me in sight but not too close, if anything happens on the way in, run and I'll deal with it."

*

Buchan could feel the weight of responsibility bearing down on him, he not only had to get Maria away from the house but also do whatever it took to keep Kerry out of the firing line.

They walked to the start of the footpath and Buchan moved ahead, it was still raining, lightly but persistent. Buchan thought this is just what he needed, he knew the guards would probably be under cover and out of the rain. He retraced his route back towards the house, pausing every couple of minutes to listen and check that Kerry was still with him. When he reached the observation point he stopped and waited for Kerry to catch up with him.

They lay together looking down at the house.

Buchan spoke in a low voice, "Take a good look round, this is the place I want you to come back to, as we go in make a mental note of anything you'll recognise on the way out. We'll go down together and I'll come with you to the front, I won't move round to the back until I'm sure you're settled and ready to go."

He pointed to the cover where he expected the guards to be sheltering, "That's where the guards are likely to be, we'll skirt round to our right and approach the house from the front through the trees. Follow me and I'll find a position for you to hide until we're ready."

Kerry appeared to him to be remarkably calm at the prospect of throwing grenades and having to escape in the darkness.

They moved slowly down the slope towards the house, Buchan was careful to avoid being skylined and moved slowly, they reached the trees without problem and moved from tree to tree until the front of the house and the two parked cars were immediately in front of them. An impressive double timber door was flanked by Corinthian columns supporting a roofed approach, four ornamental lights illuminated the scene. Buchan gripped Kerry lightly by her arm, she was trembling with excitement or nerves with action so close. He pulled her behind the trunk of a tree.

   Whispering, "It will take me fifteen minutes to get into place at the back, have the grenades ready and remember, take cover as soon as you have thrown them and then get out before they can react and don't worry, you'll be fine."

Kerry did not reply and Buchan moved quietly retracing his route back to the observation point, there was still no movement and no sign of the guards. He made his way through the grounds frequently stopping and listening. The back of the house was in darkness, he saw there was an ornate conservatory and decided he would avoid entering through that and would use a standard window to one side of it. He waited wheel brace in hand and was experiencing the familiar pre-action feelings of apprehension and nervous weakness but he knew he would be ready when he heard the first grenade explode.

Kerry Blazer

There were two BMW's and an F Pace Jaguar on the fine shale drive guarded by two stone lions in front of the house. Kerry opened her Voodoo Envy and sixty seconds later the external CCTV cameras were now showing a recorded still of the grounds. She allowed seven minutes to gauge any adverse reaction.

While she was waiting Kerry removed the shiny green spheres from her leather satchel and primed the detonators. She was using M67 magnetic fragmentation grenades with added amplification for the utmost disruption. The key to the M67s is the ability to use Wi-Fi. Kerry will be two hundred yards away the other side of the ten feet perimeter wall when the multiple explosions rip through the three vehicles.

She takes the cellophane off burner phone H and sends a SMS text message to burner phone G. It simply says: two minutes pop pop pop

Burner phone H pinged: thumbs up.

*

Kerry opened the Voodoo Envy the three parked cars show up on the home screen. She clicked the bye bye icon and seconds later the night sky was lit with a series of blinding flashes. The noise was deafening. On screen the devastation was clear to see. The cars are now unrecognisable mangled wreckage. There was no glass left in the front windows of the house.

It was over a minute before the first people arrived on the screen. Two of Scilacci's henchmen could be observed bursting out of the house. Kerry let them clear the door before clicking on the bye bye icon again. The bang that followed ensured that Kerry had given Buchan a devastating diversion. She hoped it would be enough.

Kerry took out the Kill Wings transmission blocker from the hard leather case. The red light began blinking immediately. The technology would be a double edged sword. It would prevent Scilacci or anyone involved with him summoning help but it would also mean contact with Buchan would no longer be possible.

Buchan

Exactly on time the first grenade exploded, the house alarm shrieked into life and Buchan swung the wheel brace against the glass of the window and kept smashing until the window was clear of glass. As he climbed inside he heard the second grenade explode and brought the Spider sub machine gun out of his pack and looked round. He was in what appeared to be a laundry room with washing machines and spin driers. He was sweating and already and breathing heavily, the hair on his neck was standing on end. He knew he and Maria might only have minutes to live.

He opened the door and stepped into a short corridor and moved towards the front of the house, the lights were not switched on and the alarm was screeching, echoing through his head, he had to ignore it and keep moving. Then he saw lights ahead and moved towards them. He could hear nothing over the noise of the alarm.

He had to throw caution to the winds and hope his reactions were quicker than anyone he met. Then the noise of the alarm was cut and he heard a voice shouting, it was Scilacci.

"Get to the back of the house, that's where he'll be, it's got to be Buchan, move yourselves but don't kill him, I want him."

Two men silhouetted in the faint light came into view, one behind the other, Buchan dropped to one knee and aimed, the men were carrying sawn off shotguns, the one in front skidded to a halt and started to bring his shotgun up to take aim but the second man blundered into his back.

The Scorpion rattled in his hands as Buchan fired a three round burst into the chest of the man in front who fell to the ground and Buchan fired a second burst at the second man but saw he had only been hit in the shoulder, he had one arm hanging useless by his side but he was still struggling to bring the shotgun up. Buchan fired another burst, this time accurately into his chest.

Buchan moved forward and kicked both shotguns away from the bodies, one man was moaning and gasping and Buchan knew he presented no further danger.

Buchan kept moving and entered what appeared to be the entrance hall, he could hear shouting coming from an open doorway, he recognised the voice, it was Scilacci again.

"Get out there and sort him out, that's what I pay you for, go on get out."

"But Dom, he's got a machine gun, what do you expect me to do?"

"I expect you to get out there, you get out there and face him or I'll shoot you myself."

"I'm not going, he's bombed us and now he's got a machine gun, it's a war zone, you don't pay me enough for that, I'm finished, I'm going."

*

Buchan was shocked to hear the sound of two shots, a scream and then Scilacci again.

"I warned you, why didn't you listen." There was the sound of another shot.

Buchan remained silent, it could be a trap and it was obvious Scilacci was waiting for him to walk through the door so he could shoot Buchan as soon as he showed himself. No, he thought, 'I'm not that much of a mug, I'll do it my way.'

He swiftly returned to where the Scilacci henchmen were laying, now obviously dead and picked up one of the sawn-off shotguns. He checked it and saw it was double barrelled and loaded with two cartridges. He returned to the entrance hall and hid the Scorpion behind a chair. He took the Makarov automatic out of his pocket and placed it close the door to the room where Scilacci waited. Then taking the shotgun in his hands, he steadied his breathing, he knew if he was too slow or Scilacci too fast, or too well prepared, he would be dead in five seconds and Maria would follow him a few minutes later.

Holding the shotgun at waist height he fired two shots angled at the two far corners of the room, dropped the shotgun, scooped up the Makarov and burst through the now shattered door. Scilacci had been caught in the blast of the shotgun and was staggering and holding his face. Buchan smashed him to the ground with a body charge and grabbed his gun from an unresisting hand. It was another Makarov. Looking round he saw that Scilacci had indeed shot and killed the last of his defenders.

Scilacci had small wounds, cuts on his face, one eye was closed and leaking blood, he stared up at Buchan with his working eye, "I can make you a very rich man, you don't have to kill me.

"I don't want your money, I want Maria, where is she?"

"She's in the cellar, she's had a rough time but she's OK. I'll give you and her enough money to more than make up for what I've done, what have you got to lose, why would you refuse it?"

Scilacci attempted a smile, "Do we have deal?"

Buchan looked coldly into his eye, "No, you've forgotten something, you killed both my parents."

And shot him twice in the chest, Scilacci slumped back onto the floor and blood was soon soaking into the carpet around his body, Dominic Scilacci was dead.

*

Now he had to find Maria.

He looked more closely round the room, it was the office Kerry had shown him on the computer. He eased out through the shattered door, there was no sound. He had to find the cellar and Maria and he had no means of knowing if there were any more of the Scilacci gang still in the house waiting for him to make a mistake. He retrieved the Scorpion and confirmed the magazine was half empty. He was ready.

There was a second corridor leading away from the entrance hall, he moved along it throwing doors open and passing on when he had cleared the room. He moved quickly and knew he was announcing his presence with every door he kicked open but he also knew there was no choice.

He then noticed the next door was heavier and had a more old-fashioned look, the wood was darker than the others and there were heavy metal hinges visible. He stood to one side of the door and lifted the weight of the dark metal latch and pulled. The door swung open and Buchan could see steps leading down into darkness that was relieved by a faint glow of light from below, he had found the cellar, he took one step down and then a second, he heard a muffled voice and called, "Maria, are you there?"

More muffled sounds came from below and he slowly and silently descended one step at a time. The walls of the stairway were of brick, encrusted with dust, spiders webs and grime. They appeared not to have been cleaned for a century. There was a half-opened door at the bottom, he put one toe against it and pushed, it swung slowly open and in the dim light he saw Maria. She was tied to a chair, secured by thin rope by her legs and arms. The muffled calls had come from her, she was gagged. He could see that one ear was missing and her shirt heavily blood stained. Her eyes were wide and staring and she was frantically shaking her head from side to side while making more muffled sounds, she was warning him. There was somebody in there with her.

Buchan reasoned that the obvious way for anyone to ambush him as he walked in would be from behind the door so they could attack him from the rear. He wanted to be able to move quickly in the confined space, so he put the Scorpion down at the foot of the steps and drew the Makarov. Tensing himself ready for action he kicked the door hard smashing it open and rushed through the doorway, he looked and saw there was nobody behind the door. He swung round the other way but he was too late. A shriek echoed round the cellar and a wild-eyed Francesca Scilacci was on him, stabbing. He felt a mind-numbing pain in his left shoulder and acting purely by instinct stepped back and kicked. His foot connected Francesca's thigh and she fell back.

Francesca scrambled away on her knees, leapt to her feet and crouched behind Maria, grabbed her hair and forced her head back exposing her throat while holding the blood-stained knife against Maria's throat.

"One step and she's dead" hissed Francesca.

Buchan aimed the Makarov at her, "If she dies you die."

Francesca giggled, her black hair was wildly disordered and she looked every inch the vengeful Italian Mafia woman, her dark eyes gleamed, obviously enjoying the danger and relishing the malice, Buchan realised she was mad, totally insane.

Buchan speaking slowly and keeping his voice low and calm said, "Well Francesca, looks like we've got a Mexican stand-off, what do you suggest we do?"

Francesca smiled, "Mexican stand-off, I like the sound of that, let's make it interesting. I'll make her bleed a little." And pushed the blade of the knife into the side of Maria's neck, a trickle of blood flowed down her neck and spread into her shirt. Maria's scream was muffled by the gag and Buchan was tempted to risk shooting but had no confidence he could kill Francesca before she killed Maria.

Francesca's face took on a look of obvious cunning and Buchan knew she would try to outwit him. She took the initiative, "I'll make a deal, you lay your gun down on the floor and step back to the wall, I'll run to the door and get away and you can have your bloody Maria. Do we have a deal?"

Maria was frantically shaking her head from side to side, her eyes pleading.

Buchan thought for a moment, "That could work, there's been enough killing and I don't want to have to kill you as well, I just want Maria back. I'll put the gun in front of the chair and back up against the wall."

Francesca grinned, "Get on with it then, just let me get out of here and you can do what you want with her."

Buchan stepped forward, bent his knees and without taking his eyes off Francesca, placed the Makarov on the floor a little to the right of centre in front of Maria who stared into his eyes, tears running down her cheeks. Buchan stepped slowly back to the wall and stood waiting.

Francesca edged round the chair with the knife held close to Maria's neck, she let go of the knife and dropped to the ground reaching for the Makarov, she grasped it and swung round to aim at Buchan but found she was looking down the barrel of his back-up gun, the Berretta. Francesca screamed, a scream that was cut short by Buchan when he pulled the trigger twice and she crashed to the floor. Blood sprayed from her head and pooled around her and it continued to flow while Buchan cut Maria free and removed the gag.

Maria grasped him, "I thought she was going to kill you, she would have killed us both."

Buchan smiled, "I knew she would try, that's why I carry the back-up, let's get you out of here."

Supporting each other, nursing their pain, they limped up the stairs and into the entrance hall.

As soon as they reached the entrance hall Buchan knew something was different, he could hear movement and voices outside and lights were flashing through the broken windows, the lights were blue and the phone in the office was ringing. He recognised the tactics, the police had the house surrounded and wanted to talk to him, there was no way out.

Carmen

After spending two nights in the Bed and Breakfast Accommodation, Carmen was told she had been granted a place in a safe house in Cheshire.

"A safe house, is there such a thing?" asked Carmen.

"Yes, its run by the Salvation Army," Kate, a Social services Duty Officer informed her.

"An Army!" Carmen was alarmed.

"The Salvation Army is a church. As you've agreed to help the Police with their enquiries, you will be well-cared for there, while your case is being considered," said Kate.

Carmen looked uncomfortable at the mention of a church.

"Why would they want to help me? I've been very wicked," she asked.

"It's our belief you have been violated and abused since you were brought to the UK. In the safe house you will meet other women and girls who have had similar experiences."

Carmen was beginning to realise how much her mind had been twisted with constant fear of reprisals. Survival had been the basic instinct which had kept her alive, making her act in a way completely opposite to her nature. Was it really possible that help had not been that far away?

"I will tell the Police all I know," said Carmen, "but what about Valeria? Where will she go? I have to know that she will be safe from Scilacci if I tell them everything."

Carmen was told that Valeria required some medical attention and would be sent to a safe house as soon as she had recovered.

"Will she come here?" asked Carmen

"I can't promise that" said Karen, it depends where there is a place when she's ready. But you will see her again, I can promise that. Is there something else you want to ask?" she said, sensing Carmen's agitation.

"Church," Carmen almost whispered. "Do you think I would ever be able to attend Church again after all the things I've done? I can't remember when I last went to Mass."

"Yes, Carmen, that can be arranged for you. There is a Roman Catholic Church, the Church of Our Lady, nearby and I believe the Father visits the house regularly. Would that be the right church for you?"

Carmen nodded, "How I would love to go to Church again. It's time I made my confession."

Valeria

Valeria looked at the calendar. Tomorrow she would be seventeen. She thought back to the night before her sixteenth birthday. She had been a child, determined to find a better life in England. 'How could she have aged so much in one year? She sighed.

She had been very naive to think it possible her father would ever have helped her to follow her dream. Now, a year later, she realised it was much more likely that he had sold her to Scalacci.

The year had turned out to be an unbelievable roller coaster journey of emotions. She had felt relief at being allowed to leave home but anger after discovering she had been tricked.

Her happiness at becoming friends with Ramona and Adriana in Romania had been followed by fear at realising the job centre advert had been a trap to lure them into thinking they were being taken to a language school and would be given jobs afterwards.

She still had the physical as well as the mental scars to remind her of the terror she had felt when being branded by Francesca Scalacci. The sadness she had experienced after learning Ramona and her mother had been killed seemed never to diminish and added to that was the feeling of guilt because it would never have happened if she had not come into their lives.

And, although she had never had any choice she could not help feeling disgust and shame at what she had endured. Then, after being rescued by the police there was the uncertainty about her future. Would she be sent back to her father or be allowed to stay in England? But now, her more recent emotions were surprise, joy and gratitude.

When she was told there would be compensation from the Scalacci family she wondered how that could be possible when Dominic and his sister were now dead. There had been no explanation from Maria Ross, Paul Buchan nor Kerry Blazer although they had all smiled knowingly at each other. Nevertheless she had gratefully accepted the money along with the suggestion it be used to set up a refuge for girls like her who had been tricked into sex slavery by villains like the Scallacis.

*

After searching the internet they had all agreed that The Old Vicarage was the perfect property. A five bedroomed, detached house with beautiful gardens in a little village north of Newbury on the southern slopes of the Berkshire Downs with the most stunning scenery.

They had also agreed she would be the best person to understand and help the girls who came here and she had happily assured them she would love to live and work here.

She still felt quite breathless when she remembered the price of the property but they had told her she need not worry about money. The refuge would be run by a charity they had set up and there would always be funds to pay for the running expenses. All she had to do was look after the girls and help them to recover from their ordeal.

Carmen

Carmen discovered that the safe house had previously been a convent. She could feel the sacredness in the building, the many years of praying and devotion. It was helping to restore her faith that there were good people in the world. The young woman she used to be, before she was lured to England with the promise of work, was slowly re-surfacing.

She was saddened at the age of some of the girls in the house, also seeking refuge, under twelve years old she felt sure. Some of the women wanted to talk about their abuse, some were still too traumatised. Most of them, like herself, were overjoyed to be rescued and were willing to co-operate with the Police.

She had been taken to Greater Manchester's Police Headquarters to give statements several times. On one occasion she had met Valeria, also there to give a statement. Carmen was relieved to see that the bloom on Valeria's skin had returned and she was a beautiful young woman again. They parted, not exactly best friends but there was an understanding between them.

Carmen had given the Police the address of her home in Romania, today she was hoping for news of her parents. Two female Police Officers entered the interview room introducing themselves as PC Williams and PC Carter.

"Contact has been made with your family," said Williams.

"How is my father?" asked Carmen quietly.

Williams continued. "Sadly, we have to tell you that your father passed away a few months ago. Your mother wanted you to know that his passing was peaceful. We are very sorry for your loss."

Carmen had feared this would be the news, she held back tears as she asked if they knew how her mother was coping.

"We also have good news about your family. Your mother is being cared for by your sister."

"My sister? My sister, Madelina, is with my mother?"

Carmen could hold back the tears no longer, "But how can that be? My sister was ...my sister was..."

"Married to an Englishman," said Carter

Carmen interrupted fiercely, "My sister was forced to marry the Englishman so that he could get Romanian citizenship."

"Yes," said Carter, "we are discovering that the evils of Scilacci are even more far reaching than we originally thought. Your sister's husband disappeared as soon as he was aware that the Police were onto the trail of the Scilaccis. At least your sister was in her own country with enough money to get home. He will get some credit for that when we arrest him."

"You will find him?" asked Carmen

"We have Interpol, an International Police Organisation constantly working on cases like this. However stressful it is for you, the more information you give us, the more chance we have of catching the criminals responsible for ruining good peoples' lives," said Carter.

"It has been a long time and I forced myself to forget things but as I remember them, I will tell you everything. But then, after that, do you know what will happen to me?" Carmen had a worried look on her face.

Williams looked sympathetically at Carmen. "Your case will be considered by The Home Office, a department of the British Government. It will probably take several months to gather all the evidence about the Scilaccis. In our experience, it's possible you may be allowed to go back home afterwards. Is that what you would like to happen?"

Carmen clasped her hands together. "I pray to the Blessed Mary every day for that to happen. Now I know she won't fail me. I've waited all these years, I can wait a few more months."

Buchan

Buchan knew he was beaten, the blue flashing lights, the noise and the persistent ringing of the landline telephone told him the police had arrived in force and they would have the house surrounded by trained marksmen.

He pulled Maria close, "You know what's happening don't you?"

She clung to him, even closer, "Yes, they have us trapped and they are not going to leave us any way out."

Buchan stared into her eyes, "You have done nothing wrong you were kidnapped. I'll answer the phone and tell them you're safe and that you will be coming out first, it's the only thing we can do."

"But you've just saved my life, I can't abandon you."

"You're not abandoning me, the best way you can protect me is tell them outside that I am the one who stopped Scilacci from killing you. We have to act soon, or they might come crashing in and we could both get hurt."

He kissed her softly on the lips, released her and walked into the office to pick up the phone.

"Buchan."

"Mr Buchan my name is Martin Kent and my job is to get everybody out of the house without anyone getting injured, can you tell me who is in the house with you?"

"There's just me and Maria Ross, you will obviously want to get her out first."

"Correct, do you have any firearms?"

"There are several firearms in the house but I will not be carrying one, I'll make them safe and leave them in clear view."

"You obviously know the ropes, please leave the line open and I'll brief my men to expect her and I'll tell you when we are ready."

*

Buchan laid the phone on the desk, picked up his mobile and phoned Annie Gray, she answered immediately.

"Annie this is Paul Buchan, I've been keeping you informed about Scilacci."

"Oh good, a name at last, do you have something for me?"

"Yes, write this down, I'm at Great Oaks Farm near Lymm. The house is surrounded by armed police and I am inside with Maria Ross, she's alive. Dominic Scilacci and his sister Francesca are both dead as well as three of their men."

"When did this all happen, tell me about it."

"I don't have time to go into details but you need to get out here as soon as you can, did you get all that?"

Her voice rose in pitch, "Yes, yes I did but can't you tell me more?"

"No, just get here as soon as you can and bring a camera crew if you have one."

Buchan could hear a voice on the landline and picked the phone up, Martin Kent did not sound happy, "Who were you talking to."

"My favourite newspaper reporter, I expect she'll arrive soon with a photographer and perhaps even a film crew, are you ready for Maria?"

Buchan heard him sigh but like a true professional he carried on, "Tell Maria to walk out of the door with her hands clearly in view and do exactly as she is instructed."

Buchan responded, "She knows what to do, I'll send her out now."

*

Maria had been listening, she hugged him fiercely and they kissed, she walked to the door, turned to give him one last pleading look and walked out, as she disappeared from view Buchan could hear instructions being shouted.

Martin Kent was back on the line.

"Maria's clear, time for you."

"No, I know where all the weapons are, I'll make them safe and then I'll come out."

Without waiting for a reply, he laid the phone down and collected all the firearms in the entrance hall, removed their magazines and ejected any rounds still in the weapons.

He picked up the phone again "Are you there Mr Kent."

Kent replied, "I am, the question is are you ready to come out."

"I'm ready when you are."

"OK, walk to the door and push it open, as soon as the door opens make sure your hands are in the air showing empty palms to the officers waiting. You will be told what to do, make sure you follow the instructions and do not make any sudden movements. Do you understand all of that?"

"I understand, I will be pushing the door in about thirty seconds."

There was no point in waiting, he walked to the door and pushed it open and with his hands in the air and stepped out into the glare of lights, he could see nothing beyond them.

A man's voice, "Take three steps forward."

Buchan did as he was told.

"Now, with your hands still in the air drop to your knees."

Buchan dropped to his knees and could hear people behind him, his arms were grasped from each side and another voice said, "We are going to lower you to the ground, just do what you are told and you won't get hurt."

He felt himself being pushed to the ground face first, his arms were forced behind his back and handcuffs clipped onto his wrists.

"Do you have any weapons on you?"

"No, none." He had never felt so helpless.

He was roughly and thoroughly searched before being pulled to his feet.

"What are we going to find inside, anything that we need to be careful of?"

"You will find two shotguns, three pistols and a Spider sub-machine gun, they have all been made safe and left in the entrance hall. You will also find five dead bodies; I don't know if there was anyone else hiding in the house."

"Any explosives?"

"None that I know of."

*

Buchan was led away, told he was under arrest, cautioned, seated in the back of a police vehicle and driven quickly away from Great Oaks Farm. He had succeeded in rescuing Maria but was already wondering how long it would be before he breathed fresh air again.

The journey was quickly completed, and Buchan was pulled from the vehicle the door of the police custody block was already open and waiting for him.

Buchan blinked in the bright lights and noticed the angry looks being exchanged between the waiting officers. It would not take much to set them off he would give them no excuse for violence.

Buchan was searched again and gave his personal details to the Custody Officer. When asked if he had any injuries he replied, "Yes, I've been stabbed in my left shoulder."

An hour later Buchan had been told of his rights while in police custody, been examined by a doctor, had his wound dressed, had all his clothing seized and he was now alone in a cell wearing just a blue boiler suit.

He looked round the at the metal toilet with no lid, the blank walls, the bed which consisted of a dark blue waterproof mattress on what appeared to be a solid concrete base, on that was a wrapped pack of bedding and his shoulder was throbbing.

He felt a wave of despair flow over him and wondered how many years he would have to live in places like this. He did not fear being beaten; he had noticed there were CCTV camera's everywhere. The police had treated him correctly but with tight lipped icy contempt and he was desperately worried about how Maria was coping; she had been through hell.

Every hour the hatch in the cell door would crash open, eyes would briefly appear and the hatch would crash closed. In the morning he was handed breakfast on a cardboard tray and noticed the atmosphere had changed, the officer had smiled. He also murmured "We know you got Maria out, nice one."

*

Later the cell door opened and he was led through the custody office to an interview room. He was expecting a formal interview but was simply told, "There is someone here to see you."

He desperately wanted it to be Maria but knew that was impossible. He wondered if Maria would decide he brought too much trouble in his wake and take this opportunity to finish with him. She would be interviewed by the police as soon as she was released from hospital and there was no way they would allow the two of them to communicate, even if she wanted to.

The door opened and Buchan saw his visitor was his old commanding officer from the Intelligence Corp. Out of habit and instinct Buchan leapt to his feet before remembering he was no longer in the army.

The Colonel smiled, "Relax Mr Buchan, we aren't in barracks now."

"I know sir, force of habit, what on earth are you doing here?"

"I have been asked to speak to you, it seems you have been a little busy since we last met."

"All due respect sir but I don't think I should talk to you about that, if I tell you what has happened you become a witness and they'll force you to go to court and repeat everything I've said."

"I can't blame you for being suspicious but I can tell you there is no record of us meeting in this police station and nothing we say is being recorded, I give you my word on that."

"So why are you here?"

"You seem to have caused great embarrassment, not only to Greater Manchester Police but also the government nationally, I'm here to try and minimise that embarrassment."

"I'm sorry but I have every intention of embarrassing the Greater Manchester Police. They have allowed gangsters to rule the roost and done nothing to protect young girls who are smuggled into the country and treated as little more than meat. They even protected my parents murderers, they deserve to be exposed and I'll make sure the world gets to hear about it"

The Colonel sighed. "I told them you were a man of principle, perhaps I should tell you what has happened in the last twenty-four hours."

"Do you mean they've actually woken up and done the job they are paid to do?"

"You could put it that way but for the record every suspected brothel in Manchester has been raided, they even had to bring in more police from other forces. Over a hundred girls and half a dozen boys have been released. Dozens of men, customers and enforcers have been arrested. It's been a massive operation."

"That's good to know but how many criminals will walk? Some of the police are in their pocket."

"Yes, I've been told about that. Apparently there's a Detective Inspector called Kinkaid, they know he's corrupt and has corrupted others in his department. They've been covering up, destroying evidence and obstructing every investigation they could, including the one into your parents murder."

Buchan thumped the table, "Sorry sir, I'd like to get my hands on Kinkaid for just five minutes but I know that's never going to happen."

"You may get your revenge sooner than you think, Kinkaid is a married man with three children and strange as it may seem he says he's worried about them; he doesn't want to leave them without any support. He's agreed to do a deal."

Buchan leapt to his feet; sending his chair crashing to the floor behind him. "A deal, he's as bad as the Scilaccis' he can't just walk away, he's got to go down."

The Colonel appraised Buchan through cold grey eyes, "He won't go down as you put it, we have something rather more extreme in mind for DI Kinkaid."

Buchan retrieved his chair and sat down, "And that is?"

"We know Kinkaid must have deposited a great deal of money in foreign banks, we want to trace it and take steps to recover it, then we will deal with his criminality. You have to be patient Kinkaid has agreed the deal but we don't think he has any intention of fulfilling his part of the bargain. He'll run if given half a chance"

"How do you propose to stop him and just what is this deal he's agreed to?"

"In exchange for his family being looked after, he's going to hang himself, he will be released and described to the media as being, 'under investigation'. When released he will say goodbye to his family and go down to the local woods and hang himself. He doesn't know but there will be two lads from the regiment who will ensure it gets done. Are you happy with that?"

"It sounds good to me but can you really do that?"

"You should understand, when you seriously piss off those in the highest reaches of government and I don't mean the politicians, we can do anything."

Buchan sat back shocked. He could think of no more suitable punishment for the man who had treated the killing of his parents as little more than an inconvenience. Perfect justice but now he had to think of his own future.

The Colonel might have been reading his mind, "Now we have to decide what to do about you Mr Buchan."

Buchan raised an eyebrow, "Probably a full life term as a category A prisoner."

"No, we wouldn't want that, we don't want you standing up in court and telling the world how you had to track down the people responsible for your parents murder because this one branch of the Manchester Police CID was corrupt and working with and for the criminals."

"It's nothing but the truth and I have to admit I've been looking forward to telling the judge, the jury and of course the media, how Scilacci and his gang smuggled young women into this country and forced them into prostitution and all under the noses of the authorities, people have a right to know."

"That is why I have been asked to speak to you. There will be major media interest in this whole affair to say the least. My masters in London are not too concerned about the reputation of the Manchester police, they have after all allowed corrupt police officers to flourish for far too long and they deserve criticism. What they want to avoid is too much negative publicity of the type that may reflect badly on central government. I'm talking about border controls, currency manipulation and the safety of vulnerable young people entering the country. I have been authorised to make you an offer."

"I always knew there was cynicism in the higher levels of government but do you honestly think I am going to keep quiet in exchange for what, a shorter sentence, ten years perhaps instead of life, is that what you're here to offer?"

The Colonel smiled, "No Mr Buchan, I am offering you a get out of jail free card. You will not appear in any court; you will not go to prison. If you want you can even have a new identity. Of course, there will be a price to pay."

Buchan sat back trying to take it all in, would he really be allowed to simply walk away, he knew he had committed numerous crimes involving firearms, explosives and killings.

"What is the price? Because I can tell you for nothing I'm not going to hang myself."

The Colonel stifled a laugh, "You don't have to do anything like that. No, we want you to be available to us in government. We want you from time to time to carry out unattributable operations on our behalf, operations of the type you have recently carried out so successfully on your own."

"I hope you're not suggesting I should become an assassin or something for the government."

"No of course not, we are thinking more in terms of being an addition to our current pool of talent in dealing with organised crime syndicates that have become too powerful to pursue through the courts."

"That does interest me and I confess I've developed a taste for it but what about the five bodies at Great Oaks Farm, the press will be desperate for information about what happened to them."

"I'm sure they will, the current thinking is that there was a fight between criminal gangs, one in which they all sadly died or escaped before the police arrived. The price you have to pay to walk away from this is to maintain absolute secrecy about your recent activities."

Buchan nodded he could live with that.

The Colonel continued, "If that's agreed we will leave the station now and I'll take you to a safe house where you will be fully debriefed and then you will be able spend some time with a young woman who is anxious to thank for getting out of Scilacci's clutches."

Scarlett

Scarlett had been enjoying a few days at the Tranquil Gardens Health Spa near Nantwich when she got the news that her husband and sister-in-law were dead. It had taken the police almost twenty-four hours to find where she was staying and so the bodies had already been removed from the house.

Two police officers had taken her into a small room off the reception area, their faces grave she knew it was serious. They had said she was needed to identify the bodies and was taken immediately to the city morgue.

The news had completely shocked her. She had always suspected that Dom would be 'taken out' one day but at home? That was the shocking part. He usually kept business well away from the house, she had been thankful for that. And Fran dead too. What on earth had they been up to? The officers had said they could not give her any specific details. She had not asked, she did not want to know.

They were very kind, offering to take her to a friend, a relative, trace where her daughter might be. Millie was touring the USA with a friend, Scarlett said she would prefer to contact her herself. As forensics were still gathering evidence they said she would be informed when she could return home.

*

Back in her room, she did not know whether to laugh or cry. She went to the mini-fridge and took out a small bottle of wine, chilled ready for her. She poured the contents into a glass and took several large gulps before stopping to look at the half-empty glass. Now she laughed hysterically, she would not need this anymore. With shaking hands she took it to the bathroom and tipped it down the sink.

She took a few deep breaths and watched as the wine slurped down the plug hole. This will not do she told herself 'Be calm, drink tea' remembering the red and white mug at home. She sat on the bed to ring reception and ordered a pot of herbal tea.

"Of course," said the young receptionist, "Is there anything else we can do for you Mrs Scilacci?"

"Yes," she said, "please book me in for a couple of extra nights, I can't go home just yet."

The tea did the trick, she lay on the bed feeling a lot calmer. Thoughts and plans invaded her mind, plans which had been in the back-ground for years. The house, Great Oak Farm, would it all be hers now? And Millie's of course. They would sell it, what did they want with a six bed roomed house and an indoor pool that hardly ever got used? The huge kitchen, bigger than the entire floor space of the cottage she had grown up in.

Millie would be devastated, she had always been a Daddy's girl. And to be fair, Dom had always shown affection for her. 'Love', she thought, was going too far, it was something he was incapable of. Even with his sister, Fran, there was a distance, never any hugs or kisses. There would not be any now. She still could not quite believe they had both gone.

Scarlett's dream of buying a house on the North Wales coast, maybe near the cottage she had bought for her parents a few years ago, began to surface. It would be good to back in regular contact with them. Tears began to flow as she realised how much she missed them, how she wished they were here with her now. She had to call them soon before it was all headline news, maybe it was already.

She finished the tea, dried her eyes and sat up. It was *her* time now and she had to be practical. It sounded like the house was in a mess, perhaps Chunky could organise a clear up when the police had finished doing whatever it was they did. Apparently other bodies were also on the scene, the officers said they had not been formally identified yet. She did hope one of them was not Chunky, he was the only one she felt she could trust.

Telling Millie was going to be an ordeal, hopefully it could wait until she returned home in a few days. She considered it was doubtful they would be watching any UK news. Yes, she would be heartbroken but she was a rich, young woman. Without the influences of her father and Aunt Fran, anything was possible for her. Scarlett prayed she would make good choices. Pray...that was something she had not done in a long, long time. Maybe she would start going to chapel again, maybe she would revert to her maiden name 'Hughes'. The opportunities were endless, her mind was racing again.

She checked the brochure lying on top of the bedside table. There was a slot for a full body massage this evening, with essential oils. Perfect, even the mention of it was relaxing. Tomorrow a manicure and a pedicure. Yes, this was definitely the right place for her to be for a few days while she collected her thoughts.

Maria

Maria felt the soothing, softness of her mother's hand on her own. Opening her eyes, she could make out a blurred image of that familiar face.

"Maria, Maria darling," her mother crooned. "Oh, I think she's coming round Ted, thank God. Don't try to talk darling, we're here for you, we'll always be here for you."

Maria opened her mouth but no sound came out.

"No, don't try to talk," her father's voice this time and the slightly rougher feel of his hand. "You're going to be all right, I promise you. We love you, you have to get better."

She was aware of numerous tubes attached to her body and a dull ache in her ear. She reached up a hand to touch it but a huge wodge of padding prevented her from doing so.

"Be careful, darling," her mother said, gently bringing the hand down and placing in on top of the crisp, white sheet. Maria desperately tried to ask something, a name stuck in her throat, still no words came out. Her father guessed what she wanted to know.

"I'm sorry but Paul isn't here, we haven't been able to see him. He's in Police custody. We've tried to get a message to him, to tell him that you're recovering, that you'll be all right. We thought you would want him to know that."

She closed her eyes, trying to remember those last few minutes after she and Paul knew they were surrounded by the Police. Did she tell him to run? Did she tell him she would wait for him? How long had she been unconsciousness?

Her father continued to fill in the gaps, "You've been here for three days and you've had some surgery. Your ear was damaged but its healing nicely now and the surgeon says it can be fixed. You've been so brave, my darling, we're very proud of you."

"Now you must rest," said her mother, "you're safe, you have us, you have your own bodyguard right outside the door and lots of good wishes from your colleagues." She pointed towards the door and then to an array of Get Well cards on the window-sill but Maria had closed her eyes again and drifted off to sleep.

*

It was several days before Maria regained full consciousness. Beside her parents, the surgeon was her first visitor. He told her what she already knew, her ear had been crudely severed off causing a nasty infection. Strong anti-biotics had been administered and it was now healing, but any permanent hearing loss could not be assessed yet. The good news was that, due to great strides in plastic surgery, a new ear could be constructed when all the healing was done.

Next to visit was Detective Sergeant Havers, Maria's parents reluctantly left the room.

"Maria, it's good to see you recovering but I think you know there are questions I have to ask." He didn't wait for a response.

"You were assigned to Paul Buchan as a Police Liaison Officer and I know the relationship didn't stop there. You got involved in Scilacci's evil world and didn't declare it all. Right?"

Maria nodded.

"Can you tell me how you got to be kidnapped by the Scilaccis?"

"I was helping Paul, he didn't feel we were doing enough to find his parents murderers."

"So you shared information with him, confidential information?"

"He tried to protect me, there were things he refused to tell me but I knew deep down that he had acquired weapons. I tried to keep it above board but it all got out of hand. I'm sorry I let you down but I'm not sorry Scilacci and his evil sister are dead, I can't imagine how many lives they've ruined."

"But that was no reason for you to take matters into your own hands, Maria, you do know that charges will be brought against you, don't you?"

"Yes, I do and I'm willing to come clean with everything now. Will I be able to see Paul soon?"

"That isn't possible at present. Now you must rest and regain your strength. A formal statement will be taken from you in due course. You do understand that your career might be seriously affected don't you?"

Maria did not care about her career, her biggest concern was that she could not see Paul.

"Do you think you will be able to get a message to Paul from me?"

"I'll try," said Havers.

"Tell him I'll wait for him, just tell him that."

Annie Gray

Annie's feet had not touched the ground since she received the amazing telephone call from the crusader, who had confirmed her suspicion that he was Paul Buchan.

He had sounded anxious, and though it was controlled, Annie could hear the urgency in Buchan's voice. So, poised like a greyhound in a trap waiting for a rabbit to be released onto the racing track, Annie was prepared. She was an accomplished shorthand writer and her pen sped across the page of her notebook as Buchan rapidly reeled off the greatest and exclusive news tip she is ever likely to receive.

Buchan would not tolerate any questions but Annie could hardly complain and could not believe her ears as to the weight of the facts that were coming through her mobile.

She was not going to question any of the details, knowing that information from Buchan would not only be accurate but truly trustworthy. She was flattered that he had also trusted her but more than a little concerned about his request regarding Maria. She would think about that later, first she needed to get one of the paper's photographers to go with her to Great Oaks Farm.

Head photographer, Clicker, was available but refused to ride with Annie in her Fiat. She was a tad disappointed but as there was no time to argue she agreed to go in his Land Rover. She had to concede that his 4x4 was eminently more suitable than her car for driving over the type of roads and lanes they are likely to encounter on the way to the remote farm.

They could not get close to Scilacci's house because of a police cordon and Annie knew it would be hopeless to try and get any information from the police press office. The site was crawling with police officers wearing Hi-Viz jackets but Clicker managed to take some long-range photographs. And when Annie tried to speak to officials, who were standing outside the forbidden area, she was brusquely told where to go and overheard one of them say, "she's no friend of the police, get her out of here". However, Annie was more than comfortable with the information Buchan had given her and she was going to tell all.

Annie, it's Robbie George, is it true?" Annie's phone had not stopped all morning.

"Is what true?"

"What I read in the Star yesterday, that Paul's parents have been avenged, is how you put it Annie."

"Yes it's all true Robbie. Dominic Scilacci is no more. His crumbling, criminal empire has been systematically stifled. The real baddies are dead and Scilacci's accomplices, including the corrupt police officers that enabled him to ravage Manchester are currently in custody."

"So our streets should be safer now."

"I suspect things will be very quiet for a time until some other evildoer attempts to fill what they might see as a gap in the drugs market, though they won't find it so easy. As I explained in the article, Manchester Police have vowed a zero tolerance on drugs and weapons and are pushing for a more robust stop and search order."

"Thanks for speaking out for Stretford Annie, we won't forget it."

"Your very welcome George." With a smile of satisfaction on her face Annie put down her mobile, knowing she had achieved the scoop of the year.

*

The front page headline stated, "Gangland Shoot Out-Bodies Removed from Farm" but Annie really wanted to say loud and clear, "Lone Vigilante Clears Our Streets of Vermin", which Dave Arden dismissed as being too controversial. She wanted to tell Manchester that Paul Buchan shamed the police into action, which rescued young, innocent people brought so low through drugs, sex and murder that will take years of professional healing to mend.

Annie's inbox was loaded with letters to the editor supporting the content of the article and, in a new wave of reassurance and courage, the writers each wanted their name and address to be printed. Most were from Hale Road, Stretford, where Paul Buchan's parents lived and died.

In a humbling show of gratitude Annie received bouquets of flowers and boxes of chocolates from "grateful residents of Stretford". Her part in the campaign to highlight police corruption, which added to the anxiety of law abiding citizens, was minor, compared to what she thought Paul Buchan must have endured. Annie believed it was he who ought to be showered in tributes of thanks.

Buchan's crushing thirst to avenge the unsolved, cold blooded murder of his parents came through his conversations with Annie and she was glad that retribution had finally been served.

*

Annie did not turn off the television until well after midnight, when the wind-driven rain splattered on the window of her living room. As daylight faded into night she had not bothered to switch on her lights or close the curtains. She sat in gloomy solitude with only a shaft of light streaming through the window from the streetlamp outside her house. When she finally shut out the wet remains of the day she noted that all her neighbours had gone to bed.

No matter how tired Annie felt she was unable to sleep. She could not switch off from the recent events that were crowding her thoughts - the killings, the sensational revelations of police corruption, the arrests of drugs dealers and upcoming court cases. Her main concern, though, was to do with a part of that last explosive telephone call she had taken from Paul Buchan.

Writing news stories and court reporting could be challenging but it was all part of her job and doable but what Buchan had asked her to do would take Annie out of her comfort zone. A promise is a promise, however, and Annie, who remembered her father once telling her, "Never make a promise you can't keep," will deliver it.

Buchan had told Annie that, when Maria is discharged from hospital and feels well enough, she would be staying with her parents at their house. He gave Annie the address and said, "Annie I want you to do something for me, I want you to visit Maria. I daren't risk getting in touch with her myself. I've got to disappear, don't ask questions I don't have much time, just tell me you'll do it."

Maria, who had become the most important person in Buchan's life, had helped Annie through the traumatic episode of the hit and run case and, though in the beginning of the relationship there had been animosity, the two had parted on good terms. Annie decided it was the least she could do for Buchan so she gave him her word.

The plan was that, when possible, Buchan would contact Annie to give her a message to pass on to Maria and in turn Annie would update him on Maria's progress. He told Annie to visit Maria on foot using only public transport and to "not go in that red tin box of yours". He explained it would be safer for all concerned as followers of Scilacci would have Annie's car on their radar. "I'm deadly serious Annie, please be careful," he warned. Those were his last words before the line died. For a while and still holding the phone to her ear Annie had sat motionless as she wondered what sort of shady world Buchan was heading for.

*

In the meantime she would continue writing for the Stretford Star, having successfully achieved an increase in salary, along with her new title of news editor. Dave Arden did not quibble about the salary she demanded as he knew she was being head hunted by two major newspapers. Annie was initially flattered with the attention, after all it had been her dream to work on a national daily. She decided, however, to stay with the Star, realising she was well acquainted with the people of Manchester, indeed she was one of them and she wanted to continue telling their stories and to speak up for those whose voices would otherwise not be heard.

Several of the Stretford residents learned they could trust Annie and took her into their confidence, like the single mother who lay awake with her stomach churning and feeling sick into the early hours until she heard her son close the front door. She contacted Annie and told her about her torment at not knowing where to turn as she guessed he was involved in drugs.

One night he was found with gunshot wounds lying in a dirty, cold alley way. The name of the single mum is Mrs Osman, who asked Annie to help her promote a self-help group for parents, who are or have been in the same position as herself. The group meets monthly at the Hope Church Hall. This was where Annie's heart lay.

Dave Arden sauntered up to Annie's desk and said, "you'll be able to afford a decent car now, Annie."

"No thanks Dave, my father's Fiat Panda serves me well and it has been through a lot lately so from now on I will be giving it copious amounts of TLC. She knew if her father was listening he would be pumped up with pride.

Kinkaid

9 months later...

The one thing he still had was the most precious thing of all, his freedom. The sentence handed down by Judge Malings had come as a shock to the police, the courtroom gallery and the blood hungry eager press box, all baying for blood, his blood. When the judge announced a two year custodial sentence suspended for twelve months there had been an audible hiss of astonishment by the vast majority of rubberneckers at the trial but not him.

Of course everyone else in court had not sat down to enjoy a dinner with the judge and his wife two weeks previously. He smiled to himself as he descended the wide expanse of steps that announced the courtroom's grand entrance with a renewed spring in his step. With Scilacci dead, along with his poisonous sister and his criminal organisation now dismantled, it had left him with a free ticket to rebuild his life without fear of retribution.

The funeral of Scilacci had taken place whilst Kinkaid was released on bail. He was of course persona non grata to the police officers attending. Their grudging looks were to be expected following his exposure as an informant for the Scilacci operation. Especially considering the life changing injuries to Maria Ross. Served the interfering bitch right he thought nastily.

Anyone who thought that he would find the future a struggle were sadly mistaken. He was in control of six offshore holding accounts worth in excess of seventy five million dollars. He had been careful leading up to the trial to portray a frugal existence, but now he was in the clear.

*

Lakeside Investments held the bulk of Kinkaid's illicit fortune, over sixty million pounds of it. He took the plastic wrapping off a new burner phone and opened an account in google. He entered the required fifteen digit security code 4547#3!78¥552{9 and waited for the page to load. It was time to start enjoying himself. An image of a sun kissed lake started to fill the screen top to bottom. In the bottom right hand corner was a US dollar icon, Kinkaid clicked on it and his main account loaded.

It was immediately apparent that something was drastically wrong. His brain could not compute what it was witnessing. In place of an expected eight figure balance was a sum of $1,455. Kinkaid went white. He checked and double checked but he was not mistaken.

He quickly accessed the other five accounts. He found three of them had been closed down and the other two were in the red to the lower limit of the account, forty thousand dollars. He began to sweat and swear at the same time. He only stopped ranting when he heard the ping of an incoming text on his legitimate mobile.

*

Kinkaid froze when he saw the name. He checked the number. It was impossible, he had witnessed the cremation.

He read the text in a state of terror:

We need to talk about my money. Dom xxx